G000021568

*Also by Jack Dickson*

*Erotic Fiction:*
*Still Waters*

*Thrillers:*
*Oddfellows*
*Freeform*
*Crossing Jordan*
*Banged Up*
*Some Kind of Love*

First published 2002 by Prowler Books,
part of the Millivres Prowler Group,
116-134 Bayham Street, London NW1 0BA
www.zipper.co.uk

Copyright © 2002 Jack Dickson

The following stories have been previously published:
"Ball Games", *Scotsgay*, Issue 8, 1994; "Bronco Bill", *Bunkhouse* magazine, Brush Creek Media, Spring 1998;
"Dragon's Fire", *Sex Magik II*, ed. Cecilia Tan, Circlet Press 2001; "Terminal Orgasm", *Wired Hard II*, ed. Cecilia
Tan, Circlet Press 1997; "Tripping", *Eros Ex Machina*, ed. M. Christian, Masquerade Books 1998

Jack Dickson has asserted his right to be identified as the author of this work in accordance with the Copyright,
Designs and Patents Act 1988

A catalogue record for this book is available from the British Library

ISBN 1-873741-63-4

Distributed in the UK and Europe by Airlift Book Company,
8 The Arena, Mollison Avenue, Enfield, Middlesex EN3 7NJ
Telephone: 020 8804 0400
Distributed in North America by Consortium,
1045 Westgate Drive, St Paul, MN 55114-1065
Telephone: 1 800 283 3572
Distributed in Australia by Bulldog Books,
PO Box 300, Beaconsfield, NSW 2014

Printed and bound in Finland by WS Bookwell

# OUT OF THIS WORLD

## Jack Dickson

Zipper Books

# Contents

# THE HEAD FUCK

The blackness is almost total. I say 'almost' because myriad sparkling dots shimmer before my eyes. But I know there is no way light can penetrate the leather blindfold pressing against my lids. Its thongs cut into my scalp.

The silence is almost total. I say 'almost' because there is a high-pitched whine somewhere far away. But I know there is no way sound could penetrate the wax plugs wedged in my ears.

My hard-on shudders.

How long have I been standing here? Fifteen, twenty minutes at most. I shuffle uneasily, deaf to the metallic jangle of leg irons which hold my ankles firmly in place. Chrome bracelets secure my hands overhead. The gag stuck in my mouth makes me salivate, forcing my throat into a continual swallowing motion.

A shiver teases its way across my naked body even though the room is well heated. It won't be long before they all start arriving. 'Back in half an hour, tops,' Dave had said, just before his thumbs pushed the earplugs into position.

Dave is a lecturer at the university and took me for several classes when I was there. We recognised each other as fellow faggots – Dave's choice of noun – almost immediately. Our easy, chatty friendship began then and has continued ever since, even though now I'm doing my post-grad work at another of this city's illustrious ivory towers. We run into each other occasionally. Dave restricts himself to the local leather bar, a place I only go to now and then. I'm not really into all that dressing-up and silly role-playing.

However, I do like ogling heavily tattooed, muscular arms – from a wholly aesthetic point of view, of course.

Engaged in that very activity last week, I managed to drag my attention away from a pair of ink-scarred upper arms long enough to say hello to Dave. 'How's things?' he asked. I gave him the usual student's tale of financial woe. 'Want to earn a bit of extra cash?' he enquired.

I listened, then almost choked on my drink, and said no.

'You'll be perfectly safe. A sort of... living work of art, on display in a cage but not to be touched under any circumstances.'

I thought it over, then thought about the money, and said yes.

After all, how wild an event could it be – a surprise party for the curator of the Gallery of Modern Art? And Dave would be there, Mr 'S/M Means Consent' himself.

The arrangement is exactly as he promised. I am strung up in a tubular cage of silver metal, built on a three-foot platform and positioned on the middle of the room. Around the walls are tables laden with booze. 'A harmless, eccentric party-novelty for about fifty artsy queens and their fag-hag coterie,' as Dave put it.

I am also rock-hard and have been since shortly after Dave left. That possibility hadn't been mentioned – indeed, had not even entered my mind.

Still, I don't suppose it matters, outside my own irrational embarrassment. I doubt I've ever met any of this crowd socially, or ever will. If I manage to stay hard for the whole three hours, perhaps I should ask for a bonus.

Surely half an hour has passed since Dave left. Perhaps the party's already in full swing – all animated conversation and shrill laughter, while I'm in my solitary world of silent black with a twitching hard-on. Some of the guests might be walking around the cage, amused, titillated by the muscular 23-year-old body inside, staring at the exhibit...

My rigid cock flexes in a convulsive spasm.

I try to think of something else, suddenly aware of an unexpected and very real possibility of sex. My thesis... yes, the ideal opportunity to give some serious thought to its layout.

I feel a rash of goose bumps ripple across my naked skin. The door is opened, subtly changing the currents of air within the room. My body hair bristles in response to the draft skimming over me. This is it!

My hard-on is jumping and kicking like a dying man on the end of a rope. I can feel their eyes on me, their gaze pressing against my flesh. A group has gathered around the cage. I can smell the alcohol rising off their breath and hear the muffled sound of men and women's voices.

Oh, shit! My cock is straining and pulling, desperate to find something solid in the darkness, any source of friction which might help discharge its unbearable tension. But there's nothing, only empty space. I start to undulate, thrusting my hips back and forth. I can't help myself.

There is an equally vocal and entertained group to my rear, focused on my bare arse.

Oh, God! I feel a burning rush of humiliation. One of them has noticed and is pointing something else out to the others: the way my fuckhole is opening and closing, its indiscriminate desperation for a filling, any sort of filling – a finger, a cock, a fist – any object which might plug its gaping, hollow emptiness.

Oh, Jesus! My cock is aching, flailing around in the vast darkness in search of relief, but there is none.

I'm moaning now, trying to form words behind the gag, trying to plead for mercy – for someone, anyone, to unlock the gate and touch me, to release the agonising pressure trapped within my seven inches of engorged flesh. I'm trying to tell them I will do anything they desire, fulfil their most secret yearning in exchange for the slightest touch, the lightest caress.

My gyrations become ever more agitated, my naked body

signalling by every means possible that it is available. More than available.

Desperate.

My buttocks are now the focus of attention. I can feel the crowd's concentrated gaze. I know they're watching my bare arse. I know they know what it wants. It is begging, pleading for the sharp slap of an open palm or the sting of a belt. I am aware of curling my stomach muscles, then thrusting my arse out towards them, wanting, wanting...

I shoot my load in an explosive jerk, which crashes through my whole body. I can sense, almost hear, their response – the mingled shrieks of laughter and disgust as the front-rowers search for hankies to wipe my spunk from their hair, their faces, their clothing.

My heart is thumping, my body coated in sweat. But I know the activity has attracted those who weren't previously watching. They are drawing towards the cage, swelling the number of spectators. My cock and arse are now on display to an even larger audience.

It's as if the ejaculation had never happened; everything I felt before is still there, only more intense. My hard-on is still there, reaching out towards the onlookers – an open invitation with no takers.

I hold my breath for a second and groan in appreciation. I feel a finger tracing gently down my spine and shoot my load a second time. Only in mid-spurt do I realise it's not a finger, but just a trickle of sweat disappearing into my arse crack.

Oh, Jesus! I suddenly know it will never stop. I am a human fountain shooting out a stream of never-ending spunk.

Oh please, Dave... help me. You must realise it's all gone terribly, disastrously wrong... please...

I feel anxious, agitated fingers undoing the thongs holding my blindfold in place. My eyes close in reaction to the blinding light. The plugs are pulled from my ears and I hear Dave's voice, gossiping about the museum curator.

'That fuckin' stupid old queen! Well, first of all he goes into a mood because he thinks everyone's forgotten his birthday. Then he takes a swing at his boyfriend, breaking his nose no less. We explain we were all only pretending to have forgotten –'

I open my eyes to an empty room, with everything exactly as it was when I last saw it.

'– we tell him there was going to be a surprise party later. Well, you can imagine.'

Dave reaches up to undo the arm chains and I look around the room in disbelief.

'He hears that; feels totally guilt-ridden about his boyfriend's nose; has to have a major drama and rushes off into the night, blinded by tears.'

Dave bends down to release the leg-irons and for the first time notices my drooling, semi-hard cock and the splatters of viscous globules gleaming on the carpet.

'Well, I can see you haven't been bored.'

Our eyes meet and I have the sensation of an unspoken something passing between us. He lightly slaps my arse and I have a sense of possibilities, limitless possibilities.

'Get dressed and I'll drive you home.'

I struggle into jeans, watching him use a tissue to wipe up the mess I've left on the floor. And I know with absolute conviction that Dave and I will be seeing a lot more of each other, that the leather bar might have more to offer than just colourfully decorated, over-developed forearms.

# DRAGON'S FIRE

I stared at the last glowing embers of the camp-fire, then raised my eyes to the dark sky. 'Want to hear a story?'

Johnny shifted in my lap. 'I've heard all your stories, man...'

Looking down, I smiled. 'Not this one. It's a story about the past... and the future... and maybe even the present.' I felt him shiver in the cool night air and move back against my chest. 'Interested?' I reached forward, nervously poking the dying coals with a stick.

He stretched languidly, cat-like, making himself comfortable between my thighs. 'Okay, then... I'm listening.'

As twin moons slipped into their descent, I began my tale.

*Breathing broke the humid silence – the shallow, easy breath of sleep, and the troubled, erratic inhalations of the sleepless. Saja eased Ver's arm from around his naked waist and sat up. Sweat pinpricked his brow. He frowned. Nights had been hotter than days recently. A sign?*

*He flicked the tent's door flap aside and gazed out into the night. Soon there would only be night. His eyes adjusted to the velvety pitch, Saja focused into the distance, beyond the rest of the Fini encampment to the great cimma forest... or what remained of it. Once majestic rows of tall, proud trees had stood stretching up into a lilac sky.*

*Saja focused on the sparse clumps of decaying wood and vegetation, rotted by the slow but certain climactic change. He turned away from the wasteland and glanced back into the tent. Ver was snoring gently, his pupils flitting beneath his eyelids. Saja smiled and continued to watch as Ver's chest rose and fell with an oblivious rhythm. His smile slid into a frown.*

*Ritual – the Ritual of Fire.*

*Dragon's Fire.*

*His breath caught in his throat. Old Yrad's ravaged face flashed into his mind. Saja looked up into a dark-purple heaven and cursed.*

*Fire Gods – Dragons.*

*The Old Ways.*

*He shrugged off a shiver. Change: everything ran its course. As no-mads, no one knew that more surely than the Fini. He thrust a hand through his thick black hair in frustration and scowled. Circumstances changed: change was part of life. Adaptation was the key to survival, and the Fini knew all about adapting. The tribe had survived near-extinction before, and would again.*

*He stared up into distant galaxies twinkling with life and myriad opportunities. What would happen? What did the future hold for Ver and himself? What was the best he could hope for? An icy hand gripped at his soul. The Ritual of Fire would go ahead. Yrad and the Old Ways would be proved right. He would live to a ripe old age.*

*Torrents of cold sweat poured from Saja's forehead, running into his eyes and mixing with the salty tears already forming there. He released the tent-flap and moved over to Ver's sleeping form. Manoeuvring them both into their familiar S-position, he molded himself around the golden figure and buried his face in Ver's shoulder.*

*Saja would live to a ripe old age, but would be alone forever.*

I felt Johnny's blond head resting heavily against my chest. 'You still awake?'

'Mmm...'

I smiled, and wrapped my arms around him. 'Want me to go on?'

He gave another sleepy, monosyllabic response. I sighed, and continued.

*

*Yrad bowed, made the sign of Vala, then raised cataract-clouded eyes. From his knees he stared at the 77 onyx steps which lead up to the altar. He watched the unending procession of Fini slaves as a cargo of precious cimma wood made its way to the very top. His heart swelled in his chest. At last, his tribe would have a home and Esidarap would be forced to accept his people's right to be there. For millennia his ancestors had traversed galaxies like so much rootless seed, settling wherever the wind blew – and then for only as long as their hosts would permit.*

*Generations of Fini had attempted growth in many lands. They had tried to adapt, to fit into their environment. The Old Ways had been abandoned. The Great Book and its teachings were consigned to his forebears, passed down through the generations until the knowledge and the faith – the belief in the Fire Gods – resided in Yrad and Yrad alone. Until now.*

*He stared beyond the line of industrious workers to the fading rays of Esidarap's sun. This planet was dying. No amount of thought or action, on the part of Esidarap's native intelligentsia, could change that. But he could change it. When the Great Day came, all would be forced to admit that the Old Ways were best.*

*Yrad stared at the icon, at this moment under construction by three sweating, uncomplaining slaves. Pride overwhelmed him. His heart leapt as he gave thanks to the ancient Fire Gods, who had not deserted his people in their hour of need. Through their auspices, he had received insight into young Ver's great gift; a gift that promised redemption and rebirth. A gift to replace the dying corona which was gradually fading to nothingness above Esidarap's sand-covered surface.*

*The Fini shaman inched to his feet, stretched out his gnarled arms and began the morning prayer of supplication. 'O Vala!' The workers ceased labouring, and fell to their knees. 'Thanks be to thee for guidance! Thanks be to thee for wisdom! Thanks be to thee for knowledge in our ignorance, sight in our blindness, light in our darkness. Soon, as it is written in the Great Book, Ver and Ukiro will join under your benevolent gaze.*

*Their union will be fruitful. The fruit of Ver's loins is fire; a fire which has raged unabated for one thousand cycles.'* Yrad closed his rheumy eyes, his voice soaring up through the atmosphere. *'He bears the mark of the Dragon. Dragon's Fire beats in his heart and flows in his veins. Bless this union. Give us a son!'*

'Swords and sorcery!' I heard a sleepy but familiar scepticism in Johnny's voice. 'I don't believe in all that rubbish!' His tone was suddenly sly. 'You know the type of stories I like –'

Nuzzling his neck, I made him silent. 'Shh. Listen. Listen and learn.'

*Saja smiled, watching as Ver braced his arms against the rock and submitted to the scraping. Copper skin glowed under the helion's weakening rays, shining from both the oil and the sweat, which poured from the hard body. Saja pressed the ivex scraper firmly against the muscles of Ver's back, which arched in response. As he ran the ceremonial implement down over Ver's arcing incline and onto his tightening buttocks, a sigh escaped Ver's lips. The sinewy body convulsed as tiny droplets of cimma oil leaked into the deep crevice between two hard mounds and trickled down the inside of one thigh.*

*Saja raised the scraper, running a rough finger over the dull edge where Ver's sweat and the sacred oil had collected. An aroma drifted up, filling his nostrils, his heart and his mind. He wanted Ver to fill his body. It was not to be. A groan from the rock beside him dragged Saja's mind back to his duties: the Preparation for Fire. Ver was the Chosen One. Saja shivered as the shaman's ancient phrase crept into his brain.*

*As the eldest son of the Fini tribe, Ver's candidature had been assured from birth. Lineage and legend had proclaimed his eligibility. Saja lowered his eyes to groin level. The sacred mark confirmed it.*

*The Fini had rejoiced. A Chosen One: after centuries of waiting, of wandering, the honour had fallen to one of their own. Esidarap's survival was in their hands... or, rather, Ver's loins.*

*Saja pulled his thoughts away from the inevitable and laid the slick ivex scraper on a rock ledge. He began to massage Ver's sweating shoulders with expert hands. The groans deepened as his strong fingers kneaded the hard muscle, rubbing away the tension, the apprehension, the fear. Saja reached over and kissed the back of a sweating neck, enjoying the texture, the saltiness on his lips. His lover's skin. Under his hands, Ver twisted unexpectedly and turned to face him. Saja paused, gazing into the eyes of the one who, regardless of his destiny, formed and filled his world. But the bright, auric pupils spoke another, less welcome message.*

*'The mark of the Dragon makes me special. The mark of the Dragon occurs only once in three thousand years. The Dragon is not for you.'*

*Saja smiled while his soul leaked the tears of a thousand and one empty nights. He watched as Ver blinked, lashes sparkling a little under the sun's faint rays, then returned his smile. They stood together under a lightening lilac sky until Saja lowered his eyes and took a step back, almost ashamed. Ver's body always overwhelmed him. He winced as an arrow of jealousy pierced his heart, then turned away.*

*Saja knew he was a disappointment to his family – to the entire Fini tribe. It was only through Ver's insistence that he was permitted to even associate with the Dragon, let alone steward him, the Chosen One.*

*Saja was stocky where Ver was tall; heavily muscled, where Ver possessed the streamlined sinews of a runner; hirsute, where Ver's golden body was virtually hairless; raven-haired and ebony-eyed, where Ver's blond and golden-irised characteristics were classically Fini. Saja's dark eyes darkened further with black memories. Children of his own tribe and others had teased him at school, calling him Vini – a pun on the Esidarapian word for 'dark horse' – whereas 'Fini', according to the Great Book's ancient dialect, translated as 'golden warrior'. Saja clenched his fists, as he had clenched them for years, never allowing the taunts to hurt or affect him; never complaining, never retaliating. After all, they were right, weren't they? He was an anachronism, a throw-back to a more primitive era – maybe even a prank* played by the mischievous Fire Gods who, legend told, were often eager to swap their own children for a Fini cherub.

Strong arms reached under his shoulders. Saja leant back into another sweating body, feeling the hardening buds of Ver's nipples crushed against the tufted skin around his spine. He didn't care if he was different. Ver was with him; he was with Ver. They had loved each other for as long as either could remember – as children, with a child's unquestioning, unconditional love; as youths, with youth's curious, physical love; as young adults, with an ever-increasing emotional love.

And now, as two grown men, they loved each other with all the trust and respect that sprang from a mature love. This love acknowledged all previous loves, combining and creating a love which was more than the sum of its parts – a love that burned in their hearts with the passion of fire.

Dragon's Fire.

Then Ver's slick arms languidly turned him around, pulling him against his smooth, gleaming chest. Saja sank into the embrace, pressing himself into his friend's firm flesh, loving the feel of his own rough, matted pectorals on Ver's smooth sinew. Resting his head on a well-covered collarbone, he instinctively began to rub himself up and down Ver's naked thigh as he felt Ver's hands travel down from his shoulders. Ver's fingers lingered on his waist, toying with the hide thong, which held the traditional steward's uniform in place. Saja tensed as a hard index finger worked its way beneath the the leather strip, lifting the well-filled pouch until the loose flesh within was as tight and constricted as the sun-dried leather encasing it.

He gasped into his friend's shoulder, pressing his open mouth to warm flesh. He lowered his hands down past Ver's waist, settling on two hard mounds of muscle. The pressure in his groin increased as he continued to undulate. Saja bit his bottom lip as he felt Ver release the thong, then lower both hands, fingers spreading over his hard buttocks.

Saja moved onto his toes to allow Ver deeper access. He raised his hands to Ver's neck and massaged him with his thumbs, while the other man's thumbs hooked up towards the very heart of him. The leather *pouch was held in place by the swelling of Saja's passion, its thong torn away by Ver's eager fingers. With eye-lids closed, Saja raised his head and felt Ver's teeth nibble the skin of his neck. Saja was thrusting urgently now, moaning with pleasure as Ver's thumb pressed against the tight ring of muscle, seeking entry to his hot body. Inside, another tight circle spasmed in welcome as the first wrapped itself around Ver's thumb in a pulling motion. Saja clenched his teeth as a nail's, then a knuckle's length entered him.*

*Ver's arm was around his waist, holding him tightly as the slick thumb edged back, then thrust harder, deeper into his body, slowly at first, then more vigorously. Saja felt his breath quicken, become more shallow as Ver continued to thrust passionately. Tension began to mount. Wild thoughts flashed through his mind as Ver pressed skin to skin – thoughts of Ver's fingers, thumbs, tongue; thoughts of his own body deep in Ver's sweet mouth, the feel of Ver's lips and teeth along the length of him. His mind was reeling backwards and forwards across the years, across the memories, across all he and Ver had been to each other. He thought of their perfect union, and of his own body deep inside Ver's as Ver's thumb was now deep inside his.*

*As the weakened sun of Esidarap neared its apex in the purple sky above, another stronger son of Fini neared a pinnacle of his own, on his own. His hips shuddered, thought dissolving as his body dissolved. Saja thrust forward against his friend's thigh as hot waves of milky liquid drenched the ceremonial pouch, leaking out onto hotter flesh. Lights danced on his eyelids as Ver's four fingers pressed against his buttocks, holding the thumb in place, forcing it ever deeper as Saja's muscle spasmed and sparkled like a thousand shooting stars.*

*Through the shattering orgasm, Saja was aware of the rapid beating of his heart, and of Ver's heart's slow, steady beat – and of the Dragon which lay sleeping against his own thigh.*

'What's his problem?' Johnny sounded more alert now. This was the kind of story he liked to hear.

'Whose problem?'

'The "Ver" guy! Why's he not hard?' A hand played along the inside of my thigh. 'I mean, if it was me, and some hunky guy was –'

'Shh!' I smiled, knowing I had caught him and drawn him into my story. 'I know patience isn't one of your virtues...'

*Ukiro wandered around the encampment, eyes drinking in the familiar sights she had grown up with. She wanted to see them as if for the first time, so as to imprint the minutiae of everyday life on her retinae. She wanted to take this world with her when she entered the next. It was an honour. She knew that. To be selected to receive the Dragon was a great honour. She glanced over to the tent where her life-partner, Micha, and three daughters sat sewing. So why did she not feel honoured? Why did she feel like hiding, fleeing, crying, screaming with rage at the honour that was to make her name last for ever in the hallowed halls of Esidarap's history?*

*Ver opened his eyes, focusing golden pupils on the eight inches of lifeless flesh which lay between his legs. He blinked through the gloom. Each day since puberty he had come to this cave – in the beginning to enjoy its restful qualities and the tranquillity it somehow instilled into his racing mind and pulsating body. He had come here of his own free will. Under the tutelage of Yrad, the visits had become a routine part of his instruction and induction.*

*Reaching down, Ver pulled back the hood of skin and stared at the small white circle just below the head of his thick penis. He inhaled slowly. All this – the years of control, of learning to understand his body and its special qualities; the role this bundle of sinew and veins would play in all their fates – because of something which looked like a flaw, an imperfection. Ver traced the pale circle with a smooth index finger. The heavy organ, tamed by meditation, twitched almost imperceptibly under his touch. He inhaled deeply, redirecting the frisson of pleasure that shot up his spine. He held the breath, then exhaled.*

*It was Saja who had first noticed the mark of the Dragon. Ver's penis jerked again at the memory: a night, himself sixteen years old, lying naked on the warm black sand under a glowing moon, his friend's full mouth nuzzling his own, then stopping.*

*'Oh!'*

*There had been concern in the rich, dark voice as Ver had gazed down past Saja's glossy head to a faint, vaguely circular outline on the underside of the rod of hardening flesh.*

*Ver almost laughed out loud, remembering their panic – the frantic washings, the cimma infusions, the guilt, which culminated in his first, timid visit to Yrad. Ver sobered, recalling the look of disbelief then awe that crept across the ancient shaman's face. He closed his eyes, and while absent-mindedly rubbing the sacred mark with his index finger, he remembered how he had sat cross-legged with Yrad on this very spot, listening with growing anticipation to the elder's words of explanation.*

*'There is nothing to fear, my child – you have done nothing wrong. On the contrary, you have been blessed with a wondrous gift. What lies in your loins is something of great beauty and strength, of immense wonder and spiritual power. You must not abuse that power, but learn to control it, hone and develop it because one day, the future of those whom you love – the very survival of us all – will depend on you.'*

*In the darkness of the cave, Ver inhaled slowly. The sense of pride and responsibility was heavy, tinged as it now was with more than a little fear. Ten years earlier, he had listened to the venerable sage's words, answering the strange questions with tremulous nods and shakes of his blond head. Yes, he had already received pleasure from his body: Yrad didn't seem surprised. Yes, he had become aware of a strange heat in his loins at the moment of orgasm: Yrad had nodded, enigmatically. No, he had never lain with another: Yrad had smiled, resting a craggy hand on Ver's shaking shoulder.*

*'That is good, my child. That is how it should be. The ways of ordinary men are not for you. Your destiny is as a high priest of Fini, and as such, your body is sacred. It holds the Dragon, the Fire Dragon and the*

*divine breath of the Dragon. Now that the sacred mark has appeared you must guard the Dragon and its fire.'*

Ver opened his eyes and inhaled the damp, slightly musky odour of the cave's interior. He had tried to keep faithful to the oaths he had sworn to the shaman ten years earlier. The tantric vows had not been broken. He had not spilt his seed since the sacred mark's appearance – not by his own hand, not with man, nor woman, nor beast of the field.

Ver shifted slightly on the uneven, rocky floor. A warm glow spread over his body as Saja pushed into his mind; countless purple days and nights – in their tent, under the stars, by the running water of moonlit streams – the feel of Saja's hot skin on his, the taste of Saja's sweat, the texture of hard lips, of rough dark stubble against his own hairless face, the weight of Saja's tongue twining with his own –

The fire inside increased. Ver tried to clear his mind.

– the thickness, the smell of his friend's glossy hair, the pressure of Saja's knees in his armpits, the weight of Saja's strong form on his chest as Ver took his friend into his mouth, caressing him with lips, edging his tongue under the loose sheath of darker skin, even nibbling that darker skin –

In his loins, the sleeping Dragon moved against a sweating thigh.

– and when Saja was moaning, and thrusting deep into his soft mouth, when Ver had licked and sucked so that the hard organ pressed against the back of his dry throat with unbearable urgency, he would gently ease himself away and then stare – just lie and stare at his friend's glistening, shining member as it stood up almost vertically from the impossibly tight root –

Ver became aware that his breath was losing rhythm and was coming in short, shallow pants. He knew Yrad would not be pleased, but also knew he could control the Dragon, the fire that burned deep inside his body, as he had controlled it for years.

– they moved well together, so well that the progression was superfluid, two sides of a mirrored reflection. Saja would roll from astride him, clasping tightly and taking Ver with him, until Ver was on top, *squatting over the gleaming, saliva-soaked organ. Entwining the slick fingers of one hand with his friend's, Ver would reach down and guide that member, pulling down and back until the shining, exposed head leant against the quivering entrance to his own body. Then he would pause, as he always did, pause and look down into dark, bottomless eyes. Ver received great joy from the pleasure he gave to Saja; joy by proxy, as they both knew, but any physical discomfort was eclipsed by the expression of Saja's face as Ver lowered himself, impaled himself, thighs trembling, onto the thick staff of flesh.*

*Ver cried out, so great was the desire and longing. Naked and still shining from the cimma oil, his torso shuddering with sobs, he stretched his arms upward towards the roof of the cave. In his mind's eye, his fingertips gouged through the stone and up into the clear night, wanting to pluck down a star, maybe a surplus sun from some distant solar system, and deliver it to Yrad – deliver what Esidarap lacked by mortal means – rather than suffer this curse.*

I felt the tension in Johnny's hard body.

'That's not fair!'

'What's not fair? That Ver has never experienced... ?'

'You know damn well, Ian!' He moved from my lap and settled a few yards away. 'That stuff about the white patch... on Ver's...' Johnny's eyes avoided mine as he refused to finish the sentence.

I held out my arms. 'Hey! Come on, it's only a –'

Johnny turned away, ignoring the gesture.

I stared at the back of his blond head, watching while he toyed with the fire's dying embers. 'I didn't mean to –'

'Just get on with it!' His tone was harsh.

Doubting for the first time the intention of my tale, I found my mouth was dry.

*Standing before the sacred altar as the last few lengths of cimma wood were positioned, Yrad felt a fluttering deep in his ancient chest.*

*A sign?*

*He gazed up into a hazy purple sky. The sun seemed to weaken before his eyes, flickering dully through cataracts.*

*A sign?*

*The Gods of Fire spoke to him as his heart-rhythm altered, stuttered then began again. Tingles played down his right arm, stiffening and relaxing in turns.*

*A sign.*

*Yrad fell to his knees, left arm clutching right as the beating in his chest echoed in his ears. He opened his mouth.*

*Silence.*

*Yrad evoked the shaman voice of a thousand generations of Fini shamans. Captured by the breeze, the unspoken command was carried on the wind to all corners of Esidarap.*

*The Fini heard it. Labouring in the fields, they heard it. Planting in the forests, they heard it. Talking in tents, they heard it. In her life-partner's arms, Ukiro felt the command, and her heart died. As a body, the entire Fini tribe stopped what they were doing and began the journey – whether short, whether long – towards the altar. All except two. For the power of the Fire Gods had jurisdiction over only two media: earth and air.*

*Ver loved to swim with Saja. He loved the feel of cold, clear water pouring over his face and hair. He loved its fluidity, its restrictive inertia. He loved to battle against the fullness and weight of it. He loved the way it cooled his body, deadened his mind of worry and distractions until only one thought remained. In the mountain stream, he opened his eyes as his body broke the surface skin of glacial water and looked around. No one. Nothing. Only rock and sand and scrub-land.*

*A splash beside him. Ver grinned as strong arms seized his waist, pulling him back down into the icy depths. In the clear water, Ver tried to catch his friend off-balance, wrestle him to the river bed. But Saja was too quick for him. Powerful legs were around his waist, squeezing tightly, and Ver found himself on his back, on the smooth floor of the* river, lungs bursting. Then Saja's mouth was open on his, breathing into him, into his chest, his heart, filling Ver with something other than air. Between almost-numb thighs, the sleeping Dragon began to stir. Gasping, they shot towards the surface.

His head once more in the keen air, Ver watched as Saja shook himself like a dog, scattering droplets of spray in a wide arc. Something rang in his mind, the echo of a thought. Ver smiled and shook it away like Saja shook the water from his brawny body. Glancing down, he saw the length of Saja's love for him, the measure of desire projecting up from a wiry jet-black forest. Ten years of restraint ebbed away, ten years of denied response, ten years of unfulfilment – of selflessness.

Saja was with him always. Even in the cave, Saja was increasingly there, in his mind, when that mind should be on other, more important matters. But what was more important than life and love? What was the basis of life? What – who – was the nadir and the apex of his own life? For a second, Ver considered Yrad, his family and tribe. Then he thought of Ukiro, of someone he had never met, but whose life he would end. A life for a life – a son for a sun. What was life without love? The sleeping Dragon began to uncurl.

Recklessly, selfishly, Ver pulled Saja to him, felt the hard heat of another body close on his, shadowing the solar heat which pulsed in his veins. The sleeping Dragon was stretching to full length after a decade of slumber.

He laid a hand behind his friend's neck and raised the powerful face upwards, leaning into a kiss. Saja's mouth was urgent, his tongue a familiar explorer. Ver felt strength course through his body, mixing with the fire, tempering heat with other heat. Instinctively, as Saja had done on many occasions, Ver began to undulate. The Dragon twitched its tail.

Open-eyed and open-mouthed they communicated without words, with pleasure, with joy, with their bodies. Ver gasped as the Dragon reared, then hissed. He felt his friend pause in the kiss, slowly edge away and look down to where a tiny white pearl brushed the Dragon's mouth. The fire was pulsating now, the heat of a million fires focused into one, man-made, man-oriented inferno. Ver felt his scalp tingle with a thousand tiny sparks.

*He tilted Saja's face to his own. His friend's expression was one of confusion, wonder. Ver laughed, as he had not laughed in a decade. It was time for laughter, for seizing the moment. Both knew the risks. Both knew the price. Grabbing his friend's outstretched hands, Ver led him through the cool water and onto the riverbank.*

'No!' Johnny now sat close to me, my affront to him forgotten as he was drawn into the story. He clutched at my arm. 'He's a priest! He can't! What about the planet and the Old Ways? It's not right! They're being selfish!'

'Who's selfish?'

Johnny scowled. 'Ver and the hairy guy – they're only thinking of themselves and –'

'Ver and Saja are in love, Johnny – each is thinking of the other, not himself.'

'Yeah? What's Yrad gonna say when he finds out?'

Reaching down, I hooked my hands under his arms and gently heaved him up over my body. He fitted against me eagerly, easily. 'You mentioned a sacrifice – there are many types of sacrifice...'

*In the arms of a burly slave, Yrad allowed himself to be carried to the foot of the altar where Ukiro, pale and trembling in a white ceremonial loincloth, stood waiting. Through eyes misted by the pain in his arm and chest, he watched the beautiful woman also cast a pain-drenched look to her life-partner and daughters, who stood yards away at the front of the swelling crowd. Above, the sun was fading fast, in a darkening sky. Shadows lengthened around the altar, dragging the 77 onyx steps up into infinity. Night was falling.*

*A sob from Ukiro split the silence.*

*Barely able to speak, Yrad tried to reassure her in whispers. 'Do not be afraid, my child. It will be quick, and full of joy. Ver has guarded the Fire Dragon well. There will be no pain, no regrets, nothing... only life.'*

\*

Stroking the blond head, I looked into the night sky. The two moons were almost gone and on the horizon a pinkish glow was appearing.

Muffled words breathed onto my chest hair. 'Poor Ukiro. Does this story have a happy ending? It's gotta.'

I sighed. 'Happy for whom? Happy for... ?'

He nuzzled my hardening nipple. 'Don't stop. I need to know.'

*Naked, the cool water rapidly drying on his hot skin, Saja stared at the golden Dragon, at the proud head licking upwards from a bush of saffron hair. Breath caught in his throat as the fire-beast swayed under his gaze, brushing Ver's navel, edging up the bronze stomach until it stood completely erect.*

*Ver's hands were warm on his waist. Saja flinched. Jumbled emotions rushed through his mind: guilt, lust, fear... He looked back up at Ver's handsome face, the face he had known since childhood, the face which had for the past decade been clouded with worry, with tension, with the strain of enormous responsibility. Now that face seemed younger and older at the same time. Ver's eyes were glowing, the yellow irises alive with fire. Ver looked happy. Slowly, Saja reached out a hand, brushing the burning face with his knuckles, then stretched down and stroked the Dragon's back.*

I pulled Johnny's hard body closer to mine, until I could feel the beating of his heart and feel his breath on my shoulder, his lips warm against my skin. We began to move.

*Darkness shrouded the planet. Ukiro's tread was heavy as she mounted the onyx steps, heavy as her heart was heavy, heavier than the tears which sparkled in her brown eyes and coursed down over silken cheeks.*

*Yrad watched her slow progress, while pain shivered up and down*

*his arm. Doubt glistened on the edges of his mind as his eyes flicked be-*
*tween the solitary figure on the onyx steps and the weeping Micha. He*
*pushed doubt away. It had to be. The Fire Gods had spoken. Ver must*
*have a partner and Ukiro bore that honour. The Old Ways.*

*The Old Ways were best.... best... best...*

I rolled Johnny over in the cool, black sand, enjoying the feel of
his body against mine, his hardness against mine.

'Don't stop, man. Go on.'

Story or movement? I didn't know. Was it really important anymore? But I wanted to finish what I had started, though the pink
horizon grew to a golden red. I eased myself up, and nestled
Johnny between my thighs. One arm around his waist, I pointed
to the sky.

*As the Dragon pulsed in his friend's shaking hand, calescence exploded*
*in Ver's brain. Yrad had been right. This was power – a fierce power be-*
*yond anything he had ever experienced. Tongues of flame spoke to him,*
*their voices deep in his soul as his whole body focused first into the*
*Dragon, then spread outwards towards Saja.*

*Fireworks filled his eyes. Saja gasped in the darkness as Ver's body*
*began to throb with a light that seared his vision, singed his flesh and*
*burned into the very heart of him. This was life; this was love; this was*
*his past, present and future, regardless of anything Yrad had ever said,*
*regardless of the destiny of a civilisation or the future of a world. He felt*
*selfish, achingly selfish. And selfish felt right.*

*With no regrets, Saja moved forward and pressed himself against a*
*pillar of flame. A hot mouth was open on his. Scorching breath filled his*
*lungs, choking, cauterising. Then he felt his friend's hands on his shoul-*
*ders, lowering them both to the ground.*

*On the 77th step Ukiro paused and stared over at the cimma marriage*
*bed, her funeral pyre. Silence rang a death knell in her ears. Below, the*
*crowd was swelling. Ukiro couldn't look down, dared not look down at*

*the face of her life-partner, and the children they had mothered together. Instead, she raised eyes heavenward, into the purple darkness.*

*In the distance...*

I waited and watched.

'You're a real tease, you know that, Ian?' Johnny wrestled free from my grip, spun around to face me. His legs astride my waist, his hazel eyes searched mine.

'I'm only the story-teller, I –'

'Well? Come on, man!'

*The Dragon was breathing fire now. Burning lava filled his body as Ver stared deep into ecstasy-filled eyes. With Saja's strong legs over shoulders, he pushed down, pinning his friend's body to the ground. Straining muscles stood out on Saja's thighs as Ver manoeuvred the Dragon towards the pulsating entrance to his friend's body. The Dragon inhaled, then breathed out.*

*Ten years of longing slipped away as the Dragon sank into Saja's body. Ver felt strong muscle accept, then close around the Dragon, caressing, harnessing ten years of his own passion and the power of the ancient Fire Gods. Pressing his mouth hard to Saja's, Ver thrust deeply, towards his friend's soul.*

*Amidst a shiny, auric halo the golden warrior and the dark horse were united by the Dragon.*

I moved my gaze down from Johnny's dilated pupils. Behind us, the glow threw our shadows together onto darker sand. His hands reached out for mine. Fingers entwined, we stretched our arms toward the lightening purple sky.

*Yrad blinked. At the periphery of his vision, something sparkled.*

*Breath filled the air. The crowd inhaled as one.*

*Where there had been only darkness, a golden pinprick...*

*

Johnny was staring over my shoulder. Transfixed as I was by the golden skin of his face, my words soared like birds into the dawn sky.

*Two became one, seared into a molten mass of burning flesh. As Saja's tongue flicked the inside of his mouth, Ver gripped his friend's slick waist with fire-tipped fingers and felt the Dragon throb. Golden irises stared into dark, liquid pools as Ver's body merged with Saja's. Physically, they had been one – been so close – many times. But not like this. Riding the Dragon.*

*They were burning, alight with life, love and fire. White heat soldered limb to limb – legs, arms, hands, eyes. No Ver, no Saja, no Dragon, nothing but heat and fire and love.*

*Insolence filled them, as the blaze increased. Far from taming the Dragon, Saja's body pushed up the temperature, ignited the already blazing union, drove it forward, degree by degree.*

'Yes, yes, yes...' Johnny's breathy voice filled the morning air.

*Ukiro's eyes felt rather than saw the star widen as it grew in the purple heaven. Shadow vanished as a thousand flares exploded in the sky, bringing life where there had been death, heat where there had been chill. Light, where there had been darkness.*

Heat warmed the back of my neck as twin suns rose over the horizon and the black sand sparkled with life.

*As the molten essence of Vala coursed from his soul up into his friend's body, a rush of burning air propelled Ver upward – into and away from Saja at the same time. Through scorched golden irises he could see his lover's joy; feel it as a palpable presence; feel it intensify as the*

*Dragon's breath poured into Saja's body, sealing them together in a bond of pure energy. They were together – together forever...*

Johnny was on his feet, pulling me upright. 'Look!' He raised my hand towards the horizon. 'It's Saja and Ver! It worked, didn't it?' He turned the face of a happy child towards me. 'They did it, man, they had a son – two suns, really!'

I smiled, staring down between his naked thighs. 'Love... and magic, Johnny – the magic of Ver's very difference.' I ran a gentle finger over the patch of discoloured skin which had caused him to pull away from me in shame.

Johnny flinched, then relaxed. 'I know, man, I...'

Then his mouth was on mine, his sweet mouth moving with mine as we kissed under our planet's twin suns. The heat we generated almost – but not quite – matched that of Ver and Saja and we didn't need to die to stay together.

He pulled away first, sweating under the fire of our kiss. 'Hey! What about poor old Yrad and Ukiro? What happened to them?'

I laughed, draping an arm around his broad shoulder. 'Oh, Ukiro ran safely into Micha's arms. And the Esidarapian paramedics reached Yrad in time, and he lived in Paradise to be four hundred and two!'

Johnny squealed with delight. 'Oh, man... you and your stories!'

We picked up our clothes and began to dress.

# A NIGHT ON BEAR MOUNTAIN

Paul fiddled with the toggle of his jacket and blinked. 'What?'

Alex poked the dying embers with a stick and looked across at him from the other side of the camp-fire. 'Maybe we'll meet him,' he repeated. Paul blinked again. Alex grinned. 'Big Foot – we're right slap in the middle of Big Foot country. Didn't I mention that?' The grin broadened, splitting his handsome, bearded face.

Paul gripped a cigarette tightly between thumb and forefinger, and hummed a snatch from the 'Twilight Zone'.

Alex laughed. 'Hey... there's more things on heaven and earth –'

'– than are dreamt of in your philosophy, Horatio!'

They both laughed. Alex pulled a bottle of Chardonnay from the wine-cooler and refilled Paul's cup, and then proposed a toast. 'To the most recently tenured – not to mention youngest – member of the Humanities faculty! Well done!'

Two plastic cups clunked together. Paul drained his in one gulp, and looked around.

'Beautiful, isn't it?' said Alex.

Paul stared towards where the sun was just setting behind a craggy peak and sighed. Alex was right; Bear Mountain had a smell, an atmosphere all its own, something you didn't get from maps, photographs or even movies. He switched his eyes back to Alex. His friend was staring at a clump of bushes a little to their right. Paul followed the stare. Was it the wine, or had something just moved in those bushes? He swallowed down the beginnings of panic. 'Very... picturesque.'

Alex continued to stare. 'Mmm... certainly is...'

'Anything wrong?'

'No –' Alex's eyes flicked away '– just checking out the... night life.'

Paul laughed; he could never really tell when Alex was teasing him. And that was one of the things he liked about the broad, well-muscled bear of a man sitting across the camp-fire from him. 'Tell me more about this Big Foot thing.'

Alex winked. 'Turns up in the collective unconscious of various cultures: Yeti, Abominable Snowman, Wild Man... '

Paul sniggered.

Alex shook his head solemnly and then leant forward and stirred a pattern in the ashes with the end of his stick. 'Look at Grizzly Adams! I think –' he winked across the camp-fire '– we all like the idea there will always be something beyond civilisation, something we can't tame.'

Paul snorted and refilled his glass. 'Maybe he's an alien, come to –' he laughed '– probe us.' His hand shook slightly. He took in Alex's muscular body. They'd known each other over a year, worked together for nine months. Gradually, they'd progressed from colleagues to friends. Maybe they would be more than friends. Academic aspirations and a few chaste kisses apart, Alex was still very much a closed book but if the blurb was anything to go by, the man should prove an interesting read.

Paul followed his friend's gaze back to the dense bush.

Alex grinned. 'Wonder if his feet are the only part of his anatomy on the large side!'

Paul laughed, then glanced over at the pup-tent. 'I hope that tent won't be too cramped.'

Alex chuckled. 'Hey, we'll manage – after all, isn't that what the Great Outdoors is all about? Roughing it? Making do?'

The camp-fire was dying down. A chill breeze swept over him. Paul shivered slightly, zipping up his buck-skin jacket. There was a loud hiss. He looked back to where Alex was pouring the dregs of the Chardonnay over spitting embers. Paul jumped to his feet, rubbing his hands together. 'Think I'll turn in. Coming?'

Alex grinned. 'Sure...'

Paul felt an unmistakable stirring beneath his work-pants.

As they walked towards the pup-tent, Alex lightly swatted his bum. 'Gotta protect you from Big Foot!'

Paul's cock took a little leap. He grinned, mock-punched the side of Alex's head. The hoarse, responding laugh was carried off into the dusk.


Was ground always this hard? Paul turned over for the sixth time and tried to get comfortable. Was the great outdoors always this dark? He wrenched one arm free from the sleeping-bag and illuminated the watch on his wrist: 23:54. Was it always this damn quiet? No traffic, no noise from next-door's TV, no voices...

He lay on his back, listening to the even shallow sounds of Alex's breathing. The guy obviously suffered from some sort of narcolepsy – he'd been asleep almost as soon as his head touched the ground-sheet.

And was this whole trip such a good idea? Here they were, miles from anywhere and not even a chemical toilet to remind them of civilisation. What if one of them got sick? What if there was a sudden landslide, and those majestic peaks behind them came tumbling down around their ears?

Paul turned over again, groaned and gave up. He unzipped the sleeping-bag, fumbled around until he found what he hoped were his clothes. He dressed quickly, then pulled open the Velcro door-fastening and crawled outside.

A heavier quiet. No rustlings. No sounds of birds settling down to roost. No scrapings and scurryings of rodents. It was like all wildlife deserted Bear Mountain when the sun went down.

Paul frowned, stuck a cigarette between his lips. And talking of going down... He turned towards the tent, and flicked the lighter. As they'd both undressed in semi-darkness, he'd just managed to glimpse the heavy cock which swung lazily between his friend's thighs, before Alex had leapt almost jauntily into his sleeping-bag and said good-night.

Paul's own cock started to stretch against his thigh. He strolled further away from the tent. Maybe Alex didn't find him attractive. Maybe he'd read the signals wrong. Maybe his carefully planned weekend's seduction in the wilderness was about to turn into 48 hours of blue balls. Paul sighed.

Although more quiet, it was less dark out here. He leant against the trunk of a tree and gazed into a haze of velvety blackness. The cigarette's end glowed three inches from his face. The Big Foot legend flashed into his mind. Paul laughed out loud; if the creature was up and about, he'd evidently invested in slippers. He stifled the laugh, moving away from the tent; no point in both of them being sleepless.

Then something grabbed Paul from behind. His heart stopped beating. Paul dropped the cigarette as a broad arm encircled his waist. His mouth fell open in a yell, which was cut short by a hand – or a paw.

His heart was making up for lost time now. Warm wetness trickled down the right leg of his pants. Through the adrenalin rush, Paul was vaguely aware he'd just pissed himself. He was also more than vaguely aware of something very large and very strong. He tried to wrestle free in order to get a good look, but couldn't.

His fingers scrabbled on broad, hairy biceps, digging in. And then a hard member jabbed at his left buttock. A hand pulled questioningly at him and Paul allowed himself to be encompassed in hairy arms and led away from the safety of the tent.

The large beast was pulling him through dense undergrowth now, its massive back and broad shoulders screening him from the worst of the lethal thorns and branches. Paul's heart was pounding in his ears.

One boot came loose. Then the other. His feet tripped over scrub-ground, and then rockier terrain. Ahead, ragged breathing disturbed the night's silence. Paul closed his eyes and followed blindly along, his cock getting harder and tighter with every second that passed.

When he eventually opened his eyes, he was neither dead nor in the open air. Paul stared up at the roof of the cave. A moon had appeared, and was shooting bright rays down through the spaces between the rocks. He groaned, one hand moving to rub his bruised body. Skin met skin. Paul realised he was naked.

Two yards away, eyes gazed at him out of the darkness. Paul leapt to his feet. Big Foot! He could prove to a sceptical world that the creature existed.

A paw grabbed at his ankle. Hands grasped for a grip. Fur brushed his thighs, his belly. Then his legs were pulled roughly apart, and warm breath brushed his arse-hole. Paul froze.

A rough tongue lapped at his crack. Paul roared in desire. The sound echoed around the cave, then died in the damp air. Lying face down in the beast's lap, arse in the air, Paul submitted to the Big Foot's attentions. Bristling hair burned and scraped at his arse-cheeks as the tongue continued to lap up and down, pausing at his balls, then flicking up to the base of his spine.

Paul groaned. Trapped between his thigh and a hairy belly, his cock was lengthening, growing thick against hard, hirsute flesh. He could hear snuffling as the animal continued to eat him out. Warm wetness coated the area around his hole. Paws moved from ankles to arse-cheeks.

Paul gripped the biggest pair of feet he'd ever encountered. Every muscle in his body was rigid as Big Foot spread him, then thrust a big tongue deep into his arse-hole. He moaned and clenched his sphincter. The tongue pushed easily past.

Slurping sounds filled the cave. Paul writhed and thrashed as his imprisoned cock pulsed and flexed against the taut, hairy stomach. The beast was flicking his tongue in and out of Paul's pucker like an ant-eater into a termite hill, and Paul squirmed, luxiariating in the sensations.

Then he was released. Before he could register the freedom, his head was pushed down between fuzzy loins, and Paul knew big feet were only half the story. A solid cock bumped against his face.

Paul stared at the pulsating member, wondering vaguely if one could catch any horrible diseases through unprotected sex with a myth. But as he sheathed his lips and took the large member into his mouth, Paul stopped caring. He inhaled.

Big Foot's crotch smelled of tree-bark, wet undergrowth and dark pools. The powerful, musky odour filled his head as the animal began to fuck his face. Paul took as much of the cock as he could, swirling his tongue over and under the hard shaft. He coughed as his gag kicked in, hands tightening on a bristly waist. Big Foot showed no mercy. The cock receded a little, then plunged back in.

Paul was choking, but he loved it. Something about the angle of the thrusts was stimulating his saliva-glands. His mouth and throat were filled with cock and spit. Trickles dribbled from his mouth. Then another taste: strong and salty and slightly sour. Wrenching his tongue out from under the cock, Paul flicked the tip over the large head and savoured the beast's pre-come. In his mind's eye he could see the headlines: 'I gave Big Foot a Blow-Job, says recently de-tenured Professor of Aesthetics.'

Large paws were over his ears, dulling all sound. Paul's heart pounded behind his eyes. He drew back gradually, gazing down as Big Foot's big cock slowly emerged from his mouth. Pin-pricks of moonlight pin-pointed dots on the floor of the cave. He watched the flexing, shining cock appear. The skin glistened with his spit and the animal's pre-come.

Paws slipped from ears to shoulders. Paul waited for claws to dig in.

They didn't. He continued to move backwards on all fours. The cock slid from between his lips and stayed there, a gleaming rod of pulsing, erect gristle.

Paul looked up at the shining eyes, remembering something about staring animals down. He considered holding Big Foot's gaze. He didn't get the chance. The large, fuzzy shape seemed to sigh. Then, with a speed belying its bulk, Big Foot moved behind him. Then Paul heard something that definitely sounded like a plastic packet being torn open, but surely not...

Strong fingers gripped his shoulders. Then the slick, wet rod rested against his slicker, wetter hole. The hairy body tensed once, then thrust forward.

Paul threw back his head and howled as Big Foot's big meat pushed past his clenched pucker and up into his arse. Paws gripped more tightly as his body was propelled forward, half in fear, half with the force of the thrust. Large balls impacted against his trembling arse-cheeks. Big Foot's grunt petered out into a long growl, which Paul found himself echoing from between gritted teeth. The beast's meat was almost splitting him in two, despite the diligent lubing his arse-hole had received. Paul gripped handfuls of moss and lowered his head. Big Foot began to fuck him.

As a hot throbbing cock pounded in and out of his arse-hole, the sensations resonated all over his body: the hair on the thighs behind his, the breath on his neck, the grunts in his ears, the almost unbearable pain in his guts – and the throbbing in his cock.

Big Foot's member was so large it was stretching and filling his arse. With each stroke, the head of the animal's cock stabbed at the small round gland behind Paul's bladder. He finally knew what it meant to feel pain and pleasure simultaneously.

The fuck was speeding up. Paul shuddered. The force of the thrusts spread into every muscle in his body. His fingers ripped through the moss and dug into his own palms, reopening the earlier thorn-scratches. He yelped, pushing back against the invading enormity.

His mind was seeing more ridiculous headlines:

'"Big Foot was my lover," says recently institutionalised ex-professor of Aesthetics.'

'Academic and anachronism in custody-battle over love-cub.'

Paul found himself grinning: hell – after this, being probed by aliens was back-page stuff!

A sudden increase in the force of the fucking brought him back to earth. Wet, warm fur pressed against his back. Paul yelped as teeth dug into, then broke the skin on his neck. His cock was aching. His balls felt as if they were on fire. His arse was a quivering, pulsating tunnel of bruised tissue.

Big Foot's big paws gripped his waist and pulled him back onto the beast-meat one last time. Paul screamed. His own come hit his face. And, totally exhausted, he fell immediately into a deep sleep.

Somehow, he could still walk. Somehow, he found his way back to the tent. Somehow, Alex was still snoring, the sleeping-bag rising and falling with each shallow breath.

Paul blinked, pulled the soft micro-pile up around his ears and stared up at the dim outline of the kerosene-lamp.

Four hours later, the dawn sun soaked through the walls of the pup-tent and cast the first shadow. Only then did he sleep.

When he awoke, Alex was crouching beside him, bare-chested. The handsome face frowned with worry. He held out a mug of coffee. 'You okay?'

Paul's head hurt, but that was nothing to the way his arse felt. He smiled weakly, took the mug and wondered how to phrase his first sentence.

Alex saved him the trouble. The strong fingers of one hand

brushed strands of sweat-damped hair from his forehead. The other held out what looked like a cheap gorilla-suit.

'I meant it to be a childish prank, but then you were so into it...'

Paul blinked. The mug of coffee shook.

'You've always turned me on...'

Hot liquid splashed onto the sleeping-bag and began to soak through, seeping onto Paul's thigh. He yelped.

Alex dragged the coffee-stained sleeping-bag away and pulled Paul into a bear-hug.

The press-conferences and the photo-opportunities receded. Paul laughed and snuggled into the embrace. He hugged the broad, hair-covered shoulders tightly.

'You bastard! You mean, kinky... adorable bastard!'

When they eventually pulled apart, Alex was looking less sheepish. He kissed Paul's forehead and grinned. 'You had a good time, then?'

Paul winked. 'What do you think?' He beamed innocently at his lover. 'Oh, and tell your friend – the guy who took over when you left – he's one hot stud, too!'

Like Big Foot, the expression on Alex's face had to be seen to be believed.

## SKINNER'S RULES

Leo paused outside the Pre-Fab building and took a deep breath.

Eighteen months on Kai, working the casinos, saving every credit he'd sharped from drunken, card-playing workmen, and for what? Mugged – in broad daylight! The brand new skim-jet, his clothes, all his money and most of his possessions were gone. Leo frowned: you couldn't trust anyone these days.

He fingered the cheap amulet around his neck – a souvenir from a particularly satisfying night's work. He owned only what he stood up in; his work-permit had expired, and Immigration would be up his arse within the week. He stared at the scribbled sign to the left of the entrance: Hunters' Registration.

Leo sighed. Not exactly where he'd planned to be today but he needed money, and he needed it quick. Fastening the hand-stitched drongo-skin jacket and pulling back his shoulders, he pushed open the door.

The Plaedean behind the desk didn't look up. 'Name?'

'Smith.'

A seven-fingered hand tapped at a keyboard. 'Work-permit number?'

Leo rattled off a fourteen-digit figure.

The tapping continued. 'Experience?'

Leo grinned. At 6'3" and weighing 250 lbs, his muscled bulk provided good cover in the casinos: looking like a big, dumb-fuck hunter whose wages were burning a hole in his pocket worked every time. 'Two years with the sleigh-squad on Orion.

Supplied the Gamma expedition – and got the contract when the sector was settled.'

The bald head looked up. Leo felt three eyes appraise him. The Plaedean smiled. 'The good old days, yeah?'

Leo faked a nostalgic grin. 'Yeah... is there a stalking-party leaving today?'

'Not today.'

'What is available? I can turn my hand to most things.'

'There's an auction in –' the Plaedean consulted a time-piece '– half an hour.'

Leo's brain zipped into action. Better than he'd expected. Auctions paid up-front; he could take the money and run to the nearest jet-port. 'That'll do me just fine!'

The Plaedean laughed and winked with his middle eye. 'They'll be a mixed bag – good luck!'

Thirty minutes later, he stood with another five lots. All held numbers. Leo's was six: last, but not least. He smiled.

Bidding began. Number One – a seven-foot Cyclopaedean – went quickly, and for a good price. The line moved up. So did Leo.

Number Two – a Sigma – almost caused a riot amongst the hunters, so great was the demand for his razor-teeth and psychic-tracking talents. Leo's eyes swept the crowd. They were about thirty in total – from all species.

Bidding got under way for Number Three. Leo listened to the offers: the average price was high – more than enough for a one-way ticket off this damned rock. The Troll generated so much excitement he was eventually sold jointly to two miners, who would settle terms privately.

Minutes later, Number Four – a symborg – was withdrawn, having failed to reach his reserve price.

'Number Five!'

Leo watched as a Vervain tart sashayed forward. He seemed

more organised than the others, gave a short emplo-history then stripped, revealing a well-muscled, honey-coloured body complete with the extra, much-in-demand orifice.

The bidding went on forever. Leo listening to the haggling, then got fed-up and tried to work-out from the remaining crowd who were hunters, miners, stalkers and who were meatmen. Not that it made any difference: he had conned them all, in his time.

The Plaedean's gavel struck the desk. 'Sold!'

The Vervain dressed, then walked from the podium.

'Number Six!'

Leo strode forward, grinning broadly at his potential employers. From the sea of faces, a pair of dark eyes glowered at him, then sparkled. Leo stared. Something about the eyes was vaguely familiar. His cheeks suddenly felt very hot. He looked away, focusing on a spot on the Pre-Fab's rear wall.

A low hum of conversation buzzed across the crowd, then settled into bored silence. One, then two minutes passed. Eventually, the Plaedean auctioneer took pity on him. 'Come on, guys – I know he's a little long in the tooth, but he's bound to be useful for something!'

The crowd grumbled in disagreement.

Leo's heart sank into hand-tooled boots. Even the symborg had generated more interest than this! He scanned the crowd and immediately caught the dark eyes again. Their owner raised a fist. 'I'll take him off your hands for four credits.' The voice was low, cultured, contrasting dramatically with the bedraggled appearance.

The Plaedean banged his gavel through growing laughter. 'Skinner's Rules in operation!'

Leo scowled. What the fuck were Skinner's Rules?

Someone sniggered. 'Three point seven-five!'

Why were the bids going down instead of up? He glanced across the podium to the three-eyed auctioneer.

The Plaedean winked. 'Bidder's prerogative, son!'

'Three point five!'

One of the crowd guffawed. 'For that?'

A strange prickling sensation tingled on Leo's skin.

Others joined in the laughter, which became so loud, the Plaedean was forced to bang his gavel three times. Eventually, the crowd settled down.

Leo's gaze flicked back to the dark-eyed man. The guy was hooded and wore the traditional yashmak of the planet, screening the lower half of his face. Leo knew Kais to be skilled, ruthless skinners and cold, heartless employers. He shivered and closed his eyes. His brain was still trying to make sense of Skinner's Rules when a rough hand grabbed his chin, forcing his lips apart. At first, he was too surprised to react and then too shocked. Leo stared at the Kai's ridged-forehead while his teeth were examined, then broke away, adrenalin flooding his body. 'Hey, no handling the goods!'

The Plaedean banged his gavel. 'Bidder's prerogative!' The middle eye glared at him. 'Behave yourself!'

Leo swallowed a retort, submitted to the inspection and tried to stand still. As abruptly as they'd been inserted, the fingers were withdrawn. 'Full set. Two point two!'

Leo scowled as the Kai stepped back, then flinched a little as a broad hand cupped his balls. He suddenly realised he was hard.

'Breeding-potential, I'm sure!' The Plaedean auctioneer's voice squeaked hopefully in the background. 'You got stud-experience? Pedigree?'

Leo considered bluffing, to bring in another bidder, but decided it was a bad risk. His silence spoke volumes.

'Two point two! Skinner's Rules still in operation!' The Plaedean banged his gavel. 'Any further bids?'

Leo's heart hammered. He could still feel the rough fingers in his mouth, taste the flesh of whatever beast the skinner had been despatching prior to the auction.

'Bidding stands at two point two! Last chance to acquire this... er, useful piece.'

The crowd was starting to drift away. Leo watched miners, hunters and other meatmen wander from the room until only he, the auctioneer and the Kai skinner remained.

'Sold!' The gavel fell. 'I think you've got yourself a bargain!'

The words resounded in Leo's guts as his new employer laughed and strode towards him.

The collar felt strange around his neck – another of Skinner's Rules.

The Plaedean was reading a list of conditions. Leo wasn't listening. He turned to the rangy figure at his side. 'I've not done much skinning but –'

'Sign!'

Leo bristled. 'I need to read the –'

'I said sign!' The collar dug into soft flesh.

A low chuckle echoed in Leo's ear as his face hit the ledger. Before he knew what he was doing he'd made his mark on the contract.

'Smith, huh? On the run from Immigration, more like!'

Leo clenched his fists. How the fuck did –?

The collar tugged again. Leo's head jerked back.

'Come on. Let's see what you're good for.'

Leo was already planning his escape but as he was led from the auction room, he was sure he saw the Plaedean's middle eye wink.

Leo tried to keep up, but the Kai's long strides and fast pace made this difficult.

'Not done much skinning, eh? What about fleecing?'

'Er... no, I'm more of an... entrepreneur, and I –'

'Shut up, meat!'

Leo was about to object to the title and point out that it was bad manners not to respond to a question, when the Kai stopped abruptly and Leo's head impacted in the middle of the tall man's shoulders.

'Clumsy, aren't you?'

This time Leo remained silent.

It seemed the desired response. A deep chuckle resounded in the dark. 'Skinner's Rule Number Eight, meat – learn to keep that hole shut.'

Leo tried to imagine why silence should be particularly desirable in a tannery.

'Unless, of course, it is in use at the time!'

In front, a door opened. Raucous laughter and blue light leaked out into the black night. Leo stared. This was no tannery. A rough hand pushed him forward. Leo tripped, landing heavily. He cursed, raised his face and found himself staring into pink, Vervain eyes.

'Hello again, dearie!'

Leo scrambled to his feet, turning to glower at the tall Kai. 'But I thought you were a –'

'Skinner? Sure, meat – I'm that all right. But there's all sorts of skinners... looking for all sorts of skins!'

Leo's eyes flicked around the crowded, stinking room. Someone gave a low whistle. Leo felt himself start to flush up. He tried to back away. The Kai's rangy body blocked his way. Then a soft hand patted his arm.

'Come on, dearie – I'll get you sorted.' The hand tugged him away.

His face scarlet, Leo followed wordlessly towards a door in the corner of the room.

An hour later, Leo was almost sorted – thanks to Laic, the slim Vervain. His employment apparently involved a twelve-month debenture. Two point two credits would be deducted for each month, repayable at the end of the term if and when the Boss sold him on. Leo would be eligible, of course, to bid for himself – via the reserve price option – when the time came, provided he had earned enough credits in the intervening period.

'Okay, dearie?'

Leo scowled and nodded. None of it mattered, of course. He'd slip away at the first opportunity.

Laic talked on. 'Point zero-five credits – of which the Boss takes fifty percent – for each satisfied customer. No limit on the number of customers to each meat – provided the meat's up to it.'

Leo glanced around his new room. A cot, a washing area ... no windows. The only door led to the bar.

'How many holes?'

Leo's eyes flicked back to the smiling Vervain. 'What?'

Laic elaborated. 'Three? Four? The more holes you have, the more customers you can service; the more customers you service, the more credits you can earn.'

Leo squirmed. One hole was drier than a desert, the other surprisingly moist.

Laic chuckled. 'Only two, huh? Oh well... we can't all be Swiss cheese, I suppose!'

Leo stared at the nano-thong which he was evidently expected to wear and shook his head.

The Vervain sighed sympathetically. 'I know, dearie – you're such a –' pink eyes scanned him '– big one!'

Leo glared at the flimsy garment. 'Why can't I wear one of those?' His eyes moved over the Vervain's demure rosy gown.

'Skinner's Rules, dearie!' Laic thrust the thong at him. 'Get into it, then I'll show you around.'

Leo's hand moved towards his belt. 'What is this Skinner's Rules stuff?'

Laic smiled and ignored his question. 'That's the ticket, dearie. Sooner you start working, sooner you start earning.' The Vervain's smile tightened. 'Don't want the Boss to exercise Skinner's Rules Number One and take some of those credits you owe him in kind, do you?'

Leo scowled. His skin started to prickle again.

Laic's smile relaxed and became almost teasing. 'Or do you?'

Pushing thoughts of that ridged, hard forehead and those dark, familiar eyes from his mind, Leo bent down and began to undo his boots. His fingers became tree-trunks, the laces slippery eels as he wrestled with their fastenings. Eventually, he kicked off the foot-gear, and started on his shirt.

Laic's wide eyes widened. 'Very pretty!'

Leo peeled off his hide pants and work shirt. Naked, he stared at the top of Laic's blond head as the Vervain fingered the cheap amulet which dangled between his nipples.

'Valuable?'

Moist air caressed Leo's body. He shook his head. 'Just a worthless piece of junk.' He stared at the amulet and smiled.

Laic laughed. 'How appropriate!' The Vervain stood back, arms folded while Leo struggled into the nano-thong. As he tried to cram himself into the meagre strip of fabric, Laic laughed at his efforts. Leo's fingers tightened on his half-hard cock. The uncut head poked cheekily over the waistband, despite his best efforts to tuck it inside. The more he pushed, the more Laic laughed and the more Laic laughed, the harder Leo became.

The Vervain suppressed a chuckle. 'What's wrong, dearie?'

'Nothing!' Leo wriggled, plucking at the thin strap which dug into his crack and tried to adjust the thong so he didn't feel quite as awkward.

Usually, he was in charge. As one of the slickest Minodos-sharps in this sector, Leo was accustomed to holding all the cards. Despite his discomfort, he smiled, remembering the kick of watching grown men offer him the drongo-skin jacket off their back in a desperate attempt to try to off-set their losses.

'Ah well –' Leo flinched as Laic ran a hand over his arse-cheeks and then gently patted him in the direction of the door '– let's see how you go down.'

Leo stuck closely to the slim Vervain. He was half-relieved, half-disappointed to find his presence largely ignored, although he was the only guy wearing a nano-thong. The pouch was uncomfortable. For some reason his body felt twice as naked with the garment as it would have without, but Leo found that if he stared straight ahead and didn't catch anyone's eye, he could just about manage one foot in front of the other.

As they walked, Laic murmured to him: 'Easy... hard... very hard – don't go near him, dearie – easy... and generous with it... he's a sweetheart, but he likes four holes, so he's out...'

Leo tried to absorb the info, but without actually looking at the characters under description, it didn't mean very much.

'Laic, ya three-holed bitch! How ya been?'

A good-natured, Vervain laugh tinkled in Leo's ears. 'Harl, you old fucker!'

Leo raised his eyes. Laic was embracing a dark-skinned man with a lone hackle of silver hair. The man grinned, and released the Vervain. 'What's this?'

Leo's face began to heat up. Laic chuckled. Leo felt the Vervain's arm around his shoulders. '*This* is new!'

Before Leo could move, Harl reached forward and thrust a hand between his legs. 'Is that a cock you've got there?'

Leo tried to edge back. Harl's fingers spread out and tightened. 'Whoa!'

Leo froze as a rough digit pushed against his hole, then thrust past his sphincter.

Harl chuckled. 'Good – I like my meat with a little spirit!'

Leo found himself hooked like a bowling-ball and drawn, thighs parted, towards the grinning figure. His cock throbbed, the swollen head poking over the top of the pouch.

'Am I gonna have fun with you! C'mere, ya –'

'Skinner's Rules, Harl.' Laic's soft words splattered on Leo's prickling skin. The finger withdrew itself. Leo stood there, knees bent, thighs still parted.

Scalp-locked Harl shook his head. 'Sorry... no idea...'

Leo's mind raced: Skinner's Rules...

'Hey Laic! Over here!' The familiar, cultured voice interrupted his flow of thought.

The Vervain sighed. 'Sorry, Harl – maybe later!' A hand on Leo's arse – 'Come on, dearie.'

Leo caught a smirk on Harl's face as he was steered right. The thong's strap was rubbing painfully between his arse-cheeks. He pulled at it.

A soft whisper in his ear. 'Don't – remember you're under Skinner's Rules.'

Leo sighed. They were walking in the direction of a table, at which a group of men were playing cards. A grizzly-looking guy, a melanised symborg, a shaven-headed Arcadian and a fourth player, who Leo noticed with a combination of annoyance and apprehension, was the yashmaked Boss.

He also noticed, for the first time, the long laser-panel strapped to the rangy Kai's arm.

'What's that?' Leo paused, looking down into pink eyes.

Laic's hand patted the collar around Leo's neck. 'That's employers' insurance, dearie.' The voice was a whisper against the surrounding guffaws. 'One wrong move and you're ex-meat... and the Boss gets his investment back in bone-weight. Skinner's Rules.'

Any thought of escape deserted Leo like fleas from a corpse. He followed Laic as the Vervain sauntered over and leant on the shoulder of the grizzly-looking man. 'I'll bring you luck, daddy.'

The man laughed, patting Laic's lanky arse. 'I could sure do with some!'

The Kai chuckled. 'Luck's got nothing to do with it, Mantu – this game requires skill. Don't you agree, meat?' His arm encircled Leo's waist and a finger rubbed the strap of his thong. The Kai talked on. 'Luck's a different matter altogether, Mantu. It was luck that I happened to be at that auction tonight – eh, meat?'

Lucky for whom? Leo opened his mouth – then remembered Skinner's Rule Number Eight – and swiftly closed it again.

Another low chuckle. 'Looks like I bought myself a goldfish – not got a tongue in your head, meat?'

Leo's heart began to thump. 'Of course I –' He yelped as rough fingers grabbed his hair and pulled.

In the background, more laughter. Leo bit his lip.

'Skinner's Rule Number Eight, meat – remember?' A powerful, musky smell drifted up from the Kai's body.

Leo risked a nod. His head was pulled back further.

'No movement without permission, meat – Skinner's Rule Number Five!'

Leo remembered the broad control-panel on his Kai employers' wrist. One wrong move... Leo tried to relax, to slow his heart. He couldn't. His neck ached, the roots of his hair strained. One wrong move...

After what seemed like an eternity his head was released. Leo's scalp burned painfully. He was trying to ignore the increasing tightness in the thong's scanty pouch when the grizzled man's laugh cut through the haze.

'C'mon, honey – help me get the better of this ridge-faced bastard!'

Leo took a step. A hand seized the back of his thong.

'The new meat stays with me, Mantu – Skinner's Rules,' said the Kai.

Sweat trickled from Leo's brow. Seconds later he found himself perched uncomfortably in his debentor's lap. He looked across at Laic. The tall Vervain smiled, then shrugged. A hand slipped around Leo's waist and settled on his crotch. Leo inhaled sharply.

Mantu grinned across from the other side of the table and winked. 'What's a honey like you doing in a dump like this?'

Leo frowned. Trying to work out what the hell he could do to get out.

'He's learning Skinner's Rules, aren't you, meat?' A finger eased itself into the thong's pouch.

Leo flinched. 'Yes, I'm learning –'

A hand grabbed his throat, and squeezed. 'What did I tell you about unauthorised use of a hole, meat?'

Leo looked for Laic, but the Vervain's pale face was buried somewhere in grinning Mantu's lap. Stars spangled before his eyes. His air-supply lessened under the force of the grip. Everything started to fizzle around him. Something stirred in his own lap, causing his cock to pulse against his Boss's index finger. The Boss laughed, relaxing his grip.

Leo gulped for breath, head spinning at the oxygen rush. Blood poured into his face. He swayed, then felt an arm around his waist, pulling him back against a hard, ridged stomach. Fighting the feeling he was about to pass out, he focused his attention on the Boss's cards, which danced before his eyes. He waited until the jitterbug became a more manageable foxtrot. Two pairs. Both face-cards.

Leo stared at the pile of credits on the table. The Kai pushed a further heap into the pot. 'I'm gonna take everything you've got, Mantu!'

The grizzly-face smiled. 'Ya think so?' He nudged four shining credits into the pot, equaling the stake.

The arm around his waist tightened. 'Any tips, meat?'

Leo bit his tongue and remained silent.

The Kai laughed. 'Aw... the meat's sulking!'

Mantu chuckled. 'C'mon – I'm feeling lucky tonight!'

'I've told you before, Mantu: luck's got nothing to do with it.' The voice was different: low, unlaughing.

The hand on his balls tightened, then squeezed. Leo howled,

and leapt up. Cards flew everywhere. An open palm impacted with his right cheek.

'Skinner's Rules, meat – no unauthorised use of a hole and no movement without permission!'

His face tingling, Leo fell to his knees and began to pick the cards up. A hand slapped his bare arse.

'I said no movement without permission!'

Leo froze. His arse-cheeks smarted; his balls ached. He remained there on all fours, eyes closed, while gnarled fingers gathered up the cards.

A cultured whisper in his ear: 'Skinner's Rule Number Six, meat: never forget a face!'

Groin throbbing, mind reeling, Leo remained silent.

The cultured voice was louder now. 'Want back onto my knee, meat?'

Leo wanted to crawl away into a corner.

His tormentor laughed. 'Okay – stay there then!' A booted foot prodded his arse.

Leo whimpered with pleasure. His eyes shot open. He stared. Feet. Everywhere were feet. Work boots. Trappers' sandals. Sandshoes... Leo inhaled sharply as one booted foot was raised, then planted on the other side of him. The Boss moved his feet closer together. Leo whimpered. On hands and knees, he turned his head to stare at his boss's right foot. Sixteen eyelets of weathered drongo-skin. Twelve inches of hide lacing. Four sets of buckles, which were pressing themselves into his flesh. Leo inhaled sharply. Something other than air flooded his brain.

Ten months ago, in a Pre-Fab casino on the other side of the planet, he'd admired those same boots while exchanging two useless cards with an unbeatable pair from a hollow panel in the sole of his own sabots.

A foot impacted in his guts. 'Up here, meat... you can do my boots later!'

Fingers which had executed a thousand sleights of hand shook as Leo remembered his opponent. Tall and handsome, in a rough sort of way.

'I said, up here!'

Leo's hands flew to the collar around his neck as a sharp tingling shot through his body. Seconds later, he was back in the Boss's lap.

The Kai sighed theatrically. 'Sorry about that, Mantu – meat-problems.'

A laugh from the other side of the table. 'No sweat, Boss – now, let's see that hand!'

Leo's brain was working better, after the mild electric shock: he had taken the handsome man to the cleaners that night, then taken him back to his room and extracted the outstanding balance in his own time.

Behind, a hard chest hardened further as the Kai laughed. 'Read it and weep, Mantu!' He spread the hand out on the table.

Mantu stared, then laughed good-naturedly. 'You're too good for me, Boss.'

Leo flinched as two arms reached around him, gathering up the winnings. A cultured voice in his ear: 'Yeah, I'm good – too good to need to cheat, eh meat?'

Leo's heart began to pound. Slowly, he turned his head, and found himself staring into narrow, hard eyes. He blinked.

The Kai laughed. 'And we all know what happens to cheats, don't we, meat?'

Leo gazed into blank eyes. He didn't know, but he could imagine... and that intrigued him more than the unfathomable Skinner's Rules.

The small room was dark. The words were darker. 'I think you have something which belongs to me.'

Leo grasped the cheap amulet which dangled between his nipples, tugged it free, then held it out.

A low laugh and quick fingers snatched it away. 'That's only the beginning, meat!'

Leo listened to the sounds of undressing. The smell of stale sweat drifted into his nostrils. The pouch was still uncomfortably tight. Silently, heart pounding, Leo moved back as a dark shape moved closer. 'Listen... I'll return your money as soon as I can –' he knew he was babbling '– but don't call the cops and pleased don't call Immi –' The word turned to a grunt as a hand struck his face. Leo fell from the cot.

'Skinner's Rule Number Eight, meat – hole not in use!'

His body hit loose, dirty floor-boards. A laugh in the dark. 'I don't want your money, but you do have something else that's mine!'

Face scarlet, cock aching and cramped in the tight thong, Leo spat earth from his mouth. A foot impacted on his bare back, pinning him to the floor.

'Remember that night?'

The foot pressed harder. Leo gasped.

'Remember... afterwards?'

Leo tried to wriggle away. He failed. The foot released him. Something flared in the dark. Light appeared inches in front of his face. Leo raised his head. Dark eyes smiled at him. The hood was gone. The yashmak was gone. Leo stared at the full lips that had been around his aching cock ten months earlier. He raised himself onto hands.

'You thought you took from me, didn't you?'

Leo's cock twitched at the memory.

The full mouth laughed. 'Oh no, meat... you gave!'

Confusion filled Leo's head. Blood continued to fill his cock until he felt it might burst.

The ridged forehead creased further in the light from the xenon flare. 'And you're gonna give again – as often as I want you to.'

Leo's stomach churned. His mind reeled with memories of that night.

'Because we both like games, but you don't play fair. You left without telling me your name.'

He could feel the Kai's hot breath on his face. 'The name's Leo – and I play by my own rules.' He dragged his eyes from the Kai's dark pools and glanced at the laser-panel which still covered the muscular right forearm.

The Kai followed his gaze then laughed. 'John... John Skinner – and so do I!'

Surprise was on the Kai's side as, seconds later, Leo found himself astride a hard belly. He stared down. 'What the –?' A rough finger reached up to stroke the hollow of his throat. Then a hand covered his open mouth.

'Hole not in use – remember?'

Another hand gripped Leo's waist, pulling him forwards. The rough surface of Skinner's belly caressed the skin of his arse. His balls tightened. He leant down, rubbing the length of his cock against the hard, ridged belly. Skinner trembled. Leo savoured the frisson as it tingled up his shaft. He threw back his head and moaned. The hand over his mouth tightened.

'Unauthorised use of a hole AND movement without permission!' The voice was hoarse.

Seconds passed. Minutes. Skinner's cock throbbed against the inside of Leo's thigh.

'Hole in use!'

Rough fingers tore the nano-thong from around Leo's aching shaft. He was pushed forward again, his length sheathed by a warm, soft cave. Knees buried in sweating arm-pits, he licked the hand over his mouth and laced his fingers behind Skinner's neck. The Kai moaned and began to suck.

Leo's stomach lurched. Two engorged nipples rubbed against his thighs. The xenon flare flickered and faded. Darkness. A low groan seeped into his ears.

Leo began to move, pushing into dark warmth, pulling

Skinner's head up to meet his pubes. The Kai's straining neck-muscles pulsed beneath Leo's laced fingers. A tongue moved along his shaft, then under, then around the head, pausing to flick into his slit.

Leo bit the hand over his mouth and undulated lower, grinding his balls against a bristling chin. Skinner drew Leo's cock deep into his mouth, thrusting back with his tongue in sync with the grinding.

Leo grunted, plunging downwards, until his aching balls spasmed and he shot, filling Skinner's mouth. Wet warmth splattered his arse-cheeks. The intensity of the release shocked him, draining strength from his muscles. He collapsed forward, belly impacting on the ridged forehead. Leo kissed the sweating palm as it moved from his mouth. Then fingers stroked his arse and he felt other ridges against his thigh – the laser-panel.

Limbs quivering, Leo pulled his still-hard cock from the Kai's mouth. A sharp tingle stung the back of his neck. Two strong arms held him in place as he shot a few last droplets onto the Kai's grinning face. Leo gasped. 'What was that for?' He sank into a ridged embrace.

A finger rubbed the back of his collar, then stroked his hair: 'Skinner's Rule Number Three: you give me it all!'

## BALL GAMES

Man! Why do I do this?

I wrap my arms around my chest and I try to hug myself warm. Way down the other end of the pitch, I can see a line of red and white. Don't ask me what's happening now: this weird game these guys call 'football' is a complete mystery to me.

I start to walk about a bit, trying to get my circulation going.

The whole country's a mystery to me. Been here two months and still can't understand half what the guys say. But there's one word I don't need translated: poof.

I stop walking, and kick a clump of dirt free from frost-hardened ground. Suddenly I'm real hot and sweat's prickling my face. Narrowing my eyes, I watch Shug kick the ball between the other team's goal posts. A whistle blows twice. There's a cheer and my heart sinks as two guys from our team rush up and grab him. His long red hair's come loose from the ponytail and I watch the way it flicks back and forward across his face. My mouth's dry as the two guys hug him. A couple of seconds later there's more guys around Shug and they've hoisted him onto their shoulders.

My heart's somewhere in my football boots. Ninety minutes of this, three times a week. Ninety minutes of freezing my ass off just to be near...

'Okay, Darren, intae the showers –' the coach is beside me, grinning, slapping my shoulder '– mibby ye'll see a bit more action next time – git a chance tae show aff they goalie skills!' He winks and jogs off down the pitch.

I make to follow him, then stop and pretend to tie my lace. Despite the freezing temperature, I can smell my own sweat... but no way I'm having a shower. Not yet.

By the time I reach the locker-room things have quietened down a bit. And I see it's still there – what Shug and a couple of his buddies were grinning at before the game. Someone's tried to clean it off, but the words are inscribed on my heart, ten feet high.

'Darren Young is a...'

I find a corner and start to undress. If I take my time the rest of the guys'll go. If I take my time I'll be late for lecture, but that's just the way it's gotta be.

Okay, so Dad's posting over here's only for a year. In ten months' time I'll be a high-school senior and back in sunny Greensboro, NC – back home. But no way these feelings are gonna go away, never mind where I am. And maybe I could live with that – and the loneliness – if it weren't for these stupid football games... and knowing the guy I really like really hates... poofs.

The sounds of laughter are way off in the distance. A couple of slowpokes are dressing in silence beside me. I try not to look at them, not wanting them to look at me. Eventually they leave; I take my towel and walk through to the shower-block.

The hot water stings my skin. Clouds of steam condense around me. I stretch under the jets, enjoying the burning needles on my face and shoulders. Then I grab the soap, and start to wash.

I've sort of filled out a bit over the summer, and I like touching my body when I'm alone. My nipples harden and tingle as I brush the tips... and somewhere below I can feel another tingle. Then a twitch. Closing my eyes, I think about Shug – his pale body, long muscled legs, tangled red hair... the way his chest is dusted with soft-looking ginger tufts.

I'm soaping my cock and balls, groaning as the hard shaft quivers under my slick hand. I try to draw myself back, but I can't.

Shug's face is filling my head... the way his green eyes twinkle when he smiles. But I know he'll never smile at me.

My right hand lingers on my cock, my left cupping my balls. Through the steam there's movement somewhere, but I'm miles away, stroking myself and there's only me and – another hand.

A dry hand. On my wet cock.

I nearly jump out of my skin! I take a step back and bump into something. Then the dry hand on my cock moves to cover mine, his other hand tight around my waist holding me steady. Or stopping me turning.

I moan as lips then teeth brush the skin of my neck and start to nibble. And I can feel a hard cock pressed against my ass. Before I know it, I'm grinding back against that cock while a rough hand starts to move my fingers up and down my shaft.

I gasp, shivers flying up and down my spine.

The shower's still running, pouring down onto us and lathering the soap. And over the sound of water I can hear our breathing... his and mine.

Christ, his hand's moving faster now, guiding mine, and I can feel the head of his cock dragging against the top of my ass-crack. Somewhere in the back of my mind there's thoughts – like, we're gonna get caught and who the fuck is this anyway? But the electricity in my cock and the moans in my ear sweep all that away.

He's jacking me furiously now, the arm round my waist holding me tighter. My head's against his shoulder, my free hand twining into his soaking hair and I can feel his thighs behind mine as he bends his knees, thrusting up and along my ass-crack.

Everything's just water and flesh and muscle and motion.

Then my balls spasm unexpectedly and it feels like the top of my skull's blown clean off! Man, there's come all over my fingers... and my head's everywhere and nowhere all at once.

I'm vaguely aware of his hand leaving my cock and gripping my waist as he starts to grind more vigorously against me. My other hand moves up, cupping the back of his neck. He's moaning, muttering my name.

Seconds later the body behind me tenses and, as he grabs my balls and shoots over my ass-cheeks, I bite my lip, twisting his wet hair between my white knuckles.

His mouth is open on my neck, kissing and licking – then he's gone and I collapse to my knees, warm water already starting to wash him from my body.

When I finally open my eyes, all that's left of him is a mushy feeling in my guts... and the long red hairs twined around my fingers.

# BRONCO BILL

Link wiped his face and thrust the three hundred dollars into his back pocket.

The crowd stamped their feet and cheered their appreciation as he held up the cheap trophy for their inspection. Link grinned, mentally disregarding its hock-value and toting up this summer's earnings – seven-five from Tucson; three thou in Casper, Wyoming; eight in Great Falls, Montana; and two-three already here, and it was only Day Three of the rodeo.

Link tipped the brim of his hat to the crowd and ambled down the steps. Behind, a blast of amateur brass surged into 'America the Beautiful'. He glanced briefly at the massed red-and-blue ranks of the Bismarck Junior High Majorettes, before making his way to the bar.

Link leant against the bleachers, watching the procession of steers and bulls to and from the show-corral. Tired but invigorated, he took a sip of his beer, then held the bottle against his hot face. He nodded to a couple of guys, drank some more beer and stuck a thumb into his jeans-pocket.

Surprisingly, it was the little rodeos in the holiday towns which netted the most. The prize money was high, the tourists liked a show and the competition was usually non-existent.

'Excuse me...'

Link looked up at the two middle-aged women in skimpy halter tops clutching cameras. He touched the brim of his hat respectfully. 'Ladies.'

They giggled and blushed. 'We were wondering...' Skimpy-Halter-One nudged Skimpy-Halter-Two forward and raised her camera.

Link grinned. 'My pleasure.' He draped a well-muscled arm around sunburnt shoulders and pulled the blushing woman closer. The other fist held up the calf-roping trophy. The automatic shutter whirred a couple of times. The women swapped places. Link posed patiently, smelling two brands of perfume and one of gin. When they'd finished, he pushed his hat back on his head and bowed. 'Glad to have been of service, ladies...'

After waiting until the two women were ten yards away, he retrieved their folded paper and twenty-dollar bill from his belt. He stuffed the money into his back pocket with his other winnings and glanced briefly at the name and room number. He smiled then sniffed – God, he smelled like a buffalo! Tossing the beer bottle into a bin, he strode towards the bunkhouse.

At five bucks a night, it was no better or worse than most accommodation along the summer rodeo-trail.

He glanced at two young men in cut-offs, bandannas and personal CD-players, then threw the cheap trophy onto the bunk. He dragged off his dusty hide boots and socks. The muscles in his arms ached. He struggled out of the leather vest and check shirt then stood up to unfasten the buckle of his chaps. Footsteps behind told him the two kids were heading off to whatever kids did in Bismarck, North Dakota.

Link unzipped and peeled off his sweat-stained jeans. Grabbing his kit-bag and towel from the end of the bunk, he sauntered through to the showers. Early morning was a stampede and the hot water ran out after the first fifteen bathers. Mid-afternoon? That was a different story.

Link stepped out of his boxers, scratched his balls and stepped under a faucet. As soothing water poured over his head and shoulders, he grabbed the soap and began to wash. Lathering the bar between his palms, he rubbed at the coarse hair under his arms and down on his chest.

Heat seeped into stretched sinew. His skin glowed, muscle starting to relax. Link cupped his pecs, feeling nipples stiffen under soapy palms. He tilted his head up, letting water flow over his face and into his eyes. Hands re-lathered and moved lower.

Bootsteps behind.

Link turned, rubbed soap from his eyes and blinked. Late afternoon sun was streaming in through a skylight. He wiped his eyes again and peered. In the doorway, a figure. Tall. Dressed completely in black. Sunlight was reflecting off the tiles, glinting back onto a tiny silver skull which held the man's boot-lace tie in place.

Link grinned. 'Howdy!'

The figure nodded.

Link spat a mouthful of water onto the floor of the shower and grabbed his towel. He rubbed his face, then looked back at the man. He was still standing in the doorway, saddlebags slung over a broad shoulder, staring at him. Link's eyes travelled down the heavy pecs to a hard stomach. Then lower. Under warm jets of water, his cock twitched. The man in black turned back towards the bunkhouse.

Link closed his eyes. Water trickled into his pubes, teasing his uncurling cock. He returned to soaping his balls. The silky skin felt good in his hands, sliding under the lather. Link pulled back his stretching foreskin to wash under the rim. His shaft was stiffening in his fist, lengthening and thickening as he massaged and cleaned around the bulbous head.

Link bent his knees, reaching under to soap his crack. His finger brushed his hole. He shivered, parting his thighs wider to work a good lather up and into the dark crevice. His wet forearm dragged down his shaft, pulling the delicate skin back further. His balls tightened. Under his damp fingertip his pucker spasmed.

Steam was building up in the shower block, tiny droplets of spray arcing into rainbows as the sun lowered in the sky.

His cock was throbbing now. Link opened his eyes. He turned to face the tiled wall, one hand between his legs, the other around his shaft. He held his meat loosely, dragging down towards the root. Each time he pulled his foreskin back up, arrows of pleasure pierced his guts.

His knees buckled. One hand braced against the stall wall, he jacked faster. Water coursed over his head and shoulders, flowing over his chest and back and washing a new layer of sweat from his hot skin. He could hear his own groans over the noise of the shower, feel the tension mounting in his nuts.

Fingers clenching into a fist, Link gasped and fell to his knees, shooting his load over white tile. He stayed there, breathing hard and coaxing two then three wads from his cock. The temperature of the water was dropping. With a shaking hand he reached up, and turned off the faucet.

Silence.

Then a slow hand-clap. Link felt his skin redden further. He scrambled to his feet and turned. The room was darker now, the sun having moved on. He stared into amused blue eyes.

'Ya put on a good show, boy.' The man's gloved hand slipped into his pocket, then tossed three green bills onto the floor.

Link was still scarlet-faced as the sound of lizard-skinned cowboy boots faded back into the bunkhouse.

The man was leaning against the end of a bunk, casually smoking a cigarette.

Link strode up to him. 'What's this supposed to mean?' He threw the dollar bills into a vaguely amused face.

The man laughed. 'Keep it – you earned it, like you earn all your –' his eyes flicked to the trophy '– prizes.'

Link scowled.

The man winked, and made to turn away. Link grabbed his shoulder. Muscle tensed under his hand. 'You got some sorta problem, buddy?'

Strong fingers gripped his bare arm in return. 'You're the one with the problem!' Full lips spat the word into Link's face.

Suddenly aware he was still naked and dripping, Link released the shoulder.

The man's fingers continued to grip his biceps, digging in. 'I've seenya prancing around in those shop-bought chaps and vest, playing to the crowd and charming the ladies –'

'Now just you hold on a –'

'Think being a cowboy begins with a hat and ends with a pair of boots?'

Link found himself staring into cold, blue eyes. 'Hey, I gotta livin' to make too!'

The Stetson shook slowly. 'Guys like you come and go with the tourists – ya ain't gotta clue what it's all about, have ya?'

Link shivered. Rage and embarrassment coursed through his body. 'Sure I do!'

The man snorted, relaxed his grip and flicked the cigarette from his lips. 'Leave rodeos to the real cowboys, kid.' He turned and strolled towards the door.

Link listened to the clink of spurs and the rhythmic tap of boot heels on the bunkhouse floor.

In the bar, later, the grizzled ranch-hand laughed and held out his glass for the third time. Link refilled it.

'Sounds like ya just met Bronco Bill!'

Link frowned. 'Who?

The ranch-hand winked. 'Ol' Bill's well-known round these parts, buddy. Been doin' the rodeos since he was fifteen, I guess –' the grey head bobbed up and down '– yes, sirree! Taken every bronco title in this here state for the past... twenty years!' Rheumy eyes fixed his, then flicked hopefully to the bottle of rye which sat on the bar. Link ignored the hint, fingers tightening around his own glass.

The old man rambled on. 'Ain't no one can tame a stallion like ol' Bronco Bill – the last real cowboy, guess you could say!'

The glass trembled in Link's fist. He stood up and walked from the bar.

Next day, he took prizes in three of the sharp-shooting events. Bill took the other three. He also beat Link's time in the steer-wrestling event by two seconds. Link bettered the older man by 1.01 in the roundup category. He studiously ignored Bill throughout the day.

That night, Link turned down three invitations from blowsy female horse-groupies to visit their respective motel rooms. He politely refused twenty dollars and the offer of a blow-job from a well-built ranch-owner in a pair of Levis which hardly contained the man's excitement.

Link exercised. He visited the corral, where Tornado, tomorrow's bronco, was pacing and snorting like the wild beast he was. Link watched the restless animal, staring at the foam of defiance which flecked its flaring nostrils.

Then he showered, shaved and threw himself on his bunk. Link didn't sleep for three hours. And when he did, he dreamed of tall men in black leather with glinting skull-clips and wry smiles.

At 2:15 the following afternoon Link was rubbing sweat and grime from his eyes. His thigh-muscles quivered after the strain of gripping Tornado's thrashing back. His arms felt like lead. A dull ache was building up in his shoulders from where they had impacted with the baked earth. He sat in the competitors' enclosure, trying to get his breath back.

Forty-eight seconds: a personal best. He grinned.

Fifteen yards away, a figure in black lowered himself onto

Tornado's still-bucking back. Four ranch-hands were attempting to hold the stallion still. Link stared at the steam which poured from the horse's nose, watching the way the animal tossed and quivered as Bill tried to get a grip on the flailing black mane. A silver glint caught his eye, then the buzzer sounded and the gate was open.

The crowd surged to its feet, roaring and cheering. Hands resting on knees, Link's fingers tightened as Bill and Tornado writhed and skittered around the corral.

The ten-second buzzer sounded. Encouraged or startled by the noise, Tornado reared up ninety degrees, forelegs pawing dry air. Bill was crouching low on the stallion's back, face almost pressed into the animal's mane. Even at this distance, Link could see his long hard muscles flex as the rider clenched the horse's flanks in an iron grip.

The twenty-second buzzer sounded. The crowd roared again. Link's fingers tightened on his knees. Tornado began to live up to his name. Hooves kicking in all directions, the horse went into a spin. The crowd was on its feet. Ropy arms gripped the stallion's neck more tightly. Bill flattened himself completely against the animal's back, lean hindquarters parallel with an ebony rump. Rider and mount had almost disappeared in a storm of dust and sand. Beneath denim and leather, Link's fingers found bone and dug in.

The thirty-second buzzer sounded. A swirling mass of man and horse was galloping around the corral. Tornado's snorts and whinnies of outrage soared over the cheering crowd as he tried to dislodge the man on his back. People were stamping their feet in rhythm with the frantic beat of hooves on dust.

Link barely heard the forty-minute buzzer. He watched, mesmerised. A shape appeared out of the whirling grit. The crowd gasped as Tornado lowered his head and kicked up his back legs. Bill clung on with arms alone, leather-clad legs flailing as the horse attempted to throw him again and again.

Link stared at the angle of Bill's body, the cowboy's spine twisting and thrashing. Tornado slumped to his knees, forelegs buckling in what looked like defeat. Then the horse rolled. Link leapt up, vaulted over the corral wall and charged towards the centre of the dirt-vortex. Crushed under fifteen hands of writhing stallion was no end for...

The one-minute buzzer sounded just as Bill emerged from the centre of the dust storm, fingers of his right hand twisted in the thick mane. Link stared.

The crowd was throwing hats into the air. Dollar-bills rained down around Bill as he led the bronco, head lowered, back towards its enclosure. The air was filled with the sounds of cheering, and the smell of damp, overheated horse. Link followed.

As Bill handed Tornado over to the ranch-hands, Link heard his deep voice. 'Get a blanket over him. Fast. And don't give him anything to drink until he's cooled down completely.' The grime-encrusted figure turned. Link caught a glimpse of the skull tie-clip and blazing blue eyes. He lowered his head.

The smell of Bill's body was hot in his nostrils as the man in black mounted the steps to collect the thousand-dollar prize money.

The barn dance was in full swing.

Alone in the bunkhouse, Link packed the last of his stuff into his rucksack. No point in hanging around until morning: next stop Grand Junction, Colorado. The money would have been nice – he couldn't deny that. But it wasn't the money that hurt. Link scowled and reached for his boots.

'How much you made this summer?'

The voice made him jump. Link looked up at the tall, bare-chest figure. His throat was suddenly desert-dry.

Bill produced a thick bundle of bills and laid them on the bunk. 'Fifteen thou here. Wanna wager everything in one last event?'

Anger flared in Link's guts. He unzipped his money-belt, tossed fourteen thousand dollars in cheques and bills beside the other bundle.

A low laugh. 'You're a spirited colt. But you're no Tornado. Throw me, and it's all yours.'

Link's cock pulsed against the seam of his jeans.

'I break you –' his ice-blue eyes stared into Link's '– and it's all mine.' Bill began to pull off his boots.

Link clenched his fists, watching. The guy was a good ten years older, skin and muscle weathered by countless summers and countless rodeos. His pecs were sculpted bronze, the sinew tailing down over a ridged belly to a patch of dark hair which sprouted from the unzipped V of his jeans. Beneath, the swollen, bisected head of a thick cock loomed up at him. Link laughed. 'The last real cowboy, eh?' His fingers tore at his vest then his shirt.

Seconds later, they both stood naked, each staring at the other's body. The kiss took Link by surprise. Shoved back against the bunkhouse wall, a hot tongue explored his open mouth while six hard inches pressed into his belly. Bill was holding him there with his weight, rough hands running up and down his body.

Link cupped Bill's solid ass-cheeks and returned the kiss. He pushed forward, levering himself from the wall. Hips thrust against hips. Bill's hands paused on Link's waist, gripping hard flesh. He tore his mouth from Link's.

They stood there, inches apart, cock brushing cock. Link's heart felt like it was about to leap out of his chest. He looked down at Bill's meat. The fat rod of flesh stretched up defiantly towards him. Link released an ass-cheek and seized the challenge, eyes on Bill's face. The weather-beaten features contorted to something neither a scowl or a smile.

The cock pulsed in Link's fist. He grinned, increasing the pressure of his grip. Then he felt something hot and tight on his chest. His back arched and he moaned as strong fingers began to twist his nipples. Link stared into ice-blue eyes. His own cock was so hard it hurt.

Bill laughed through clenched teeth. 'Not so tough now, are ya?'

Link scowled, sliding his fist down six inches of throbbing gristle to large, tight balls. The laugh was cut short.

Link's nipples burned. Then his legs were kicked from under him and his ass hit the bunkhouse floor. Bill pinned both his arms above his head with one large hand. The other was gripping Link's cock, pulling the meat out and away from his tight belly, rolling a rubber over the shaft. Bill held him there, thighs clenching his flanks, then slowly lowered himself onto Link's cock. Link stared, watching the last real cowboy take the top of the large, damp head. Bill's eyes were closed, features frozen in concentration. Link grinned, and bucked his hips. The tip of Link's meat plunged into Bill's ass-hole.

Trying to ignore the sensations in his shaft, Link laughed and twisted in Bill's iron grip, the first around his wrists, the second clenched around his cock. Bill frowned, easing the next two, four, then all six inches into his ass. Then Bill's rough hands separated Link's wrists, pinning his arms a yard apart. He stared up at the sweating figure impaled on his cock. Beneath his spine, the bunkhouse floor was warm and wet.

Ice-blue eyes fixed his. 'C'mon then, cowboy. Buck me!'

Link arched his back, feeling his balls press against the cheeks of Bill's ass. Arms pinned to the ground, he began to thrust with his hips. Bill rode him like he'd ridden Tornado, gripping on with muscle and sheer determination.

Link tried not register the way Bill's ass-muscles caressed and teased his aching shaft as he reared up against the quivering, weather-beaten body. Every now and then, his tensed abs brushed the head of the other swollen cock. Link's thighs trembled with the effort of control. His ass-cheeks were two boulders against the bunkhouse floor as he clenched his muscles, trying to buck the last real cowboy with violent, unrestrained movements.

Bill was drooling pre-come from his slit. A ribbon of transparent lust joined the head of his cock with the skin of Link's belly.

Link smiled, thinking about the fifteen thousand dollars. Then pain screamed through his chest. Link gasped. His wrists now free, he tried to wriggle away from the fingers pinching his nipples. His chest and shoulders sprang up from the bunkhouse floor. Something tightened in his guts.

Then he remembered Tornado. Seizing Bill's sweating shoulders, Link gripped tightly and rolled. In seconds, Bill was under him, legs over his shoulders. Bill laughed, leaning up to snatch a kiss before gripping Link's ass-cheeks and rolling again.

Nostrils flaring, spit flying from furious lips, Link strained upwards, massaging the head of Bill's engorged cock with his belly as he heaved and flexed. His heels and shoulders were the only parts left in contact with the bunkhouse floor. The body above him stiffened. Link felt rippling deep in Bill's ass. He forced his mind onto the fifteen thousand.

Bill's hands gripped Link's ass-cheeks more tightly. Link closed his eyes, feeling his balls knit together. One of his fists moved to close around Bill's twitching cock and the other rolled a rubber over his own stiff length. Two moans echoed in the empty bunkhouse as a callused finger thrust itself into Link's ass. He thrust forward into a hot, pulsing tunnel. Bill's vicelike calves squeezed Link's thighs while his fingers pulled and tortured Link's left nipple. Link stared up at his rider, watching as Bill was thrown up and down the length of his cock.

Link's balls were spasming uncontrollably now. The fifteen thousand was retreating before him. He jacked Bill's meat furiously, first pulling off the condom and then pulling the foreskin right back until grim determination turned to unbridled pleasure on the bronzed face. His cock pounded up and into the ass of the man straddling him, wanting to split him in two, wanting to break him the way Bill had broken Tornado.

The hard brown body slammed down, flattening itself against him and trapping Link's fist around the shuddering cock. He could feel Bill's breath on his hair, on his face, in his open mouth. Then the warm air brushed his nostrils. Link howled and shot his load into the rubber inside Bill's ass. Hips convulsed under hips. Link shot again, breath still tickling his nose. His heart was pounding. His guts churned.

Warm stickiness oozed through the fingers of his cramping right fist.

Minutes later, Bill dismounted.

Link couldn't look into the ice-blue eyes. Sweat cooled on his hot skin. He watched the tall figure walk unsteadily toward his bunk, and the pile of stake-money. Bill seized the edge of the blanket, whipped it from the cot. Dollar bills fluttered around them. Link closed his eyes, shivering as Bill knelt beside him, draping rough fabric around his shoulders. Then an arm joined the blanket. Fingers stroked his hair. Link's limbs were rubber. He slumped into the embrace, sweating face resting against a hard shoulder, which began to tremble. Link frowned. Bad enough to be defeated – now he was being laughed at!

Bill chuckled. 'First thing ya learn as a farrier: if ya wanna tame anything, blow gently up its nose! Second thing ya learn: always look after your mount!'

Bill's arms tightened around him. Link scowled. 'You won – you broke me. Take the money.'

Bill kissed the top of his head. 'Third thing ya learn: no one really wins, 'cause there's always another event!'

The heat from Bill's body seeping through the blanket felt good. Link sighed.

'You've got a lot to learn, cowboy,' Bill said. 'And I think I might enjoy teaching ya!'

Link's sore cock twitched. He tilted his face upwards.

Ice-blue eyes twinkled down at him. 'Tell ya what – after you've cooled down, I'll buy ya a drink, an' we'll talk about it!'

# EVERY INCH A LADY

He hit the door with his shoulder and moved out of glaring mid-day light.

'Jimmy's' was quiet, and comfortable, and cool – everything Bruce wasn't. The wad of hundred-dollar bills squirmed in his pocket. He rubbed his face, running his hands up onto his scalp. Cold sweat had gathered in his ponytail, trickling an icy trail down the back of his neck.

Dry-mouthed, Bruce narrowed his eyes and scanned the smoky gloom. Three bulky figures in plaid shirts lounging at the bar; Jimmy herself, polishing glasses; a couple in the far corner. His eyes travelled on over to the pool-table. Two players. One specta-tor – green dress; long, glossy red hair; scarlet lips slashed across an impossibly pale face. And the eyes – opaque, almost bakelite. She perched on a barstool smoking, one smooth leg slung over the other, apparently oblivious.

Bruce covered the ground between them, trying to keep his strides long and easy. The muscle-bound pool-players might be convinced she only had eyes for their game but Bruce knew better. Part of another game, part of the cool. He was sweating more than ever.

They'd been on his tail all day. He ran a hand over his soaking hair and scowled. 'They': he was thinking like some paranoid freak, but he couldn't help it. Some weird sixth sense was telling him someone was onto him, even though he knew he'd been careful.

Bruce focused on the lipstick-slash, as he strolled on through her line of vision and past the pool players. By the time he reached the wall, his cock was already up and around.

'Hello, baby.' Jade continued to watch the pool players.

Bruce let her voice waft into his ears over the click-click of white-on-blue-then-pink. The low drawl had a tranquillising effect, like the best high-grade junk. He studied the creamy outline of her breasts peeking over the low-cut neckline. Just enough to tantalise, not enough to tease.

Jade was every inch a lady.

He levered himself off the wall and moved a little closer. Even at this distance he could smell her perfume – that weird, sickly combination of sweet and slightly rotting flowers she always wore – Easter lilies and small, warm rooms. He inhaled and let the stink fill his head.

A low, husky laugh. 'It's been too long, baby...' She leant forward over green baize, elbows resting on the wooden surround.

He lowered his gaze and his voice, his eyes lingering on the curve of her ass beneath tight-fitting green silk. 'I need to -'

'Seems to me -' bakelite eyes flashed a warning at him over a flawless shoulder '- ya only ever come around when ya need somethin'.'

One of the pool players sniggered. 'Ain't that the truth, girl.' She winked at her opponent and wandered round the table. Bruce tried to chill. He watched the woman drape a huge arm around Jade's slim shoulders. 'Stick with us, honey -' meaty fingers pressed light imprints into shimmering silk '- an' maybe we'll let ya play!'

'An' maybe I'll let ya win again, Bobbie!' Jade laughed and wriggled away.

Bruce liked the way the silk wriggled with her, following every curve of her shape like a well-paid bodyguard. He liked lots of things about Jade, but knew there was one thing Jade didn't like about herself.

Bobbie and her friend grinned and exchanged glances, then resumed their game. Jade swayed over to the bar, six-inch heels clack-clacking on concrete. The sound called his cock to heel. Bruce followed.

'Everythin' okay?' He tried to keep the desperation out of his voice: Jade could read him like the cheap paperback he was. Bruce watched scarlet lips sip straight Jack Daniels through a candy-striped straw. It looked like Mountain Dew and she drank it that way. The red slash was an 'o' shape now, and every time the 'o' tightened, his hard-on inched a little further up his belly.

'Everythin's cool, baby.'

Bruce leaned forward, lifted his beer glass and wondered when his hand had started shaking. Warmth from Jade's body spread into his. He caught Jimmy's eye. She grinned. Bruce returned his gaze to Jade. He had no idea why she liked to hang around with dykes. He'd never seen her go off with any woman. Maybe she just liked the company. Maybe it was a female thing. He sat his beer on the bar, slid his hands onto her waist then down over her ass. 'Ya ain't... noticed anythin'? Anythin'... weird?'

'Baby, you worry too much.' The words seeped into his ears. 'Chill a little.'

He breathed in lungfulls of the sweet/sour perfume. Soft orange hair tickled his sweating face as he licked her neck. His mouth edged up towards a pink earlobe. 'I need to see it, Jade. I need to –'

'It's there.' The laugh came from so deep he could feel it tremble in her belly and spread into his own. Large, immaculately manicured hands settled around his neck. Fingers played with his ponytail. 'Don't ya trust me, baby?' A single nail traced a track up over his scalp.

'Everythin' okay, guys?' Jimmy's voice cut into his thoughts. His heart hiccuped. The blonde bartender grinned and eyed Bruce's barely touched bourbon.

Jade breathed excuses onto his panic-itchy skin. 'Too hot to drink. That right, baby?'

His cock fought with the waistband of his pants and it wasn't a fair fight. He was choking on rotten lilies. She moved her body in small circles, massaging his scalp with scarlet-tipped fingers. Hard, warm nipples pressed through the fabric of her dress and etched an outline on his shirt.

'We could go somewhere... cooler,' she said.

He could have sworn his cock nodded. His head followed seconds behind. When she pulled away he could still feel her imprint. Bruce swallowed a dry lump in his throat and tried to ignore the other hard lump two feet lower.

Jade exchanged a few low words with Jimmy. The tall blonde nodded imperceptibly. Jimmy liked her customers to be discreet, and ladies were always discreet. Jade finished her drink and took his hand in hers: it was soft and warm, and had one thing in common with the contents of his pants.

Bruce gulped down the rest of his bourbon and wished he could taste it.

Jimmy kept a couple of back-rooms for friends, and business. Bruce was never quite sure which category he and Jade fitted into. He strolled towards the familiar cot with its stained, multicoloured throw-over and sat down. He watched as she locked the door, placing the key on a glass-ringed night stand.

Bruce pulled the wad of damp dollar bills from his back pocket, slapping the money beside the key.

Today had been the last time. Forty thousand they needed. Forty thousand – give or take a hundred bucks or so – was what they had. Jade lifted the banded bills, flicked the wad in front of her face like a fan, then knelt. He stared at her green-silk ass.

Bruce had worked the numbers for Big Mac over two years now. Bruce was trusted. Mac never checked. Hell, he had a share

in half-a-dozen cheap clip-joints, plus other more legitimate busi-
nesses. Bruce knew Jade had worked hostess for him a while back.
She knew Mac's interests ran to unions, dope, hit-jobs... blow-
jobs. What was forty thou to a big shot like Mac? Bruce rubbed a
damp palm over his even damper face. He watched scarlet-tipped
fingers roll back the stained rug, lift the loose section of floor-
board and remove the tin cash-box. Taking a small key from between her breasts, Jade opened the cheap lock.

Bruce stared. Bakelite eyes raised to his. 'Tickets, passports –'
she smiled '– we're on our way, baby.' She pulled out a bundle of
notes and threw them into the air. 'All right!'

Portraits of past presidents fluttered in front of Bruce's face.
Jade threw another bundle above her head, just as his hand
grabbed her wrist.

'Whatcha doin'?' he said, alarmed.

'S'only money, baby! Let it fall!'

Green rectangles littered the faded rug. His guts turned over.
Bruce tried to smile. The money was hers – it was all for her. If this
was what she wanted...

The heat in the room and the closeness of her body was cook-
ing fear and panic into lust.

Jade laughed like a child, then began to gather the bills into her
lap. Green on green. Bruce focused on the smooth stretch of leg
between green hem-line and red ankle-strap, watching her calf-
muscle contract and relax. His eyes swept upwards. Everything
had a price. Jade didn't come cheap. What Jade wanted didn't
come cheap either. 'I did good for ya, yeah?'

She turned her head, fingers pausing. She laughed, and it
sounded different. 'Baby, you did real good.'

Bruce knew what his guts were telling him.

'Want me ta tell ya how good?'

It wasn't words he was looking for. And she knew it.

A smile played a familiar melody on the red slash. Jade stood up, towering over him. Scarlet-tipped fingers reached behind and began to lower the full-length back zip.

His mouth was drier than ever. Bruce took off his jacket, fingers fumbling like a schoolboy's as he tried to unbutton his shirt. He'd never seen her naked. When she blew him, they were usually both fully dressed. He felt honoured. His hand and paused on his belt-buckle.

The green sheath slithered to the floor.

Bruce grinned. Some women said he kept his brains in his pants. Maybe he did, but Jade didn't give a fuck about his brains now. Beneath stubby fingers, his cock pulsed like a second heart. And that was the way he liked it.

Bakelite eyes locked with his. Bruce tried to see behind the green, and failed. Every inch a lady, he never knew quite what Jade was thinking; if she was laughing at him or even thinking about him at all. And he kinda liked that too.

She stepped out of the dress and turned her back. The teddy's spaghetti-straps hung loose on her milky shoulders. His eyes drank in the silky fabric, then drifted down to her ass. Two pert mounds moved beneath satin. Light played on muscle as she leant forward to drape the dress over a chair.

His fingers remembered what they were supposed to be doing; Bruce ripped down his zipper and pulled out his cock. The hard meat bucked against his palm. A laugh drifted into his ears.

'No rush, baby – let me peel ya...' She walked over, knelt between his splayed thighs and began to ease his arms free of his shirtsleeves. Her voice made his nipples tighten and his heart dance a flamenco behind his ribs. Shirt-cuffs slipped over his wrists. Bruce raised his hands in surrender. Warm palms met his. Fingers twined. She drew him to his feet. His pants bagged around his thighs then his knees. The swollen head of his cock managed to find the fly of his boxers all on its own. Bruce looked down at the straining member, then back at Jade.

Milky skin and the flesh-coloured teddy merged into one smooth lake of cream. His skin tingled and crawled with ache for her.

Jade laughed again, pulling back as his mouth lunged for hers. A red curtain of hair swayed from one side to the other. 'Not yet, baby...'

His fingers tightened into fists.

She dropped to her knees and grabbed the root of his cock. A pink tongue flicked out, snaking over the sensitive, uncut head.

He clenched his teeth. Breath hissed from his lungs. Her bakelite eyes looked up at him through a veil of spider lashes. The tip of her tongue played around his slit. She darted forward, then withdrew just as quickly.

He shivered.

Her hands gripped the waistband of his boxers, easing up and over his shaft, then down past his thighs. Legs trembling, Bruce fell back onto the cot. The tops of her breasts sparkled with a sheen of perspiration. She whipped off the rest of his clothes then crawled towards him.

He was panting now, moisture trickling from his pits, soaking his dense hair. His balls were sweating, pulled up tight and sore at the base of his cock.

She passed her palm over his shaft, skimming skin by a fraction of an inch. He groaned, trying to thrust himself into her hand. Jade repeated the movement, tugging the invisible thread which joined her palm and his cock, forcing it to twitch upwards with every motion of the red-tipped hand.

She laughed, grasped his thighs and lowered her mouth onto him. His fingers dug deep into the thick scarlet mane. She licked him greedily root to tip, like he was a popsicle and she was hot and thirsty. Then she licked down again. Her tongue was flat and smooth as she lapped at his ball-sac, cradling each of his nuts in turn, then flicking down towards his ass-hole before sweeping back up to the tip. He was thawing in her heat. Tiny drops of pre-come leaked from his slit and the softness of her hair trickled through his fingers.

The flat tongue became a point. One hand slid down his shaft, dragging the foreskin back. His slit popped open as she squeezed, widening to admit the tip of her probing tongue. Bruce closed his eyes and wrapped his legs around her waist. The tongue flicked. He opened his mouth in a silent groan.

The tongue flicked again, pausing to explore the fleshy hole more thoroughly. Bruce thrust blindly upwards, thighs sliding on slippery satin.

One hand moved to his solid waist, holding him as she licked and sucked. He watched his cock disappear into then reappear out of her mouth. Spit coated his shaft like varnish. His balls knitted together and he gripped her head tighter, wanting to fuck her face till she screamed for his come.

But Jade was every inch a lady, and Bruce knew he'd come when she wanted him to and not before. She was crooning now, humming onto his cock through closed lips. The vibrations drove him wild. Bruce twined his fists in her hair as her tongue began the popsicle stuff again.

'Gotta get you real wet, baby...' She smiled up at him then kissed the large wormy vein on the under side of his shaft. 'We want that sweet cock of yours all nice and smooth.' She licked her lips, then removed a curl of pubic hair from between pearly front teeth.

He couldn't wait. Bruce growled, fingers tearing at the flimsy teddy. Tethered breasts sprang free, a breathy laugh following in their wake. Nipples buried themselves in the mat of his chest-hair. His arms went around her slim back; his lips searched desperately for hers.

Jade took his hot tongue into her mouth, sucking on it, feeding on him. Skin brushed skin. Bruce tasted pre-come and his cock took another leap. He shifted the kiss, grinding three days' growth against a smooth neck. His crotch thrust against a satin-encased belly. He could feel her heat, smell the lilies over the stench of his own sweat.

She pulled away, dragging herself down his body until her mouth found a nipple, and his cock found the warm valley between solid breasts. She began to rock, teeth nipping the delicate flesh, elbows braced against her sides. Jade fucked his shaft with her tits until he could hardly breath. 'Like that, baby?'

The answer remained in his lungs. Bruce knew he was losing it. She was fucking every part of him, head included. A hard nipple brushed against his glans. Something twisted and turned in his guts as adrenalin soared through his veins. He wanted to run... stay... run...

Next thing he knew, the floor hit his spine and Jade was on all fours in front of him, the scarlet curtain falling over her face and shoulders. George Washington stared at him from the back of her left thigh. Bruce tore the bill free. His cock stuck straight up. He was never as hard with anyone as he was with Jade.

Bruce wanted her on her back, vulnerable under him. But that wasn't Jade's way. He wanted to watch her face as he fucked her. But she'd never let him... not yet.

Bruce stared at her ass, still encased in cream-coloured satin. She swivelled her hips, thrusting back, then circling. The fabric gleamed in fifty-watt gloom, its contents hard and soft at the same time.

Bruce spat into the palm of his hand, coated his still-sticky shaft and rolled on a rubber, and then at last raised the wide-cut leg of her panties. Doggy-style. He leant the head of his cock against her hole. She moaned, pressing back onto him.

He gripped her waist, hands slipping up to clasp her breasts. He used his weight to enter her, pushing on in until his balls kissed rumpled satin. Jade sighed like a balloon with a slow leak. Deep in her ass, his prick inflated further. Iron muscles clamped like a vice, constricting and pumping him up at the same time. She felt good and tight around him, rippling over his cock like a tunnel of love.

She ground her hips, pushing back against his thighs. He nuzzled her neck and got a mouthful of scarlet hair.

'Fuck me, baby...'

Bruce was lost in a surge of lust. Nipples hardened further against his palms as he gripped her tits and started to move. He withdrew slowly, teasing himself and her, until the ring of muscle around the head of his cock was the only thing holding them together. She was breathing more easily, trying to follow his cock's retreat. He held her steady, then slammed back into the tight circle.

Jade liked her fucks man-rough. Sweat pouring from his forehead, he fucked her on a bed of America's greatest. He fucked her hard, long-dicking the tight hole with firm strokes until his cock hurt and salt stung his eyes.

His left leg was cramping. Bruce changed position, altering the angle of his thrusts to hit the small gland behind her bladder. He rammed the head of his cock against her prostate and felt the pleasure ripple up through her ass-muscles.

'Baby... oh baby...' Her voice was low, almost a whisper.

Bees hummed in his head. His balls were sore and hard. Bruce sank back onto his knees, pulling Jade onto his lap and fucking her there while she writhed in his arms.

His cock was burning. Rotten lilies merged with the stink of their bodies and became the sweetest scent on earth. Everything was hard and wet and warm and motion and... banging –

Bruce ignored the sound. His balls were about to explode. He buried his face in sweat-soaked scarlet hair and thrust into her one last time.

Then the door disintegrated and everything dissolved. Jade leapt from his lap. Bruce spurted into the rubber – except his cock wasn't inside her; it was mid-air. As his mind came back from orbit he turned his head to where the door had been. A pair of very large legs stood in its place. Bruce whipped off the rubber as fast as he could, spilling a bit, and raised semi-focused eyes up enormous thighs to a massive beer-belly and barrel-chest.

'Mac! What...?'

'Shut it, faggot! You!'

Bruce stared at his boss's huge, furious face.

'Yeah, you – ya piece a shit! You been skimming, shit face!'

Bruce considered denial. He looked down at the smear of come which dripped from Benjamin Franklin's bald head and decided against it.

'You fucked me over, piece o' shit!' The giant legs took a step forward.

Bruce gazed up. Mac himself seemed unarmed, but the two goons flanking him both held baseball bats in hair-trigger fists. Green flashed past his eyes.

Jade grabbed the dress from the chair, holding it in front of her breasts.

The giant legs took another step forward. 'Don't bother – we've all seen those silicon tits before. Still savin' up for the cock-job, freak? Not thinkin' of payin' for it with my money, are ya?' A hand whipped through the air.

Bruce found himself thinking it strange that someone Big Mac's size could move so quickly. Jade's scream cut the thought short. Bruce lunged at the massive man's massive knees. Big Mac swayed, caught unawares. Bruce held on, then something hit him. And hit him again. Through the agony he could hear more screams, but they sounded different, angrier.

Bruce released Mac's knees, covered his head and rolled into a ball in a dark cloud of pain. He was trying to get away when he heard the first shot.

Something large fell on him, trapping his legs. Bruce howled and tried to push it off. The second and third shots filled the room with noise and cordite, then silence. The crying started again.

Bruce managed to drag himself out from under Big Mac's dead weight. He crawled towards the sobs, palms sliding on the mixture of blood and come and dead presidents which covered the floor. He raised his head.

Jade was slumped against a wall, legs drawn up to her chin. Cream-coloured panties were ripped at the crotch. He glimpsed her cock, a small pink snail curled sleepily on top of plucked, hairless balls, like she plucked every hair on her beautiful she-male body. Between scarlet-tipped fingers, the pearl-handled revolver was still smoking.

Bruce pulled her to him. She cowered against him.

'I'm not a faggot! I'm not a freak! He shouldn't have... he shouldn't have...'

Bruce stroked her hair. 'Sweetie, you are – we both are – but who gives a flyin' fuck?' He was wondering if maybe he slipped Jimmy a couple of hundred she and the girls could get rid of the garbage before the cops came sniffing round.

The scarlet head turned from left to right. She started to sob again.

'Shh...' He held her tightly, tasting iron in his mouth. Bruce managed a bruised smile.

Jade wasn't quite every inch a lady.

His fingers slipped down to the pink snail and cradled two of those hormone-reduced inches.

Ladies didn't lose their temper and shoot people. He glanced one last time at the inert bodies of Big Mac and his henchmen. 'C'mon, sweetie. We got a plane to catch.'

# THE F-MACHINE

Sam flipped the eye-shield into place and checked the gas-mix. Fierce blue honed to a roaring transparency. Flame flooded his vision and seared his chest. He smiled, and pulled on the protective gloves. The smell of singeing hair joined with a muskier, unwashed odour. Sweat leaked from his pores, sheening the heavy musculature of his fore-arms and highlighting the throbbing veins in his neck.

Sam gripped the oxyacetylene torch and moved forward. He stared at the towering construction – ten feet of moulded, hand-hammered iron; five hundred astro-pounds of copper-coloured power. He hefted the rivet in the palm of his hand, inhaling the stench of newly forged metal: better than flesh; harder, more reli-able. Flesh let you down. Metal never would.

He tossed the rivet in the air and caught it. The iron nail was six inches long, designed and hand-wrought. Gripping the rod be-tween his teeth, Sam stared at the hole: one-inch diameter; wider than a man's tight circle of muscle; maybe as strong.

Sam pushed the thought from his mind, then spat the rivet from his mouth. Holding the head between thumb and forefinger, he kissed the cavity then slid the iron spike into the hole – a per-fect fit – and out again. In – Sam watched the forged rod caress the smooth circumference of the orifice – and out. In – sweat trickled from a dark pit – and out. In – tightening in his chest – and out.

He stared at his Machine – the mettle of a man – then slammed the rivet into place, and turned the flame up full. Showers of white-blue light sparkled from the dull metal and pierced the hide of his protective apron. Underneath, his pecs were pitted with dark freckles.

Iron began to liquefy. Sam seized the hammer. The tool felt good in his fist: well-balanced and satisfying. He raised his arm, drawing the shaft back over one glistening shoulder and held it there, enjoying the weight. Dark copper rose to red under the flame; then orange; then yellow. He felt the hammer's power deep in his guts. As the rivet bleached to a blistering white, Sam flicked the flame aside and brought the sledge down on the semi-molten head. The impact shimmered up his arm, fizzing in his shoulder and neck. The sound echoed around the forge – metal on metal.

Sam lifted his arm and delivered a second blow; a third; and a fourth. Muscle absorbed the clash. Tremors spread over his shoulders and onto his chest. Sam breathed heavily, the stench of ferrous heat and sweat flaring in his nostrils. The rivet blushed, its flattened, bruised head pounded seamlessly into the main body of the F-Machine.

Sam flicked the torch-control. The flame spluttered back to a fierce, colourless hiss. Metal cooled further, dulling the smashed rivet-head. After a few seconds, it was as if it had always been there.

Nipple tingling, he dropped the smith's hammer, switched off the oxyacetylene torch and moved back. Complete. He flicked-up the protective visor, removed the gloves and stretched out a blackened fingertip to stroke the still-warm surface. 'Beautiful. Hard and strong and...'

Sam gripped the wheels of his chair, spun round and hauled himself towards the door.

Sam lay on the bed, fists clenched by his sides.

The masseur's hands moved over his scarred body, from shoulders to chest. There was a faint tingling in his scorched nipple. He was reduced to this – agency-sluts: guys with strong stomachs and hard hearts.

'You're very tense.' The voice was surprisingly soft, soothing. It washed over Sam, an acid bath.

Long, skilled fingers paused at his abdomen, kneading the taut sinew. A muscle twitched, then began to pulsate in his belly.

A warm palm pressed itself against the throbbing area. 'Come on... relax.'

Sam balled his fists tighter, stubby nails digging into hard flesh. He glanced at the figure kneeling by his side. He was younger than the usual guys – nineteen, maybe twenty. White, flawless skin, narrow shoulders tapering down to a lean, lightly muscled back. Ponytailed, ginger hair which swept over one arm as his hands moved lower. Sensation ceased. As the boy continued to do his job, Sam tried to do his, and failed. Tendrils of tension twined into heavy ropes of rage.

Ten years ago in the fiery, sulphurous pits of Epsilon, he had a future, career-prospects. In the foundries, a man was judged by his output, his quota, the work he produced. A man was what he made.

Dull shadows of almost forgotten dreams teased his mind. Sam frowned. He wasn't a man. Not anymore. On the scrap-heap at thirty, so much unwanted, useless slag. White, arched-shaped circles were forming on the palms of his hands. No one's fault, according to the Medical Investigator's report. Just one of those things.

The sound of flesh on flesh filled the room as capable hands smacked and pummelled his body. Sam heard his legs eased apart. Flesh on flesh. Metal on metal. Iron had been his life. Iron and... men. Now he had neither.

A palm slapped his chest. 'Good! You're starting to unwind.'

Sam remembered other times, harder times, when his cock had pierced the bodies of men, a giant steam-hammer punching ingots out of semi-solid metal.

'You're tensing up again.'

Now men turned away from his useless flesh.

'Get loose.'

Sam bit his lip. The medics had been sympathetic, but unhelp-ful. He'd been offered drugs, then surgery, then prostheses – light-weight, easy to handle, labour-saving, comfort-giving.

Blood leaked from arc-shaped wounds on his palms. Sam had rejected their sops. If nothing else, he would still piss and shit like a man: no low-density, high-durability synthetic devices were gonna take that away from him.

The chair had taken two months to build. New legs... of iron. A man's metal. Now the F-Machine was complete – the mettle of a man.

'Ready?'

Sam opened his eyes. The boy was kneeling between his thighs. Large nipples the size of half-dollars shone with sweat. Sam wanted to look away from the symmetry but couldn't. The boy un-tied his ponytail. A shower of scarlet hair fell forward over a too-perfect face. He smiled, licked a finger and began to trace circles around his right nipple. Green pupils bored into Sam's. He broke the gaze, stared at the nipple, which was stiffening, stretching up from the pink surround. He switched his gaze to the rest of kid's underdeveloped pecs: hairless, like all the Agency-sluts.

'Do I turn you on?' The kid was circling both nipples now, pale lips parted in desire – two-hundred-Astro-dollars-an-hour desire. 'You turn *me* on...'

Sam's stomach began to pulse. He raised rough hands and clasped each side of the boyish waist. The skin was satin beneath scorched and cauterised fingertips. White thighs and belly framed a thatch of rust-coloured hair. Slim hips began to rotate.

'Touch me –' warm fingers grasped his hands and moved them lower '– here.'

Heavy muscle throbbed in Sam's forearms as his shaking hands settled around the boy's slim cock. The pulse in his stomach beat a drunken tattoo. The flesh was alien, unreal. Smooth. Perfect.

Sam thought of his own rod, of seven thick, flaccid inches which had become almost a foot of iron flesh when erect. He stared at the flawless torso, watched the slow, expertly paced lap-dance as the boy began to grind his balls against his scorched belly. Soft fingers released blackened flesh. Sam clasped the slick cock in one fist. A manicured index finger traced the blackened stump of his right nipple.

Sam scowled: this boy was good! Then a pink tongue flicked over charred flesh, silken hair wisping over his chest. Sam flinched: there was a time when that would have driven him wild. He stared at the crown of a ginger head, the kid's hard cock flexing in his fist.

Wetness traced a slick line towards his remaining nipple, as the kid sucked and tongued reluctant tissue and fused fur. Flesh on flesh. Metal on metal. Sam pressed his free hand against the gleaming head and pushed. Teeth grazed as the kid inhaled sharply. Sam felt the nip, and almost smiled.

The expert mouth edged down over his belly. A lightly muscled thigh swept over his arm. In one smooth, three-second movement Sam found himself staring at the kid's hole.

His wet nipple leapt to attention. Sam wound fingers in ginger silk, tightened his grip and dragged the mouth from between his useless thighs. The kid backed up onto his knees, the white, perfectly formed arse and crack looming closer to Sam's face. He continued to pull the kid back until the spasming pucker was almost directly over his nose. He inhaled. Man-smell.

His stomach tightened. Sam released the hair, seized the slim waist and positioned the kid. A smooth ball-sac caressed his chin. He rubbed three days' growth against delicate skin, registering the young man's flinch. He closed his eyes and lowered the arse. Flesh met flesh.

His hands slipped down, ten printless fingers spreading over two soft mounds, pushing, opening. Tight muscle thrust against tighter muscle. The kid's sphincter quivered, then bowed under the assault. Sam rammed his tongue deep into the hole. Flesh into flesh. Metal into metal... sweat... musk. Sam withdrew, spread the boy further and thrust again. Tingling mixed with knots of tension.

The kid was gyrating now, grinding onto heat-seared skin. Sam gripped white thighs, raised the arse and spat into a hairless crack. Catching the trickle of warm saliva with his tongue, he dove back into the hole, coating the warm tunnel with something of his own. Flesh into flesh. Metal into metal.

The kid began to writhe. Sam grasped a slick waist, set and kept the pace. He moved steadily in and out of the flexing muscle, tongue-fucking the ring with firm, relentless strokes. In the pit of his stomach, stirring. He frowned, thumbs moving, widening. Lips on arse-lips. Flesh on flesh.

Something wet dripped onto his chest. Sam slid his thumbs from the moist tunnel. The boy who sat astride his face hissed, then began to pant. Sam clamped his mouth around the spasming orifice, jack-hammering upwards. The kid jerked, then screamed. Molten protein splattered Sam's chest and belly as a tight ring of muscle clamped around his tongue.

'What's your name, kid?' A dry mouth licked come from his nipple.

'Josh.' A pale face looked up.

Sam stared into two green eyes.

'I still get paid, right?'

'Why wouldn't you?'

Josh hesitated. 'Because you haven't –'

'Didn't they tell you about me?'

Josh draped a slender thigh over an inert limb in a movement Sam watched, but didn't feel. 'I'm new – transferred over from Gamma. A few of the guys said you were weird, but harmless –' sigh '– I was expecting something kinkier.'

Sam grinned. The unfamiliar expression hurt his face. 'Sorry to disappoint you.'

'Oh, I didn't mean... I mean, I –'

Sam slapped a soft shoulder. 'Forget it!' Surprisingly strong arms wrapped themselves around his chest.

'How long you been like this?'

Sam blinked. No one else had ever asked. 'Three years.'

A ginger head flicked up. 'Man, no wonder you're tense!'

Sam tried to look away from the piercing green gaze but couldn't.

Josh raised an eyebrow, then winked. 'Tell me what you're really into, and we can go again – special rate!'

Sam frowned, levered himself up off the bed, dragging Josh with him. He stared at the limp, spark-scarred cock between his thighs.

'Oh....'

Sam waited for the sympathy.

It didn't appear. 'That's a relief!' Josh laughed. 'I though it was me – that you didn't like me. I got my rep to think of – the Agency keeps me for the pervs, deformeds... and the weirdoes. '

Sam scowled. Something twisted in the pit of his stomach.

'Listen. I'm good – I'll get you off.'

He could smell Josh's body, taste him on his lips. The F-Machine's ferrous scent called to him from the forge. Agency-sluts were usually obliging, especially those who specialised in deformeds – Sam's hands slipped down to rest on his inert thighs – especially if the price was right. He dragged his body over to the side of the bed, easing his legs back into the chair. 'You give a good massage.'

Josh grinned. 'That's not all I can do!'

Sam touched blackened fingertips to hairless chin and tilted the boy's face upwards. 'I don't want you for sex, kid.'

The perfect face scowled and tried to pull away.

Sam gripped his chin. 'You up for a little extra-curricular activity?' He stared at lowered eyelids.

The ginger head nodded. 'That's why they keep me for...'

The deformed. Weirdoes. Pervs. Sam frowned, his hand slipping to grip the boy's throat. An Adam's Apple pulsed against his palm:

'Let me do you...' The words vibrated into his fist. Then soft hands gripped his forearms and Josh twisted free. 'I got my quota to make!'

The strength surprised Sam. The familiar phrase surprised him even more. 'You worked on Epsi?'

'Six months.' Josh rubbed his throat.

Sam laughed. 'Which department?' He stared into rich, green irises.

Josh raised an eyebrow.

'Welder? Rivet-man? Smelter? Stoker?'

Josh reddened. 'Er... kitchen. Then Admin.'

Sam laughed. 'A real man.' He watched the boy flinch, but hold his ground in silence. His mind flicked to the ten-foot structure waiting in the forge. The words almost stuck in his throat. 'I need help, Josh.'

'You sure do!' Pink lips parted in a smile. 'Whatever you want, I'm up for it.'

'Get dressed.' Sam spun the chair round and drove towards the door.


'Wow! What is it – some sort of art?'

Sam stared at his creation. 'Not art.' Though forged by an artisan.

'Can I touch it?'

Sam glanced from one set of perfect features to another. 'Go ahead.' He moved back, allowing full access to the construction. His eyes narrowed.

The boy moved like a sheet-steel feeder, efficient and graceful. Josh circled the F-Machine, pausing to finger a bolt, stroke a section of particularly smooth iron. He touched each flank, then sank onto his hunkers to caress the configuration of angles which made up the feet.

Something familiar and almost forgotten rose in Sam's chest – pride. A foundryman was what he produced. A man was what he made.

Josh ran fingers over the forged bonds and slender straps that would hold the participant in place. Pale hands moulded themselves around the ten-inch cylinder. The boy moved back, groping for foot-grips, then turned his head, peering back over a muslin-draped shoulder. His thighs were clamped astride the projection, soft fingers gripping an iron waist.

'He's amazing!'

Sam bowed his head, accepting the compliment.

'Kinda like... occupational therapy?'

Sam shook his head. 'More than that.'

The boy slipped from the restraints and strolled back to behind the chair. Sam felt hands on his shoulders.

'You're tensing up –'

He shivered. 'You want to help me or not?'

Strong fingers kneaded knots of iron.

'Sure – let's see the colour of your money.'

The forge sparkled with light and cold fire.

Sam hunched naked over the anvil. The cylinder turned red. Sam smiled, raised the smith's hammer then brought a solid sledge of iron down hard. A shower of crimson sparks flared then oxidised to smoky dust. Stray spray flicked across his chest and neck. Fiery fragments sizzled on skin, filling the air with the smell of burning protein.

Sam turned the tongs, rotating the hollow tube through one hundred and eighty degrees, then flicked the flame to the lower side of the ten-inch metal dildo and pounded a second time. Colours shimmered, rising in a cloud of ferrous haze which singed his brows. Tiny specs clung to his torso, pushing their way through the already-blackened upper layers of his skin.

Sam blinked through a mist of steam, and redirected the flame. The iron sledge quivered in mid-air before it fell again – metal on metal – sending cascades of fire over Josh's pale arms. Sam watched tiny speckles sizzle and sparkle on flawless skin. The boy didn't flinch. Metal on flesh. Flesh on flesh. Sam's nipple ached. The tube glowed.

Sam dropped the hammer and extinguished the flame. 'Now!'

Powerful hands slipped under sweating thighs and heaved.

Progress was slow. Sam was heavy, the design of the codpiece elaborate.

One fist clenched, the other guided gloved fingers down between his legs. The sizzle of still-hot metal on flesh. Sam responded to the sound, nostrils flaring with the stench of smouldering. Josh's hands eased flaccid flesh into place, buckling metal straps around his waist. Something tingled in Sam's belly. Then a voice in his ear:

'Five hundred, you said?'

Sam managed a nod. For the first time in three years, he felt... whole. The smells. The sounds of metal on metal ringing in his ears. The rigid feel of something hard and powerful between his thighs. The overwhelming presence of... the F-Machine.

Josh's ponytail brushed his face. 'What next?'

Sam smiled. 'Second lever – just behind you.'

Bolts slammed into the concrete floor, pinning the chair in position. Chains raised, pulling his arms rigid. Sam checked as the boy secured iron struts across heat-seared pecs, then shivered.

'Okay? What do I do now?'

Fire pulsed in Sam's belly: he had waited three years for this. 'Now you can get outta here.' His hands gripped the cold steel, slicking and warming the smooth metal. He looked up at ten feet of metal man, then across at Josh's slender outline.

A ginger eyebrow raised itself over an amused green eye.

'Your money's over there.' Sam indicated the worktable. 'Take it and go.'

Josh laughed, flicked the tip of Sam's bud with a finger. 'I'm not going anywhere.'

Sam stared at the worktable. Beside a pile of purple currency – the remote control. In the heat of the moment, he had omitted to... his head whipped back to the Agency-slut.

Josh smiled. 'Told you – I got my quota to make!'

Sam watched the elegant figure stroll over, and lift the device. He scowled. 'Give it to me.'

Josh turned the black rectangle over and over in his pale hands. 'Come and get it!' He threw the device into the air, catching it effortlessly.

Sam arched his back. Straps dug into his wrists and his fingers clenched around the hard metal of his armrests.

Josh walked towards him, waving the remote-control. 'You can't, can you?'

Sam lunged forward, responding to the sneer. Bonds of iron dug into the pitted flesh of his heaving chest.

Josh grinned. 'Know what they call me on Gamma?' One hand moved to filmy shoulder-straps. Guts throbbing, Sam watched as the muslin garment slipped to the ground. 'The Fuck Machine.' Josh traced a line down a smooth, hairless belly.

Moulded iron struts tightened across his chest. Sam bit his lip.

Josh sauntered closer, trailed a finger along the cylinder of iron strapped between Sam's thighs.

Tightening in his guts.

Josh smiled. 'They say I can raise the dead –' fingers crawled over Sam's fuzzy belly '– coax come from a stone –' a damp palm covered the burnt-out remnant of a nipple '– make iron from the limpest dick.' The damp palm began to circle, then five fingers flexed. 'You and your stupid machine.' Sam bucked as nails dug into his skin. 'You and your stupid iron cock!' Josh laughed and skipped away.

Sam was panting, pools of sweat forming, overflowing and trickling from flesh onto metal. The more he struggled, the more the strange sensation in his guts increased. Pins-and-needles prickled between his thighs. Josh was behind him now, rubbing the hard flesh of his ore-blackened shoulders. Sam heard rustling. He knew the boy was undressing completely. Something wet, warm and solid poked the back of his neck. A slim, well-manicured hand dangled a black rectangle in front of his eyes.

'Think this is gonna do it for you?'

Sam made a grab with his lips.

Josh snatched his hand away. 'Think HE'S gonna do it for you?' He nodded toward ten feet of metal muscle, then tapped Sam's nose with the remote device and sniggered. 'Oh no, Mister Foundryman.'

A vein pulsed in Sam's neck.

Josh aimed the remote device at the F-Machine and pressed. Metal ground on metal. One iron strut slid slowly forward.

A laugh. 'He's some mover... NOT!' Josh turned, aimed the remote a second time. 'Hey, this works you too?'

Sam's head spun. Iron struts flicked smoothly past his vision as the chair's back rest slid through ninety degrees.

A low voice in his ear. 'You're quite a pair!'

Sam lay on his back, feet and wrists secured, legs raised above his head.

'I ask for defos – wanna know why, Mister Big-Butch-Foundryman?'

Sam flinched, sweat trickling up bulging forearms. He couldn't take his eyes from the ten-inch metal dildo lying on his belly. He could see his balls, two swollen sacs of rage and frustration pressed against a smooth curve of moulded iron. A ginger-haired vision slipped between his exposed arse and the F-Machine.

Josh tapped a pale forehead. 'Cos with defos, it's all up here –' he smiled '– and that's where I fuck best!'

Sam scowled. Josh giggled, and aimed the remote. Sam found himself upright again.

The boy was strolling around the construction now, running the remote device over the F-Machine's ribs. He slapped hard iron buttocks, drumming the black rectangle against broad, metal pecs. Sound reverberated around the forge. Josh's voice rose above the cacophony.

'Just another cage, man – like you think that stupid body of yours is.'

Sam tried to twist his neck and look away, but straps held

him fast.

'What were you gonna do – fuck it? Fuck yourself?'

The voice was everywhere.

'It's already done that – really fucked you, Mister Foundryman!'

Something pulsed in Sam's brain, reverberating in his nipple. Everything was too tight! Wrist-restraints bit into flesh; the straps across his chest buried themselves in melted hair.

'So... we're not gonna need this.' Josh tossed the remote device over his shoulder. The intricate, state-of-the-art instrument bounced then shattered on a concrete floor. Josh laughed. 'Or this!' He leant over and began to unbuckle the iron codpiece. Sam's nipple tingled as damp balls brushed against his thigh. Deft fingers slid metal from metal, then eased the cylinder up. He inhaled the stench of burning flesh and a deeper, muskier smell. Josh swung the ten-inch cylinder back and forth in front of his face mockingly, then let go. The hollow dildo slammed off a steel wall.

Sam's fists quivered. He squeezed his eyelids shut. No... No... Then sound filled the air. New sound... old sound. Metal against metal. A thud shuddered over his aching body.

'And we sure don't need this!'

Sam's eyelids shot open. He watched as Josh staggered under the weight of the sledgehammer then struck the F-Machine a second time.

'Do we, Mister Foundryman?'

Sam's hips thrust upwards. 'No!' Three years' work. Another thud. Then the scream of buckling metal.

'No!' His chest tightened. Three years of sweat and pain. 'No!' Punishing blows trembled up through bolts as the boy continued to pound the F-Machine. Metal on metal. Flesh on metal on metal. Each stroke buffeted Sam's body, rippling up the pulsating flesh. Blood sang an angry song in his ears then flowed away. He felt light-headed, dizzy. 'No!'

'Yes!' Josh's voice synced with his, with each fall of the hammer.

Sam watched helplessly as the F-Machine quivered under the assault. The iron head slowly twisted, shuddering then cleaving from the body. A groan tore itself loose from fused and soldered joints. In the background, Josh's laboured breathing mixed with his own. Something boiled in his stomach, then overflowed. Lower.

Pale thighs leapt into his vision. Sam stared at Josh's naked, sweating form; watched muscle ripple up and down the strong back. The boy held the hammer high above his head, sinew shimmering over pink, sheened skin. He swayed unsteadily. Metal groaned in iron death-throes. Josh pulled the hammer back further, staggering to one side. Sam thrust upwards, mouth open as the burning sensation increased.

The final blow smashed the foot-long projection that stuck out from beneath a headless metal torso. The ersatz cock dangled in a crumpled concertina, swinging limply from a thin thread of metal. Sam stared, unable to believe his eyes as Josh brought the hammer up between the F-Machine's iron thighs. A final clatter. Then only breathing.

Every muscle in Sam's body was rigid with rage.

*Every* muscle.

A teasing laugh. 'Well, whaddaya know?' Josh's grinning face appeared between his splayed thighs. 'Mister Foundryman's dick does work after all!'

Sam stared at the ten-inch rod of blackened, pulsating iron which stuck up from once-singed pubic hair. He felt his face crack into a smile.

Josh laughed, leant down and kissed the straining head. 'Told you I'd make my quota!' He raised one white thigh and straddled Sam's belly. 'Now let's see you make yours!'

## ORTARIAN HOSPITALITY

'Better luck next time, kid!'

I crouch, release the catch on Jackie's lead and watch the small, white pig-dog with the black-patched eye bound off. Yesterday's brush-off still echoes in my ears as I straighten up and follow paw prints across the bridge into the swamps.

So what? So what if I didn't make it onto the team?

I kick at a piece of verd-scrub. Overhead, birds circle, screaming down at me: 'So what... so what?' I stare towards the dunes and shield my eyes against the sun. So what? The spinball team was my last chance – that's what! Ahead, Jackie's pulling at a lump of aqua-weed. I frown and walk on.

For as long as I can remember, I've been the new kid. My family's always moving around: Dad's research job sees to that. Two years ago it was Pluto. Last year on Delta Five, I finished high school and started college. Delta was cool – I had lots of friends there. Four months ago, Dad was posted to Ortaria, guest lecturing in Cybernautics at the Sector Three University. So even though I was in college, me, Mom and Jackie did what we always did: packed up our bags and shuttled down here to join him.

Usually, being the new kid doesn't bother me. Usually it doesn't take me long to settle down and fit in. This time is different. Maybe it's the fact that I've transferred straight into second year college and everyone's a bit older than me. Maybe it's the climate: it's so damn hot on Ortaria, even in September. My pale skin seems to stand out among the other kids' red faces. Maybe it's the way I talk:

we spent a couple of years on Mars when I was eight, so I've got an unusual accent. No one's ever had any trouble deciphering what I say... but I find it hard to understand people around here. They talk strangely, slow and sort of lazy. Sometimes I don't catch what the guys are saying.

I scowl, and break into a run. But there's one word I can always make out: molly. I catch up with Jackie, who's pulling a long strand of aqua-weed along the purple sand. I grab the trailing end and pull, trying to get it away from her, trying to forget the taunt, pretending it doesn't matter. Jackie doesn't let go; neither does the taunt, gripping my throat and making my heart pound. The weed drops from my hand and Jackie drags it off towards the aqua. I watch her, my mind returning to yesterday and the trials.

Back in high school I was okay at sports: ran track for a couple of years, made the aqua-team, even took a few prizes last year. These days I get uncomfortable – I think it's the locker-room after a game. That buddy-buddy jock-stuff is so... Suddenly I find myself smiling. Seems weird to me – all the guys naked, hugging and kissing each other in the showers, and I'm the one they call a molly! I shrug, and walk on.

Anyway, that's what yesterday was all about: my attempt to fit in with this planet's way of doing things. Down here, seems it's not enough to be smart (which I am, but it doesn't make me a better person – right?). It's not enough to be well-mannered and friendly (which I am – just the way I was brought up, I guess). And it's not enough to be fairly easy on the eyes (I'm not boasting, but I have been told I'm quite handsome – for an Earthie). Nope... what makes you fit in around here is if you're a regular guy... and regular guys play spinball.

The air's really heating up now. I pull off my skinshirt and tie it around my waist. Jackie comes galloping up from her aqua-dip, shaking water everywhere. I laugh, jumping back from the spray. Then I hear something – grunting. Jackie hears it too. The hackles go up and she plants her stocky little pig-dog legs firmly in the sand, ready to repel intruders in her swamp. I grin and rub her ears. 'Me and you against the world, eh girl?'

The grunting's getting closer. I shade my eyes and scan the clumps of verdus which rise up over the dunes. The silica-swamp's usually quiet – that's why I come here. Nope, no one in sight. I sit down. The sun's blazing down on the top of my head. I look up, stare out towards the horizon...

See... there's this guy in my Ancient Lit class, this guy I like – I mean really like. His name's Mitch. He's tall – taller than me – and way better built. Plus he's a couple of years older, and he's got these cute stripey eyes. Mitch was another reason I tried out for the spinball team: he's captain.

In AL, he always sits at the back, but I've caught his eye a couple of times, passing in the corridor. After I read my term paper on Whitman to the class, he gave me a look I thought was friendly, so I smiled at him – boy, was that a mistake! Ever since then he's been avoiding me. I think maybe it tipped the balance when it came to me joining the team. Don't know what I said or did that offended him so much... or maybe I do. Let's just say that even though both Whitman and AIDS are confined to the latter centuries of the second millennium, prejudices associated with them are not.

See, Mitch is one of the molly-haters – at least, he hangs out with them. Man, if I'm honest, I guess that hurts most of all.

I stretch out in the purple sand, cover my eyes with my hand. What a disaster! What a mess! I hate this stupid planet and all the stupid people at the stupid school. My other hand flaps out towards Jackie and I stroke her still-damp coat. 'Just as well we've got each other, eh girl?'

I lie there for a while, enjoying the heat of the sun on my chest. Then I hear a low snuffle, at least, I feel it rising up from Jackie's throat. Can't hear any grunting, this time, so I guess it's just a bird or something, picking around in the aqua-weed, that's got her attention. Then the snuffle becomes a growl.

'Shhh, Jackie!' I pat her head half-heartedly. The sun and the heat and sand are lulling me towards sleep. Here, in my swamp, nothing really matters. I can forget about the jerks at school and just dream about...

I'm close to dozing off when Jackie grunts in my ear and I almost jump out of my cut-offs. 'Man, don't do –'

'Well, lookee here, guys. It's the molly!'

My skin cools down real quickly, my eyes spring open and I'm on my feet.

'All alone, molly-boy?'

There's three of them: two I recognise from the spinball team. The other's this older-looking guy with greasy black hair. My eyes dart between all three. Jackie's grunting and snarling, jumping forward then leaping back behind my legs. I stare back at Greasy-hair, who's looking at me like I've let off a bad smell.

'Aw... all alone except for his molly-looking dog!'

The spinboys snigger and Greasy-hair aims a kick at Jackie. She leaps away, his big foot missing her by inches.

'Here, girl!' I bend down and she scrambles into my arms. Crouching there, stroking Jackie's ears, I'm not really scared, though I know I should be: there's three of them, and they're all bigger than me.

Greasy-hair snorts, then spits onto the sand. 'What kinda dog is that anyway, molly-boy?'

I stand up, still holding Jackie. 'She's a pig-dog – you know, from Delta Five?'

'A pig-dog... Delta Five!' Greasy-hair makes this pathetic attempt to mimic my accent and the two spinboys chortle. One of them moves towards me.

'You're the one who tried out for the team, ain'tcha, meatsucker?'

'Yeah... and you're the one spends most of the time with his face in the line-backer's arse, ain'tcha?' Don't know what makes me say this, same way I don't know why I start to grin.

The spinboy scowls. 'Smart-mouthed Earthie!'

He takes a step towards me but Greasy-hair grabs his arm. 'Take it easy, Joe. Let's show molly-boy here some real Ortarian hospitality.'

He smiles, and I almost relax. Then I see the blade and my body goes rigid. I start to back away. Jackie's wriggling and squealing like a piglet, so I let her down and she runs off, just missing another kick from one of the jocks.

'Your rich poppa works for the government, doesn't he, molly?' Greasy-hair's walking towards me.

I take another step back. 'Yeah – so?'

'Got any dosh on ya?' Greasy-hair's flicking the blade back and forth in front of me.

I pat the pockets of my sandsuit, then make this fake-apologetic face. 'Well gee, guys! I seem to have left home without my gold Remex card!' My grin's even broader 'cause I know those years of track haven't been wasted. So I give this goofy shrug, then turn and take off. But Greasy-hair's too close. Next thing I know someone's spinball-tackled me and I'm lying with my face in a mound of verdus. My heart's hammering in my ears and I'm chewing on purple grit. Then the feet start.

'This is what we do to meatsuckers!'

Kick. Kick. First my ribs and kidneys, then my head. I roll into a sort of ball, but the feet just keep on coming. The steel toes of Greasy-hair's boots are impacting on my legs, then arms... One kick hits the side of my face, but there's no pain, 'cause it's all happening so fast. Everything's just breathing, and grunts, and laughing.

'Not so lippy now, are ya, molly-boy?'

Then there's this buzzing in my ears and I know I'm about to pass out. Somewhere in the distance a pig-dog grunts, and overhead the aqua-rooks are screaming at me to keep my stupid mouth shut in future. Then it all stops. Everything goes quiet, except for this fuzzy white noise in my ears. I know I should run, get up and get out of here, but I don't think I can. I lift my arms from around my head and blink. My face is wet. Whether it's sweat or tears I don't know.

'The meatsucker's bleeding... watch ya don't git any of his dirty molly-blood on ya, guys.'

Then a new voice. 'Oi!'

I look round, and there's Jackie and this other pig-dog whimpering and grunting around this big pair of high-topped swamp boots.

I hear Greasy-hair laugh. 'Hey, man! Just in time to help finish off the molly!'

I raise my eyes upwards from the swamp boots, up a pair of scarlet legs, cut-off sand-pants and I see Mitch. My heart really starts to pound. A hand grips me by the shoulder, drags me to my feet.

More sniggering from the spinboys. 'Hold him tight, Mitch. We're gonna teach him a lesson he ain't never gonna –'

A voice in my ear: 'You okay?'

My heart almost stops, but I manage a nod. Mitch is holding me firmly. I look into bright pink- and green-striped eyes, which flick away over my shoulder.

'You buncha swamp-rats got nothing better to do with your time?' His voice is low, quiet.

I turn, stare at Greasy-hair and the two spinboys, who look surprised.

'But he's a dirty, meatsucking molly, Mitch, and –'

'So what?'

A set of six, broad fingertips gently squeeze my biceps. A tingle flows through my whole body and the adrenalin ebbs away. Staring at the three white-necks, I see surprise sink into puzzlement, then sheepishness.

'We was only havin' a bitta fun, man –'

'We wouldn't really have –'

Mitch laughs. 'Get back to yer circle-jerks, ya jerks!'

I watch amazed as the three turn on their heels and shuffle away without a word. Me and Mitch stand there for a few minutes, his arm around my shoulder, me sort of nestling in against him. My head's still spinning from the kicks, but I can feel his body, warm from the sun, and the hair on his broad chest is soft against my wet face. Jackie and the other pig-dog chase after the three guys, snorting and grunting, then lose interest and start playing around in the sand.

About five minutes pass and I know I should say something. 'You like pig-dogs?'

His arm drops and I'm kind of disappointed. Mitch sits down on the sand, a few feet away from me. 'Yeah... his name's Taffy. Your bitch came and got us. I was wonderin' what was –'

'Er... thanks, man.' My legs are wobbly and my heart's still beating fast, but for a different reason. 'I'll just get on my –'

'How old is she?'

I pause, surprised. 'Nearly three.'

He laughs, a different, warmer sound. 'Nice markings – I like the black eye...'

I turn around.

He's smiling at me. 'Looks like her master is gonna have one to match tomorrow!'

My hand moves to my face, and I wince as my fingers make contact with the swollen, bruised flesh around my right eye.

'Seems to me like you could use an aqua-dip, buddy – cool down and clean up a bit. I got some towels and stuff the other side of that silt-dune.'

I bend down, pick up my sand-sneaker, then straighten up just in time to see Mitch striding off through the verdus. So I follow him, not really knowing why. And the pig-dogs follow me. On the other side of the dune I see a rucksack, a couple of towels and a six-pack of Nano-beer. Seems weird to me that this guy – this big, popular guy – spends his weekends in the swamp.

My eyes never leave Mitch as he steps out of the cut-off sand-pants and strips down to black speedos. My throat's dry and I think I'm more scared than I was back there with the spinboys. Then he turns, smiles at me so relaxed and easy that I start to smile back. He winks, runs down onto the sand, Jackie and Taffy flying at his heels. I'm still smiling after him, then... what the hell, why not? And I limp slowly down to join them.

Mitch is right. The aqua feels good, lapping round my sore legs. I rinse my face – my nose seems to have stopped bleeding – then watch his red, muscular body dive into the waves, a couple of yards out from the shore. The two pig-dogs are snuffling and splashing around him, and I don't know if it's relief or something else, but I suddenly feel more comfortable than I have in months. Plunging into the warm aqua, I swim out to join Mitch, Jackie and her new playmate.

Half an hour later the hogs are snoozing and we're lying on our backs, inches apart, the sun drying aqua to silica-crystals on our skins. I raise myself up on one elbow to sneak a glance over at Mitch, admiring his well-muscled stomach.

'Help yourself to a Nano-beer, man.' His voice is lazy, languid. Same accent as the rest of the kids down here, but really warm and friendly. The six-pack is a bit away, and I have to reach over him to get to it. My cut-offs brush against the flesh of his red chest. I swallow hard, sort of wobble. His hands are on my waist, steadying me.

'Sorry, man!' A blush, which starts somewhere inside my cut-offs, spreads over my face as I unhook a Nano, then try to get back to where I was. But his twelve fingers are lingering on my skin, thumbs kneading. Then one hand brushes my arse.

He laughs. 'Man, these things are still soaking. Take them off –

they'll dry quicker.' He laughs again. 'And get me a beer while you're over there.'

The Nano-tubes slurp against each other as I try to stop my hands shaking. I look down, and he's still lying on his back, eyes closed. So I thrust a luke-warm beer into his huge hand, and wedge mine in the silt. Suddenly I'm not thirsty anymore.

'Thanks, bud.'

My fingers fumble with the verco-fasteners. I want to get my stuff off and thrown over a clump of verdus before he opens his eyes. My cock's twitching, starting to stretch itself against the damp fabric of the cut-offs as I wrench verco from verco. My shorts come next – I hadn't realised how wet they were – and it feels good as I drag the jersey down over my arse and thighs. I half-turn, stepping out of my shorts and lean over to spread them and the cut-offs on a patch of verdus.

I hear spray as Mitch pops his Nano. My balls are tingling, my pubes have got all caught up round the head of my swelling cock, my skin's burning and I know it's not just the sun. I'm just reaching for a towel when:

'That's a nasty bruise, buddy – let me take a look.'

His voice is soft, his fingers real gentle as he touches the imprint left by one of Greasy-hair's kicks. Christ, I don't know where to look. My palms are sweating as Mitch examines the bruise on my thigh and I almost wish I was back with the spin-boys getting the shit kicked out of me – wish I was anywhere rather than here.

'Mmm... nothing too serious. How's the face?'

Before I know what's happening, he's on his feet, turning me around. Mitch tilts my head up and looks into my half-shut eye. He doesn't seem to notice the full-blown hard-on poking at the front of his speedos. I'm frozen with... a mixture of fear, horror, embarrassment, but more turned-on than I've ever been. While he pats the swollen flesh around my eye, his other hand moves to my side and he's sort of holding me still, six fingers massaging my waist. Then something happens and my arms are around his neck, my mouth opening under his.

He tastes of silt and Nano, his ribbed tongue flicking around my mouth. My guts turn to mush and my cock twitches against my belly... and I feel another cock twitch back – a cock still encased in black spandex. I groan as his lips harden and he pulls me closer, kissing me almost angrily. Our cocks are bumping and sliding off each other and I'm kissing him furiously, trying to get my tongue as far down his throat as I can. Then he's pulling away, leaving my lips slick with his Nano spit.

I'm too shocked to do much, so I just stand there and watch as Mitch peels off his speedos. Man, his cock just leaps out. It's thick, and purplish against his red skin. I see he's cut, like a lot of the guys down here. Christ, I want to touch that cock, stroke the thick head.

Then everything blurs and he's kissing me again, dragging me down onto the sand. Next thing I know, I'm half-sitting, half-lying between his legs, my head resting just in front of his right shoulder. His knees are up and I'm clutching the backs of his hairy thighs. His big, cut cock leans against the base of my spine and my back arches. I want to press that cock against my arse. I want to hold that cock. I want to taste that cock.

'Chris...' He nuzzles the back of my neck, one hand moving to play with my nipples and taking my mind off the fact he knows my name. 'I've wanted to do this since the first time I saw you.'

His long green hair's against my shoulder and I want to reach up and stroke it, say something back, but my mouth and brain don't seem to be working too well. So I just lie between Mitch's legs, his hard-on rubbing up and down my spine, my heart pounding like a jack-hammer. The adrenalin's back. My head turns and I start to nibble his salty-tasting pec. There's a moan from somewhere deep in his chest... or mine.

His other hand's moving lower, down over my abs and onto my dick. Man, the only hand that's ever been there is mine, and now this way cool guy, captain of the spinball team, is stroking my balls, running his index finger up the underside of my cock and playing with my nipples!

Mitch is still talking, but it's just a rumble in the background, a vibration in my neck. All I can really hear is my moans and the rasp of sandy flesh against sandy flesh. Then his fingers curl around my cock and he's starting to pump, slowly at first. He pulls the foreskin way down, way back, then brings his fist up the length of my cock to the head. There's sand on his palm, and the grittiness against my cock feels weird, but good-weird.

I'm going wild, grinding back against him, feeling the skin of his balls brush against the top of my arse-crack, gripping those strong thighs like my life depended on it. And I know Mitch is getting off on it too, I can feel my sandy back dampening as it drags up and down against his cock.

He groans and opens his legs wider and I spread mine too, rubbing my calves against his ankles. His other hand's stroking the weird bit of skin between my balls and... I bite my lip as his fingers travel back and upward, under my arse. And the hand that's pumping me slows, the tension subsiding a little. I put my weight on my feet, lifting my arse up off the sand so Mitch can reach my hole, which is opening and closing like an aquafish's mouth. I grab his neck, turning my face round to meet his.

There's this weird pain... then his tongue is in my mouth, his finger up my arse and his right hand starts to pump my cock again. The muscles in my calves are starting to tremble, because I'm in a sort of crab-position... but I don't care. Mitch's finger is exploring my arse and it feels better than I ever imagined. Just as my legs start to buckle he quickens the pace, pumping my cock furiously. His finger's tickling something in my arse, something real sensitive... and it feels like the top of my head's blown clean off.

Man, my body jerks like someone's passed 20,000 giga-volts through it! Then there's come everywhere – on my cheeks, in my eyes, dribbling into my open mouth.

I've almost forgotten Mitch is there till his finger moves out of my arse. Then his hands grip my waist and he's dragging his sticky cock up and down the crack of my arse and biting my neck. Man, there's even sand in his mouth!

My own cock's just recovering and my balls are starting to relax again when there's another wave. Mitch digs his fingers into my sides, squeezes a bruise and I yelp, but it's the same weird pain as before. His teeth are sort of hurting too and that turns me on even more than the pain in my side and the noises he's making.

His body tenses behind mine as he thrusts along my arse-crack one last time. Just as the come's starting to tighten on my hot, sweaty skin Mitch shoots against me and a warm river spurts over my arse-cheeks. His heart's pounding real fast against my back and when he grabs my balls I come for a second time, my screams drowning out the bird-cries. I'm twitching and bucking again... until I collapse back against him, our bodies cemented together by come, sweat and sand.

Then he pulls me round and we lie there for what seems like ages, until our breathing gets back to normal...

I must have dozed off, because next thing I know someone's licking my forehead. I try to open my eyes, but one's glued shut. So I open the other. Jackie's white face with its one, black-circled eye stares into mine. I laugh, push her away, then look around for Mitch. He's sitting a few inches away, still naked, Taffy curled up against his legs. He's drinking Nano, sort of watching me. Then he smiles, holds out the tube. I try to grin back, though I feel a bit awkward.

But Mitch continues to smile. 'Your first time?'

I take the tube, chug from it then wipe my mouth with a sandy forearm. 'Yeah.'

'Me too!'

Don't know why I'm surprised, but I am.

Mitch crawls over to me, leans his big green head against my stomach and sighs. I drape one arm over his chest and find myself fingering tufts of hair. I sense he wants to talk and, to be honest, I could do with some answers. This guy who's just jacked me off seems a million miles from the guy who hangs around with the molly-haters.

'Man, I'm sorry you didn't make the team – you were real good – and I'm sorry about the molly-stuff.' His voice is low and sort of sad. 'You've no idea what it's like down here – your family know you're homo?'

'Mmm...' I nuzzle his ear.

'God, I admire you so much – I ain't told no one. Thought you were real cool the first time I saw you and when you wrote that term paper on Whitman for AL...'

I smile, and my hand moves down to trace the crinkly trails of dark, Ortarian come on his hard stomach.

'Guess I'm not as... brave as you, Chris. Man, I've been so lonely. But I'm glad you're here!'

I feel this big grin splitting my face. I'm lying here naked, with the captain of the spinball team, and I just know we're gonna be seeing a lot more of each other.

Suddenly Ortarian hospitality doesn't look quite so bad.

# THE INQUISITION GAME

'I think we need a recap. Get his disc.'

Brad closed stinging, xenon-strained eyes and listened to footsteps, machine hum, beeps... more beeps.

'Read to me, Erol!'

Throat clearing. 'Bradford Nicols. Born Earth, 21-9-23.6. Relocated to Alpha Centauri 43.6. Design analyst and programmer. Three years on Mina, six months Otora, two years Ursa Minor... moved about a lot, apparently.'

Low laugh. 'Quite the little gypsy.'

Brad squeezed his eyelids shut.

'Apprehended... er, 4-7-51.3, in D Sector. Violations of Codes 3, 5 and 6 – suspected violation Code 43.'

Through the heavy work shirt, probing fingers located his right nipple and tugged. 'This one's broken every rule in the book, 43 or no 43.'

Brad inhaled sharply.

'Now... names!' The fingers released his nipple.

'I don't know anything!' Brad braced his body against metal restraints and waited for the now-familiar assault. Nothing. Just the now-familiar voice:

'I think you do.'

Pain ricocheted down the left side of Brad's face.

'I think you know only too well.'

Another slap. Brad tried to twist away but the leather band around his neck held him firm.

'But out of some kind of misplaced –' laugh, slap '– loyalty –'

Brad could feel blood trickling from the cut left by his interrogator's rings. His head lolled forward and he felt himself losing consciousness.

'– you have decided –' slap; cold fingers twined into his hair, dragging his face upwards '– not to tell me!'

The faint odour of cologne and a less-pleasant metallic scent seeped into his nostrils. Had it been hours or days or weeks? Every muscle and sinew in his body ached and wanted sleep. His skin crawled with a thousand tiny insects. Each breath fought its way out of his lungs only to be dragged back with each touch of the hand, each turn of the screw.

Brad opened one swollen eye and stared into a flesh-coloured blur. He had never seen the Interrogator's face – at least, not when he was in any condition to remember his features – never dared raise his head. He tried to focus on the fuzzy mass which swam before his dissolving vision.

Another laugh. 'He's giving me the glad eye, Erol!'

Fingers twisted his hair. Brad gasped, but refused to cry out. The face was impossibly close, breath brushing his cheek. He clenched his teeth as a handful of blond hair tore loose from its roots.

'Don't think your tricks will work with me. You know, all right… and one way or another, you're going to tell me!' The hand struck and Brad's head fell forward, silver strands raining down onto the regulation work shirt.

'Take him away, Erol…let him –' laugh '– consider his position!'

On the edges of sensation, Brad felt himself unstrapped from the chair, seized by a pair of strong arms and manhandled to his feet. A zinging noise filled his head as the laser manacles fired into place, pinning his arms behind his back. He was only vaguely aware of a cold pressure around his neck as the collar and leash were attached. His legs were sandbags dragging behind him as the guard pulled his numb body out of the room towards the cells.

His brain was far from numb. I don't know… I don't know… I

don't know... But I wish I did!

He stumbled, found himself pushed and pulled down endless corridors. It was over – for today. The thought thawed icy nerve-endings and caused his hard cock to twitch under regulation work-shorts.

The place was deserted, as always. Were there others here? Where was 'here', anyway?

The guard was in front, moving with measured strides. Brad quickened his pace.

'Make it easy on yourself: tell him what he wants to know.'

Brad stared at the back of Erol's neck, noticing a small scar just under the collar of his guard's tight-fitting tunic. Smooth titanium slicked the soles of his bare feet. He could feel a drying trickle of blood tight on his cheek, as he took in other details. His eyes lowered down a well-muscled back, lingering on the hard buttocks encased in blue-grey leather, before settling on long, athletic legs.

'He's gonna break you eventually – we both know that.' The lead tugged.

Beneath the words Brad sensed other, less physical information: Erol held the leather-coated handle tightly, like a novice – although Brad knew the guard must have had several years' experience to be allowed to take part in an inquisition. But he also knew Erol was right: Brad would be broken... or he would not get out of here alive.

He recognised his cell by smell alone. A comforting smell: the smell of his own body, and the bodies of countless other men before him.

The leash was removed. The security-screen hummed into action. Brad gulped in the stench, stumbled blindly towards a pile of dirty straw and collapsed onto it face first. Slowly, the pounding in his chest lessened and blood drained away from his cock. He lay sweating, his balls were heavy and aching with undischarged spunk.

That he could live with – hadn't he always? Stiff stalks chafed his sweating calves as he burrowed down, wanting to lose himself in his own filth, wanting to ease the longing and to blot out the hate.

Wanting to forget – and remember. Brad knew why he was hated: his kind was abhorred throughout six solar systems. But it had not always been this way. There were still reams of material, if you knew where to look. In his youth, Brad had pored over ancient vids, stomach churning, cock in hand, marvelling at the beauty of the acts, of strong bodies kneeling before stronger bodies, of torsos decorated by pain and love. He had read of times when his kind had found a covert kind of tolerance, if not quite approval. Back in the late twentieth century, when fear of infection had curtailed almost any physiological contact, many had sought the comfort of his 'perversion'. There was even state-approval, as governments world-wide came to realise the usefulness of *BLANK* as a means of both population and disease control.

Popularity grew, and the imagery of *BLANK* began to permeate world-culture, becoming a mind-set, a way of looking at things. After all, couldn't everything be reduced to *BLANK*?

A century ago, after the Wars of Peace, when the Christian Fundamentalist Alliance had triumphed, 'a threat to stability' was the official reason *BLANK* had been outlawed. Unofficially – instinctively – Brad knew *BLANK* struck a chord inside the core of the Alliance itself.

*BLANK*: even the name had been stolen, as if erasing the word could cancel the impulse.

Inhaling the pungent animal scent, Brad plunged into sleep.

Searching...

Searching the face of countless planets for the underground; hearing whispers in the backrooms of countless government-approved establishments, snatches of hurried conversations, which immediately ceased the moment he showed interest.

Brad moaned, rolling over in the straw, willing the laser mana-cles to somehow dissolve and give him access to his body.

Twelve long years ago, Brad had known what he wanted, and was determined to get it. The homosex had been relatively easy to come by. A recognised alternative, activists welcomed him. He even lived in a same-sex co-op for a while, exploring what was available there with a variety of attractive young men.

His eyelids fluttered in REM.

But his various homo encounters – while satisfying physically – had only served to increase, not slake his thirst. He longed to find an oasis. Ironically, it had been a woman who had brought him out. A het-woman. A cleaner – attached to one of the inter-planetary squads detailed to the large office block in Mina's capi-tal, where Brad worked as an architect. The encounter was etched on his soul.

Nearly midnight... working late on the plans for a new decon-tamination-unit, so absorbed was he in the minutiae of the draughting, he hadn't heard her enter the office:

'Whatcha doin' there, boy?'

The pencil skittered across days of careful work. Something in the voice demanded attention. Brad had given it. And more. When she left laughing two hours later, having taken all he had – which was nothing compared to what she had given – Brad lay naked and sweating on the floor of his office, physically drained but mind and emotions fully alive for the first time.

He had worked late the following evening, and every evening for the next month. She never came back

He was still half-sleep when he felt the foot.

'Get your arse in gear, sleeping-beauty!'

Adrenalin kicked in. Brad retreated further into the heap of straw, his head slamming into the cell wall.

'Move, shit-for-brains!'

Rustling. A gloved hand grabbed the collar and Brad felt himself dragged upright. His heart was pounding, fists clenched rigid behind his back. Still hard from the dream, his warm cock twitched. Brad raised his head and stared.

Erol.

The guard twisted his fingers in the collar. Ignoring the growing pressure on his windpipe, Brad continued to stare at his captor, looking deep into those eyes.

Erol was young – five, maybe six years younger than Brad. Blond, blue-eyed, lightly tanned skin, he had the look of one who hid behind the blue-grey leather of his SexPolice uniform. Brad knew that look: a combination of appalled fascination and gut-wrenching confusion. Men like Erol were drawn to the Interrogation Squads like bugs to fly-paper, acting on impulses they didn't dare think about.

The realisation made him reckless. Despite the pain in his aching limbs, Brad stretched languorously, raising his laser-manacled wrists as far up his back as he could. A forearm brushed the gloved hand which held his collar. Brad felt the grip slacken, then watched as something flickered in the small, blue eyes. He had seen that look many times over the past five years. The contempt, the disgust, the – longing?

The guard loaded up the syringe. Brad leaned back a little and presented his right leg. He watched Erol flinch at his ease of movement, at the arrogance of the stance of one who should, under the circumstances, be anything but arrogant. Blue eyes flicked to the prominent vein on the hairless inside of his thigh. Coldness. Then the guard began to feed him.

As the protein and no-doubt drug-rich solution seeped into the vein, Brad looked down. Erol was crouching at his feet, the tight leather of the SexPolice uniform wrinkling over an amply endowed crotch. Brad stared at the bulge, wondering if the man was hard. Laser manacles singed his wrists as he fought against the bonds. If those hands were free? Brad flinched as the needle jerked in his vein.

Erol's fingers were shaking, large, hair-dusted knuckles trembling as he knelt before Brad. His hands were tied, but his mouth wasn't. Brad tutted.

Erol's fingers jerked again. 'Sorry, er... I'm sorry I...'

Brad's cock strained, responding to the guard's discomfort. He gazed beyond the syringe at tightening blue-grey leather. The guy was hard as a rock! A spark of anger flashed up Brad's spine. If his hands were free, he would... The spell broke as Erol emptied the dregs of the syringe, wiped the needle on the leg of Brad's shorts then retreated.

The familiar septonin rush flowed through his veins, mixing with adrenalin, dulling sensation. Brad watched through a haze as the guard checked the laser manacles, then reattached the niobium leash to his collar. He met blue eyes, which held his gaze. Brad's heart raced. He stood there, 6'4", erect, proud and felt...?

'Come on, he's waiting.' The leash tugged.

Brad resisted. He knew most SexPolice officers were handpicked for certain qualities: disinterest, impartiality, Christian Fundamentalist Alliance-orientation, and a superhuman ability to avoid any type of self-examination.

Manacled hands resting in the small of his back, he raised his head and frowned. In his own time, setting the pace, Brad allowed himself to be led from the cell, wondering who was the real prisoner here.


He was back in the chair, legs spread and secured, arms strapped to metal supports, head held upright by the neck band. Under dull xenon light, Brad examined each line of mortar on a bare brick wall.

Erol's cool hands fumbled on bare flesh as he checked the restraints then shrank back, as though touch contaminated. Brad

Jack Dickson

flexed his biceps, then flinched as a hand grasped his shoulder.

'How many last night?' The voice came from behind, directed over his head.

Strong fingers dug into flesh. Brad tensed. Somewhere to his left, an uncertain laugh:

'Ten.'

The hand removed itself. On the periphery of his vision, Brad caught a glimpse of hard, heavy flesh in smooth leather. He lowered his eyes as the Interrogator walked in front of him, focusing on polished leather. The Interrogator chuckled:

'Successfully tagged?'

Erol's laugh died in his throat. 'Almost. The last two insisted they be despatched together. We couldn't prise them apart. It was –'

'Convenient of them to allow us to save on the laser, I would say – eh, Erol?' The boots passed out of sight.

'I... suppose so.'

Brad stared at bare brick.

'You sound a little uncertain.'

'No! Not at all! It's just –'

'It is a crime, Erol – more than a crime: a sickness. It is our job to cure that sickness and eradicate the disease before it infects us all.'

Brad's mind screened out the words and concentrated on the Interrogator's voice, its rich timbre and resonance. Low baritone notes seeped into his brain. He absorbed them greedily. Around heavy-gauge niobium rings his nipples hardened further and began to ache. Brad knew every inflection of that voice, every diphthong, each precisely formed consonant. You could tell a lot about a man by his voice – how he thought, how he acted, what he was capable of. This was a capable voice – a voice used to asking questions – 'We must find the source of infection, yes?' – and to getting answers.

'Of course!'

The conversation continued. Brad only half-listened, his mind torn between what had evidently taken place last night and what could well be waiting for him tonight, tomorrow night, and the night after. The thought did strange things to him. Beneath the heavy, regulation work shirt, his permanently erect nipples strained against rough fabric.

Those nipples had been his downfall, the reason he was here. Caught in a restricted area after curfew, indulging – or attempting to indulge (they had no proof of either, he was sure) – in proscribed acts. His body had given him away: there were some things you couldn't argue with – like the contradictory signals Erol gave out each time this interrogation game – the ignoring game – was enacted.

Somewhere in the background, the guard attempted a laugh but Brad was years away, in a dimly lit room, chest bared, waiting.

The piercer had been a thin, ascetic-looking man in a well-cut suit. He evidently augmented his already-huge salary as a government-approved security-tagger and implanter with a little extra-curricular activity.

'I could lose my licence doing this,' he had remarked as Brad had solemnly handed over the exorbitant fee.

I could lose my life, Brad had thought, but hadn't said.

'Got the insertion?' The doctor had casually dabbed Brad's right nipple with something cold, then aligned the barrel of the piercing-gun with the root of an already erect bud. The man had been well practiced. Brad had thought even then of inquiring about those who had sat in this chair before him. But he had known better.

'The insertion!'

As Brad's fingers had tightened on the slim metal ring in his palm, a sharpness had stung his flesh. His cock had twitched as he heard the bolt retract. Then:

'Well, give it here... unless you want to...?'

He had looked down, had watched a tiny trickle of blood leak from a scarlet hole. Hands trembling, Brad had wrenched the ring open, pressed the slimmer end to the puncture and pushed. Breath had caught in his throat as dull metal slid through slick flesh. He had snapped the hoop shut then pulled, angling the ring to lie flat, the lower edge just resting on his areola.

A disapproving voice in the background had shattered the moment. 'Hmm ... hope that was sterile – don't expect sympathy from me if there's any infection. And I don't do refunds!'

Surgical steel had pressed against his right nipple. Brad smiled at the memory. Okay, so it wasn't the most erotic experience of his life – unlike self-piercing, when he had slipped the needle though the paper-thin skin along the back of his cock. The sense of power then had been electrifying, almost overwhelming.

And when he had attached the chain and led it down between...

'You smell something, Erol?'

A hand on his shoulder brought Brad crashing back into the present. He flinched as strong fingers tightened through the heavy work shirt. Nipples already erect strained forward, the downward-facing rings brushing his chest.

A laugh – Erol's laugh. 'Yeah... I smell shit!'

Fingers rubbed Brad's shoulder, then moved down to unbutton his shirt. 'Inhale a little deeper.'

Eyes focusing on the wall, Brad watched a pair of leather-clad legs drift into, then out of, view.

'Sweat? The dirty animal never washes and –'

'Go deeper – what do you find?'

Brad blinked as the work shirt was wrenched down from his shoulders, exposing chest and upper arms. His cock poked at the front of the work shorts, fighting the fabric.

'Er... fear?'

Brad frowned, empathising with the guard's confusion and discomfort, feeding on it... and wanting more than life itself to be alone with...

'Excitement, Erol – can't you feel it?'

A hand clamped on each bare shoulder. Rings dug into Brad's sweating skin. Inches below, two other rings quivered in their fleshy sockets... and below that his balls contracted, the guiche rubbing uncomfortably against delicate skin. Brad continued to stare at bare brick as septonin began to course through his veins. Something fizzed before his eyes.

'This excites him.' The Interrogator's voice was low and controlled, all the more terrifying for its lack of emotion.

Brad's fingers tightened around the arms of the chair, knuckles whitening. Sinew was piano-wire, stretched and twisted almost to breaking point.

'Don't you see, Erol?' The hands moved away. Disappointment tingled Brad's scalp. Then they reached over his shoulders and seized nipple-rings. 'This one is beyond any cure. Codes 3, 5 and 6.'

He couldn't deny his crimes even if he wanted to: Code 3: insertion of foreign body above the waist; Code 5: insertion of foreign body below the waist;

Code 6...

Brad almost bit through his lower lip as fingers tightened and pulled harder. Flesh began to strain. Agony flashed over his chest. Then the hoops were released and smooth hands were pulling at the waistband of his work shorts. The fingers were efficient and confident as they wrenched his buttons open. Cool air brushed his cock and balls.

Code 6: reversal of circumcision procedure.

'Wow!'

Brad's body swelled with pride. While he wanted to cower before the Interrogator, Erol's awe made him want to flaunt himself, exhibit his body in all its glory.

'Doesn't it... hurt?'

Soft laugh as a hard hand touched his harder cock, fingering the ring which pierced his foreskin. 'I think you're missing the point!'

Brad managed to resist the urge to thrust forward, push his aching cock against the ringed hand, feeling metal brush metal.

'Some regard it as... enhancement, Erol.'

Brad searched for the sarcasm in the rich, low voice and found none.

'He'll tell me what I want to know – when I've finished with him, he'll be begging to tell me.'

A nervous laugh. 'It's the most –' poorly disguised envy leaked into the guard's delivery, only to be drowned by more words '– if you'll excuse me, I need to make a –'

Noise filled his ears: quick, measured footsteps, a door opening... then kicked shut. Brad remained motionless, hardly daring to breathe. He had no idea where Erol had gone, but he had an inkling why: his instinct had been right – not that it did Brad any good. Words swirled in his brain: 'He'll tell me... tell me... tell me...'

Seconds, minutes passed. The Interrogator didn't speak, but continued to finger the foreskin-ring, turning it slowly, almost gently, with large fingers. Every muscle tensed in anticipation. Then movement behind him. Slow, easy movement... and the sound of a zip lowering. And footsteps. Brad closed his eyes. Dull xenon light dulled further.

Something warm and hard began to slap his face – gently at first, then more forcibly. Brad flinched, struggling against the neck restraint. A ringed hand moved from his groin and grabbed a handful of sweat-soaked hair, holding his head steady. The cock-whipping continued. The man's meat was solid, contacting painfully with his sore face. Brad felt wetness... the cut on his cheek, or something else? His heart pounded in his rib-cage as the slaps increased in strength, rhythmic and measured... then slowed, becoming drags... almost caresses.

A velvet cock-head brushed his mouth. Brad gasped, tongue flicking out from between dry lips but the fingers in his hair held him rigid, like the arm restraints and the leg restraints – rigid like the pierced rod of flesh which curved up and out from the work shorts, pulsing as the head of another cock traced the curves of his face, rubbing over the bristly growth on his chin and upper lip.

Brad saw the cock as it brushed across his trembling half-shut eyelids. Seven, eight inches of hard gristle pressed to his cheek. Tightly stretched skin dragged along that cheek, pulling the large, circumcised head back down towards his lips. Along the under-side, a worm-like vein shivered, mirroring a shiver in Brad's balls as the guiche was pulled tighter.

Then the head of that cock was ploughing between his dry lips as the Interrogator slammed his length into Brad's mouth. Brad's fingers tightened under the restraints. Every muscle in his thighs strained as the huge head pushed past lip-covered teeth towards the back of his throat.

Brad gasped, choking as the gag-reflex kicked-in. Dense pubic hair almost cut off his breathing completely. He began to panic. Stars danced on his eyelids, then the motion stopped. The gag-reflex slowed to a series of gentle spasms... then faded. Brad inhaled the masculine smell of his Interrogator's crotch and the sour scent of his own sweat.

Everything was still, the only motion a twitching in the cock filling his mouth... and his own cock brushing his belly. Brad flicked his tongue and moaned. Then the Interrogator began to thrust. And Brad began to suck. Greedy lips stroked the cock's hard length as the large head struck the back of his throat with each thrust. Wiry hair brushed his lower lip and Brad opened his mouth wider, wanting to take the man's balls, wanting to feel their full-ness, coat the musky flesh with his spit.

The room was silent, the silence broken only occasionally by his own moans and the liquid sounds of love. The speed of the face-fucking increased. Brad longed to feel the man explode into him, taste the sour, salty spunk, let it fill his mouth then slowly trickle down his throat.

But his body betrayed him... again. A familiar tingling in his balls – the guiche was rubbing against the seat of the chair – Brad screamed, the Interrogator's hard cock cutting off most of the sound as his body jerked and twisted against the restraints. Then wetness on his stomach... warm wetness... and more twisting, like a thousand laser shocks passing through his cock. Tears stung as Brad opened his eyes.

Another moistness trickled down his hot face as the cock was removed from his mouth. Brad blinked into blue-grey leather and began to sob. He watched as his Interrogator pushed a spit-sheened cock back into his pants and re-zipped, one handed. Then the ringed hand released his hair and began to undo his arm-re-straints. Brad's heart hammered. Leg-manacles came next. Brad groaned as the neck-brace was removed. He stood up, legs shaking as the work shirt fell away. Spunk crystallising on his belly, Brad fell to his knees.

A ringed hand rested on his shoulder. 'We've come a long way, you and I.' The voice was unchanged.

Brad lowered his head to the toes of leather boots, watching a tear first fall and then roll from the highly polished surface.

'These past weeks have been –'

'Look – I don't know anything!' Brad's voice cracked, his throat remembering the fullness of the man's cock. 'Never made contact. I searched... okay, punish me for the piercings, but I know nothing of where *BLANK* operates out of.'

'I know you don't.' A hand cupped his chin, raising him to his feet. Then the same hand was brushing away tears. 'You're lucky you got me, and not some random sadist –' fingers paused '– or maybe I'm the lucky one.'

Brad stood up, found himself staring into a pale, angular face studded with dark growth and framed by a bristling crew-cut.

'Go.' The face nodded towards a door in the corner of the room. 'There's a supply-truck leaving in five minutes. It has been searched.' Heavily ringed fingers handed him the work shirt.

Brad stared. He didn't understand.

'Just go, Brad.' The handsome, angular face creased. 'Eighteen Mercy Street, Thursday nights after ten.'

Brad pulled up his work shorts then took the shirt, and struggled into it. 'But... why?'

The crease became a smile. 'Maybe we'll see Erol there. Some day.' Slowly, the Interrogator unzipped his own leather tunic, exposing his right nipple. Amidst a sea of thick hair, a tiny silver barbell shone in the room's dull, xenon light.

# IN SAFE HANDS

Small rooms have always kind of scared the shit out of me. The fact that this one is down at police headquarters an' has two glarin' cops standin' over me ain't helpin'. Between one thing an' another, I've got to know this pair real well over the last couple of months.

'Jesus, Buck! What the fuck did ya think ya were up to?' Bob growls at me. He's a big-built black guy, cropped hair, the way he moves lettin' you know that bulk of his is solid muscle.

I just looks at him.

'Ya were told to keep a low profile, drop out of sight till Monday,' Don tells me. He's white, short sandy hair, athletic build, real clean-cut an' regular lookin', like he might be a college boy or somethin'.

'Hell! I've been holed-up for weeks,' I shouts. 'I ain't hardly left that fuckin' room. I was startin' to crack up, man, just had to get out for some air. Anyways, they've obviously found me. The guy who fired that shot followed me from the motel, I'm sure.'

'Shit!' Bob spits. 'We're gonna have to find ya somewhere else. The Narducci brothers are real nervous 'bout what you gonna say in court.'

'They're nervous?' I asks. 'I'm fuckin' terrified!'

Suddenly, they're both towerin' over me, crotches at eye level.

'Not thinkin' of changin' your mind,' Don asks, his voice low, 'about givin' evidence, about makin' sure those two bastards get put away?'

A picture floats into my head: Paul an' me, both naked, his lips meetin' mine. Another picture: six months ago, the morgue, him still naked, but now with a bullet hole between his shoulder blades, an' all because the brothers found him with his fingers in the petty-cash.

'Hey! Don't worry 'bout it. I got a personal score to settle with the brothers.'

The two cops loosen up.

'So what are ya gonna do?' I asks.

'About what?' Don says, knowin' fine full well.

'The deal was immunity *and* protection. If I'm taken out before Monday, then you ain't got no case!'

'Yeah, we know,' Bob agrees. 'Ya took their money for close on ten years, quite happily did their dirty-work, an' then all of a sudden you're in here singin' your heart out, talkin' about turnin' state's evidence. Single-handed, you give us more on those gangsters than we managed to collect in twenty years.'

'An' that makes me real important to you, real dangerous to them. So, you two just go get me twenty-four-hour police protection – the live-in kind.'

Ten minutes later an' they're back.

'So, where you puttin' me?' I asks.

Don answers: 'Takin' ya to a safe house out in the sticks.'

'What about the protection?' I asks, eyes flashin' that way someone once told me looked real mean.

'Yeah, ya got that as well. Looks like that candy ass of yours is considered a valuable commodity, at least for the next couple of days.'

Bob chimes in: 'An' guess who got the job of lookin' after it, every minute of every day?'

'Oh Jesus! Not you two fuckin' baboons?'

'Right first time!' Don announces, quiz-show host style, grinnin' from ear to ear.

Bob's smile slides from his face, his expression turnin' real intense. 'We're gonna stick so close to you, Buck, ya ain't gonna be able to take a crap without one o' us there to tell ya when to stop wipin'. You read me, pretty-boy?'

'Hey! The chance that one of you two might take a bullet for me? Now, that really appeals! So you two stay close as ya want.'

'Yeah,' Don says, eyes narrowin'. 'Think of it... just the three of us... all alone... gettin' real intimate... our very own little love nest...'

I feel somethin' flutterin' in my belly. 'Oh jeez! Just hurry an' get me there before I die of boredom, will ya?'

I just follow them to the car, my balls tinglin'.

The house ain't nothin' much to look at from the outside, an' even less from the inside. It's small, not much more than a shack really, surrounded by acres of empty land. There's a kitchen big enough to hold a table an' four chairs. The rest of the place consists of two tiny bedrooms an' a john with a shower in it.

Me an' the cops ain't hardly exchanged two words the whole journey. But every time I look at their ugly mugs they seem to be smirkin', like they're sharin' a private joke or somethin'. This time ain't no different.

'We'll take this one,' Don says, sittin' himself down on the room's single bed. Bob nods.

'That'll be cozy for the two of you,' I says, standin' in the doorway.

Bob smiles. 'Listen, any night ya wanna drag that candy ass of yours in here, feel free, pretty-boy.'

Don thinks this is real funny.

Instead of sayin' somethin' back, I feels myself blush an' walk through to the kitchen. I can still hear the two of them guffawin' and whisperin'. Thing is, I know they're talkin' about me, laughin' at me, plannin' somethin' to do with...

'How's about some coffee?' Don asks, the two of them appearin' at my heels, both havin' problems wipin' the grins off their faces.

'Yeah,' Bob agrees, 'sure could do with some.'

'Fuck off!' I snarls. 'Just remember who's supposed to be lookin' after who here.'

Their smiles drop away real quick, both of them comin' over to where I'm standin', their faces only inches from mine.

'What was that?' Bob asks.

I see his fists are clenched, arms rigid. 'OK, man! Loosen up.' The two of them back away an' I feel myself heavin' a sigh of re-lief. They sit themselves down at the table while I start workin' out the cooker, findin' cups an' the like. The ice-box is well stocked, more than enough for our weekend stay, beers stacked three deep.

'Milk, two sugars,' Don says.

'Milk, an' hold the sugar,' Bob says.

I place each of their cups in front of them an' sit down with mine. Both of them got their jackets off. They're wearin' shoulder holsters, guns on the left side, the black leather straps tight against their white cotton shirts.

'So,' Don says, 'here we are.'

'Yip,' Bob agrees, 'here we are.'

I feel that current runnin' between them stronger than ever.

'Just the three of us,' Bob continues. 'No phone, no TV, no radio, nuthin' around for miles.'

'What we gonna do for entertainment?' Don asks.

Bob turns to me. 'You got any ideas, pretty-boy, how two guys might entertain themselves?'

I swallow a mouthful of coffee. 'Maybe you could play with yourself. Even better, play with each other. A pair of ass-hole bud-dies like you two must be well used to that!'

Don sighs real heavy and then... At first I can't hardly believe it.

'You really think Frank Henderson'll get that promotion?' Bob asks Don, actin' as if nuthin's happened... But the achin' sting on the side of my face tells me somethin' did happen: Don just smacked me. I sit there, too surprised to react.

'Yeah, sure he will. That bastard's been brown-nosin' ever since he first joined the department.'

Don turns to me. 'An that's just a taste, pretty-boy. From now on you gonna show some respect! You read me?'

His eyes are borin' holes into mine, 'cept I can't see him too clearly on account of the tears I'm tryin' to hold back. I nod.

'What was that, pretty-boy? I ain't hearin' you too well,' Bob says, cuppin' a hand behind one of his ears.

'Yeah, OK. No sweat,' I says, my voice soundin' all choked.

'But ain't Jack in with a good chance of gettin' the job?' Bob asks Don.

'Think I'll go shower,' I tell them, headin' towards the door, legs like jelly, a hammerin' in my ears.

'Naw! Jack's blotted his copy-book once too often. An' don't forget...'

Their voices fade to a distant rumble behind me. In the john I splash cold water onto my face and wonder if it's gonna bruise. An explosion of laughter erupts in the kitchen as I gets stripped-off. The water is cold an' the soap is old an' cracked but I gets in anyway.

I start washin', close my eyes, an' listen to the sound of their voices: sometimes shouts, sometimes whispers, but always laughin'. Before I knows it, there's a full-blown hard-on risin' up out of white, frothy suds. I tug myself slow an' easy, likin' the icy water runnin' down my spine and into my ass crack. My eyes go to the door, which ain't got no lock, an' I thinks how either one of them could just walk right in any moment.

That single thought sends a shudder right through me, pushes me over the edge. It feels like my entire insides are tryin' to squeeze themself out of my piss slit. I slide to my knees, come pumpin' all over my chest, the white globules turnin' solid under the cold water. I stays there for a while, all curled up on the stall's plastic floor. It's like my brain just can't cope with the mix of feelings rushin' through it: pure pleasure an'... gut-tightenin' fear. A loud thump on the door makes me jump, sets my heart gallopin'.

'Jesus Christ! You OK in there?'

'Yeah ... Don. Sure, no problem.'

I stagger out from under the water. My skin's gone scarlet with the cold an' I'm shiverin' like I might shake somethin' loose. A brisk rub down gets my circulation movin' again. I hear the two of them still laughin' as I head for my bedroom. I dress real slow, both wantin' and not-wantin' to go back into the kitchen.

The chatterin' an' hee-hawin' stops dead the minute I open the door. There's a long silence, me standin' awkward just inside the door.

Finally, Don speaks. 'Us guys are hungry, pretty-boy!'

They start their cop-talk again an' I get rummagin' in the ice-box.

'Man, am tellin' ya, that woman got big connections down-town and she puts out like ya wouldn't believe!' Bob says.

'Get out of here!'

'God's honest! She was beggin' for it, slobberin' over my cock like she ain't seen of piece of meat in months!'

'Steak OK?' I ask, not turnin' round.

'Yo!' Bob snaps. I feel my balls drawin' up tight. 'Come here!' he says.

I walk over, not darin' to look him in the eye, worried he might guess about the hard-on growin' fast in my pants.

'Who you think you're talkin' to?'

I stare at my shoes, the muscles in my throat so tense I can hear myself swallow.

'You're talkin' to two officers of the law, pretty-boy. Like I told ya before, that means ya gotta show some respect. You address me an' my partner here as "Sir". You understand?'

'Yes... Sir.' My dick's now stretched full length, pushin' hard against the blue denim of my jeans.

'That's a good boy,' Don says, his hand lightly smackin' my butt. My cock twitches so hard it hurts. 'Now go an' finish makin' our meal. And yeah, steak's fine.'

I turn back towards the sink, face burnin', sweat tricklin' down under my arm. The two of them talk on about 'the division' while I busy myself cookin'. Thing is, the hard-on just won't let up, has got itself all tangled up in my pubes. Every time I moves, another clump of hair gets pulled out by the roots.

The steak turns out real well, an' I serve it with some boiled potatoes and carrots. Neither of them so much as looks at me as I set the plates down in front of them.

'Where's yours?' Don asks.

'I don't feel hungry... Sir,' I tell him, which is true, excitement always havin' that effect on me.

'Bring us some beers!' Bob orders.

I does like he says, realisin' that I'm supposed to wait table. Standin' behind them, I watch as they guzzle down the food. I look down an' feel a blush spreadin' over me: that bulgin' cock of mine is outlined clear as day in my pants. O sweet Jesus, don't let either of them notice, I thinks, tryin' to get my mind onto somethin' else. But... it just ain't no use.

'What you reckon, Don?'

'Bit over done, Bob.'

My cock flexes, the broad smiles passin' between them sendin' jolts through it.

'Yeah?'

I take a sharp intake of breath as Don turns an' looks at me.

'OK, pretty-boy,' he says, 'ASSUME THE POSITION!'

I back away as he stands up, feeling the blood drainin' from my face. Judgin' by the activity inside my pants, I knows just where it's goin'.

'NOW!' he growls, those eyes of his starin' out his head, like he might be thinkin' of tearin' me limb from limb instead. Bob is chucklin' away in the background. I turn round, spread-eagle myself on the nearest wall.

'Get those legs apart!'

I feel his right foot kickin' at my ankles. Half-turnin', I see him drawin' a thin belt from the loops of his pants. By now I can't hardly breathe, spots in front of my eyes, a cold sweat sweepin' over me.

'Know why you're gettin' this?' he asks.

'Yes... Sir,' I says, amazed that I can say anythin' at all.

'Why?'

'I didn't cook the meal right, Sir.'

'An' what do pretty-boys who fuck up get?' He can't hardly keep the amusement out of his voice now.

'They... get their asses whipped, Sir.'

This has Bob laughin' hard enough to crack a rib.

I wonder maybe if I'm gonna pass out. I can't rightly put names to all the emotions runnin' through me: excitement, pleasure, fear, humiliation.

'This'll make sure you don't let it happen again!' Don says.

Suddenly, I'm aware of my butt, the way it's stickin' out behind me, just waitin'. The beatin' is short and vicious, the blows rainin' down fast and furious. My cock jumps an' kicks... an' for a minute, I almost think...

'OK,' Don says, 'bring us another couple of beers.'

I glance down at myself. The hard-on is still showin' through, obvious as ever, but no, I ain't come. They take the drinks off me without a word. Bob's been laughin' so much, he's wipin' tears from his eyes.

'Get the washin' up done!' he says.

'Yes, Sir.'

One of them produces a deck of cards an' they deal for poker, dollar bets on the table. I gets the dishes into a basin an' heats some water. My ass is really stingin', the boner round front ragin'.

Every so often I hears them sniggerin', both of them shootin' long, side-ways glances in my direction.

'That's them done, Sir,' I report. They stand up an' come towards me. I back away till my butt hits the sink. The two of them have their faces stuck in mine, their breath stinkin' of beer. Both got those real scary expressions an' I start gettin' fidgety.

'You don't look in too good shape, Buck!' Don says, an evil grin on his face.

I don't say nuthin', heart poundin'.

'I think pretty-boy here could do with a work-out, Don.'

Next thing I knows, Don's pullin' up the hem of my T-shirt, me raisin' my arms over my head so he can pull it off. Bob undoes the buckle of my belt an' says, 'Down to your shorts!'

'Yes, Sir,' I tell him, hearin' the fear in my voice.

Bob and Don sit themselves back at the table, gulpin' down big mouthfuls of their beers.

I stumble out of the rest of my stuff, insides churnin'. Finally, I peels off the socks an' stand before them in my jockeys. Now there ain't anyway they can't notice my hard-on, its purple top peekin' out over the elastic. I close my eyes, my whole body burnin' with shame. I can feel their gaze goin' from the rigid slab of flesh to my face an' back again.

'Well, well, well...' says Bob.

The two of them exchange glances like they can't hardly believe what they're seein'.

'We had no idea you felt that way about us, Buck,' Don says, real sarcastic-like.

'Bastards!' I mumble, hatin' them both, my cock managin' to pump itself up even further. But the two of them are laughin' so much they don't hear.

After a while, Bob gets enough wind to speak. 'Right, a ten says pretty-boy here can't manage twenty push-ups.'

'Naw! A twenty says he can.'

Jack Dickson

'Get that ass in motion, cocksucker!'

I hits the floor and starts. I never detested two people so much in my whole life. But I ain't never known my cock this excited, neither. An' now it's gettin' to the point where I don't know where one feelin' begins an' the other ends.

'Good boy!' Don shouts, seein' as he won.

But now Bob wants a chance to get his money back an' I realise they gonna spend the rest of the night bettin' on me instead of them cards. My balls pull together.

It goes on for what seems like forever: do ten of this; do fifteen of that; do twenty of the next thing. After a while, I see the two of them are smirkin' at somethin'. Then I notice my jockeys are workin' their way down, that the whole top half of my cock is stickin' clean out. I try to cover myself up but this just amuses them all the more. Bob gets up, takes a slug of his beer, then comes over an' stands in front of me.

'I lost a lot of dough on you tonight, pretty-boy.'

I try to stop my body tremblin' but can't.

'An' someone's gotta pay, don't they?'

I nod.

'Get naked!' he bellows, pullin' at the thin fabric of my jockeys.

I slides them down, staggerin' a bit as I gets them over my feet. The size of the boner pushin' out in front of me just gotta be seen to be believed, its head throbbin', the skin on its shaft stretched tight and shinin'.

'An' I'm gonna make sure you do pay, pretty-boy.'

He speaks real low, the look in his eyes sendin' shivers through me, my cock quiverin' in mid-air. I let out a yelp of surprise as he grabs my balls, then a groan of pain as he starts to squeeze.

'What the fuck?' Don shouts from the table, a clatterin' trash-can still echoin' in our ears.

All three of us freeze, our brains registerin' what we just heard, rememberin' why we're here.

136

'Shit!' Bob says, lettin' go of my nuts.

In an instant they've both got their guns drawn an' the overhead light off. Bob pushes me into a corner of the darkened room, stands in front of me, presses his back flush against me. I can feel the white cotton of his shirt an' the leather straps of his holster diggin' into my chest, the rough fabric of his black pants against my belly an' hard-on.

'Don't see nuthin',' Don says, standin' side-on to the window, peerin' into the blackness. 'I'll go out an' take a look,' he adds.

I watch over Bob's shoulder as his partner moves towards the door. The two of us stay put, him rammed up against me like a human shield, listenin'.

One shot, then another.

'Oh Jesus!' I mumble to the back of his neck.

'Hey, you're OK, man. Anyone out there gonna have to get through me an' Don before gettin' to you.'

I relax a bit, suddenly feelin' real safe an' secure crushed in behind those massive shoulders of his. Bob's gun is pointed at the door as it swings slowly open.

'It's me,' Don tells us before steppin' into the room.

Bob's arm drops back down by his side. 'Anythin'?'

'Somethin' movin', but I couldn't see what.'

Both make for the window, stand with their backs to the wall on opposite sides, and look sideways into the night.

'Could just be a cat,' Bob suggests.

Don nods, then looks at me. 'He's gonna be safer through in the bedroom. I don't want him under foot if anythin' does happen.'

'Yeah,' Bob agrees, turnin' to me. 'Git through to bed!' he rasps.

Only when I move do I realise my hard-on's gone. As I pass them, I feel the toe of Don's shoe land in my ass crack.

'We'll get back to you in the mornin'!' Bob says.

By the time I slip between the sheets I'm hard again. I starts tuggin' myself straight away, so built-up I let shoot in seconds. Couple of minutes later, an' I'm ready to go again. Pretty quick, I lose count of how many times my cock spits come all over me.

Durin' the night I wakes up to the sound of Bob an' Don: their voices, their footsteps. It gives me real nice feelin' inside, knowin' they're so close, knowin' they'll protect me. All the worry of the last months just seems to fall away an' I slip back to sleep feelin' a lot happier than I done in a long time.

'OK, pretty-boy, let's have you on your feet!'

I open my eyes, two men standin' over me, white shirts under their leather holsters. At first, I don't rightly recollect where I am or even who these guys are.

'An' I mean NOW!' the black one says, bendin' down, whippin' back the blanket.

I feel my balls react, an' then I remember. My cock manages to get standin' just a couple of seconds before me.

'Oh, Jesus Christ!' Don laughs, his hand swattin' my hard-on. 'I don't believe this!'

'Me neither,' Bob agrees, smilin' an' shakin' his head real slow.

'Look at the state of him,' Don says, pointin'.

I glances down an' sees the flakin' remains of dried come on my belly an' chest.

Bob nods, eyein' me. 'Well, like the big-boss man downtown said: he's our responsibility.'

'You don't mean... ?'

'Yip! Sorry ol' buddy, but we gonna have to clean him up. It ain't a pleasant prospect but I'm sure they warned ya in trainin' school – there's a lot of real dirty jobs that us cops gotta do!'

'OK then,' Don agrees, makin' for the door, 'but you deal with his ass-hole!'

Bob grabs a hold of my hard-on, and pulls me along behind him. 'Like hell I will! Remember, I got three months more service than you do. That gives me seniority.'

'Anyone ever call you a fuckin' ugly jerk, Bob?'

'Don't reckon anyone has, Don. An' if they ever did, I'd make the guy who said it eat his own liver.'

'Just as well you ain't never heard anyone say it then.'

'It sure is, Don.'

The double act is chucklin' at its own material. They push me into the shower, Bob turnin' on the water. Next they roll up their sleeves an' take off their watches, now jokin' 'bout someone they busted a couple of weeks back. Both have hands like shovels, hair sproutin' from the knuckles, the skin on their arms ripplin' with every movement.

'We gonna need somethin' to scrub him down with,' Bob says.

'Times like this, I realise why you're the senior officer.'

'Brains before beauty, Don, every time.'

'An' I suppose you want me to go an' find this somethin'?'

'Rank's got its privileges, buddy-boy!'

Don mumbles somethin' an' then marches off. Bob yawns, stretches, looks around himself... I just stands there, the cold water runnin' over me, a dot of pre-come decoratin' seven inches of hard reality. There just ain't no way I can deny what I'm feelin', the pleasure it's givin' me. I want to be their source of entertainment, my whole body just achin' to be used. Don reappears holdin' two floor-scrubbin' brushes: Bob grins and my hard-on flexes.

'Right,' Bob says, 'let's get to work!'

I yelps as they grabs a hold of my arms, push me about this way then that. The wire bristles are harsh and stingin' against my skin. Back, chest, thighs... every bit of me is set alight in turn, dull burnin' suddenly ignitin' into scorchin' pain. After a while, I lose track of whose hand is where, just roll with the fireball blastin' through my head.

Suddenly, one of them has got me by the scruff of the neck, pushes my head down towards my knees. They each start scrubbin'

Jack Dickson

at an ass-cheek: my rigid cock vibrates, sends tremors up into my belly, an' then...

'Jesus!' Don spits, both of them leapin' back as I jerk my head up an' shoot streams of white come all round.

Bob's eyes narrow as he steps towards me. 'Fuckin' hell, man,' he says, his open palm thunderin' down on my already raw ass, 'we ain't ever gonna get you clean if ya keep doin' that!'

My balls pull themselves tight... an' then I shoots a second load straight onto Don.

'Shit!' he says, lookin' down at his shirt, disgusted, then lookin' at me, even more disgusted. Bob tries to say somethin' but can't on account of the fact he's laughin' so much.

'Suppose you think that was funny?' he asks Bob.

All Bob can do is nod, tears runnin' down his face.

'Jeeze-o,' Don sighs, unbuttonin' his shirt as he walks out the door.

'Hey man!' Bob says to me, smilin'. 'We might make that our party piece.'

He jiggles my cock, bringin' my hard-on back full-force. I worry for a minute that he might be about to get a sprayin' as well.

'Get the filthy bastard out into the yard!' Don shouts from wherever he is, soundin' real pissed.

Bob grabs my cock an' pulls me out of the shower, drags me into a small, grass-covered field at the back of the house. I feel cold despite the brilliant sunshine, the heat of the day already startin' to build. They've got some rope an' clothes pins on the ground. I feel tightness in my chest, a weakness in my knees, an eagerness in my cock.

'Right, pretty-boy,' says Don, appearin' behind us, restrappin' his holster over a clean white shirt, 'on all fours!'

I does like he says, the grass damp beneath my palms an' knees.

'Head back an' open that cocksuckin' mouth!' he snarls. 'Now me an' Bob are gonna teach you a lesson you ain't never gonna forget.'

140

They talk to each other but their words don't mean nuthin' to me. The only thing I'm aware off is my two openin's, both gapin' wide, both greedy for the fillin' they're gonna get. I sort of think of myself as nuthin' but a long tube with a hole at either end. I wait for what seems like forever, my mouth an' ass beggin', desperate.

They start to undress an' I feel my heart racin', my balls slippin' up inside of me, my throat an' ass-ring startin' to spasm. Bob's black, hair-covered shins are suddenly standin' before me. I crane my head backward, him towerin' over me, thick muscles shinin'. I do a double-take on his cock, start whimperin' at the sight of the condom-wrapped shaft reachin' up to touch his belly-button.

He drops to his knees an' at the same moment Don is wedgin' himself between my calves. Bob's hard-on is the same length as my face, his balls swingin' below my chin. In a way, I'm glad I ain't able to see what Don's gonna give me up the ass, my brain already reelin' from what's goin' in my mouth.

'Oh boy!' Bob says. 'Am I ever gonna enjoy this!' He smiles over at his partner. 'You ready back there?' he shouts.

'Sure am boss!' comes the reply.

Bob's cock touches my lips and Don's presses against my ring. Real slow, they start forcin' their way in. The pain up my ass is worse, but worryin' about suffocatin' round front kind of takes my mind off it. Both of them are pushin' those cocks in so deep I gets to thinkin' that they gonna meet up somewhere inside of me.

I soon develops a rhythm, tiltin' back on my knees to help ease Don in, then leanin' forward onto the rod slippin' into my gullet. Workin' like that, pretty quick I got them both all the way inside, my throat an' ass stretched to burstin' point. The agony is like nuthin' I ever felt before, makes me think my brain gonna explode.

But strange thing is, I don't ever remember bein' this happy. Sure, the pleasure runnin' through my dick's got somethin' to do with it, but it's more than that. It's like for the first time in my life those two holes of mine finally know what they're for. Both ends of me are plugged tight an' it's the nearest thing to heaven I ever found.

'Now you gonna get it!' Bob whispers.

I see him throwin' a hard, tight-lipped smile in the direction of his buddy. I brace myself, then both of them let rip. They batter into my holes full-force, pump all the violence inside of them into me.

Couple of times I think I'm gonna flake out, gotta fight like billy-o to stay with it. Don rammin' my ass sends me hurtlin' onto Bob's throbbin' cock, his thrusts throw me back onto the hot flesh impalin' my ass. Back an' forth I go, bouncin' between the two of them, a skewer drivin' into me at either end.

They starts gettin' faster, thumpin' in with so much force I just know they gonna bust me wide open. I can feel the tension mountin' in both their bodies. My own cock is fair buildin' as well, Don rubbin' that gland way up in my ass. But I ain't really interested in that, only in those two holes of mine, an' what's hammerin' into them.

The three of us explode in a howlin' torrent of grunts an' come. The two of them fall away onto the grass, me still on all fours, shakin' an' sobbin'. I hear them laughin', talkin', slappin' each other on the back. My ass-hole an' throat are hurtin' bad. But in a way, they feel empty, like somethin' that belonged there was just amputated.

Wipin' tears away from my eyes, I see two white legs covered in blond hair standin' in front of me. I look up an' see Don pullin' off a condom. He unrolls a fresh one over a bulgin' cock which ain't gonna be any easier to swallow than the last one. As he kneels down, I feel Bob gettin' in behind me. I open my mouth, relax my ass, both my holes even hungrier than before, both cryin' out to be fed.

The two cops start pushin' themselves inside me again. Straight away, they're pumpin' me hell-for-leather, each of them already havin' broken-in the other's hole.

'OK! STICK 'EM UP!'

Snigger, snigger. 'Oh... yeah! Good one, Tony.'

The sound of two guys laughin'.

At first, I can't hardly believe my ears. I feel the shock shoot through Bob an' Don, those grindin' cocks of theirs stoppin' stone-cold dead.

'Just don't move a muscle, any of you.'

I crane my head round an' see a pair of gorillas in badly-fittin' suits: Tony an' Sam, two of the Narducci brothers' hired guns. They're standin' feet away and pointin' shotguns in our direction.

'Jesus!' Tony says, dumb as an ox, but a regular Einstein compared to Sam. 'An' this is "protective" custody?'

Sniggers. 'Good one, Tony.'

'You first, black-boy! Pull yourself out of him an' get over here.'

'You round front, get yourself out of his mouth.'

Don does like he's told an' slowly gets to his feet. I see Sam's got a length of rope. He pushes the two cops together, chest-to-chest, half-hard dick crushed against half-hard dick. Next, he binds them together real tight, wrappin' the rope round an' round.

Meanwhile, Tony's lookin' me over, but standin' behind me where I can't rightly see him. I feel the barrel of his gun slidin' past my balls an' proddin' at my rigid cock.

'Well, they obviously ain't be doin' nothin' that you ain't been enjoyin',' he says. 'Looks like you gonna be takin' that boner with you into the next world. You didn't really think we was gonna let you testify at that trial, did you?'

I shake my head, and try to stand up, my legs bucklin' under me.

'Just you stay like you were!' Tony shouts, his heel grindin' into my arse. 'I think maybe me an' Sam might like some fun before blastin' you an' your two cop-buddies straight to hell.'

I get back onto all fours an' feel cold metal bein' drawn up an' down my ass crack. It hovers round my hole for a second, then starts to work its way up. Sam comes an' stands in front of me, pushes the barrel of his shooter into my mouth.

'Oh, me an' Sam here are gonna give you a fuckin' that's just gonna blow you away!'

Snigger, snigger. 'That's a good one, Sam.'

The two barrels push in deeper an' deeper, the one in my mouth forcin' me onto the one up my ass, it doin' the same in reverse. At first I'm likin' it, but then my hard-on shrivels and I start shakin', a kind of blank terror fillin' me, just waitin', knowin' death's just minutes away. Before long I got a good six inches of each barrel in me.

'OK, Sam, on the count of three.'

I close my eyes, already imaginin' the sound of those muffled bangs that are gonna turn me inside out ...

'One... two... THREE!'

The guns don't go off on account of the fact they musta been winkin' at each other or somethin', but I feel hot piss runnin' down the front of my thighs, watery shit runnin' down the back.

'Oh fuckin' hell!' Tony shouts, pullin' the barrel out of my ass. 'He's just gone an' shat all over my gun!'

Snigger, snigger. Sam pulls his gun out as well.

Tony starts kickin' my ass, sending me sprawlin' onto my belly. 'You disgustin' sick fuck!' Snigger, snigger.

Sam decides to deliver the same treatment to my face. It goes on an' on, me slippin' in an' out of consciousness...

'Hey, pussies? How about lettin' us make your dreams come true, same as we did for ole Buck there!' Bob shouts over.

I watch the two pairs of shoes walk away.

'Know somethin', Sam? I always fancied myself a piece of cop-ass.'

I fights hard to stop blackin' out, forces my eyes to stay focused. Don an' Bob are standin' a couple of yards away, still roped together, stuck front on to one another flush as can be. Sam trains his shotgun on them while Tony pulls down his zipper, a hard cock springin' out. He mimes two fingers up Bob's ass, driving them in an' out real vicious. I catch Don's eye over his partner's shoulder an' it's like he's willin' me strength, tryin' to tell me what to do.

'This is just a taste of what you gonna get, just to get you opened up a little.'

I looks around an' sees the two piles of clothes belongin' to Bob an' Don. Each of those heaps has a holster buried in there, I thinks, an' in each holster...

I start to crawl, every part of me, inside an' out, red-hot with pain. The ground spinnin', black holes openin' an' closin' before my eyes, my hand gropes for the feel of crisp white cotton, finds somethin' hard, pulls it towards me ...

'Hey!' Sam shouts, takin' aim.

For a split-second I think I ain't gonna have the strength to squeeze the hand-gun's trigger... There's a sound like a whip crackin' an' I wonder if maybe I've got a new hole in me. It's only when I see Sam topple that I know I ain't. Tony bends down for the gun lyin' at his feet. I look at my hand, will it to fire the gun... nuthin' happens, every part me feelin' numb. Tony smiles, points his shotgun towards me. I hear Bob and Don's shoutin' 'SHOOT!' An' it's like my body's gotten so used to doin' like they tell it, they got better control over it than me. Tony looks surprised more than anythin' as he hits the ground.

'Good goin', Buck!' Don shouts over.

'Hey! We owe you one,' Bob says, beamin' that smile of his.

Managin' to get onto my hands an' knees, I stagger over to where they are, every movement feelin' like it's gonna be my last. I starts undoin' the knots, everythin' gettin' further an' further away... till finally... it just ain't there no more.

When I comes to, Bob an' Don have got an arm each round my waist. They hoist me to my feet, their naked bodies supportin' my full weight.

'C'mon, pretty-boy, let's get you cleaned up,' Bob says, his voice low an' gentle.

Real careful, they carry me back towards the house.

'You done good back there, pretty-boy,' Don says, lookin' at me with a new respect in his eyes. I press my lips to his cheek, then turn an' do the same to Bob.

'Hey!' Bob says sharply. 'It's OK this once, but if us three are gonna be a long-term thing, then don't be doin' that in public.'

'Yeah,' Bob agrees, 'we got our reputation down at the precinct to think about!'

# PUSSY-BOY

The lights at New York State's only boot camp for young offenders go out at 9:30 pm, sharp. Barrack room 6A houses twelve of us seventeen-year-olds, six cots lined up on either side. I been in and out of reform schools since I was ten. But it don't matter where I am, one thing don't ever change: Johnny Stone is top cock, numero uno, Big Daddy second to none.

You see, I quickly realised I got the build – 6'4" since I was fourteen – and I got the balls. Ain't no one treats me like a cocksucking pussy and lives to enjoy it. Like the guy who put me in here, the guy who made me take a razor to his face: he just didn't have no respect, thought he could get away with takin' a rise out of ol' Johnny-boy. Well, he soon learned different: that's one mistake he ain't never gonna make again.

Bein' Big Daddy means there's certain things you gotta do. In a place like this, for example, ya gotta get yourself a real-live fuckboy. Who's gonna respect a Big Daddy without a fag to service his dick?

Now, don't get me wrong there! When I use the word 'fag' I ain't talkin' about your actual 'homosexual'. Jeez man, I met homos who were M-E-A-N with a capital M; the kind of guys who get R-E-S-P-E-C-T with a capital R; the kind of guys ol' Johnny-boy be proud to call his buddies. Those guys ain't fags, no way.

When I say 'fag', I mean guys that can't take care of themselves, the ones with chicken and shit-scared written all over them. It's just the way of the world, when you think about it. I bet even you guys who got those really smart executive jobs know what I'm talkin' about: the look of pleasure on the Big-Boss-Man's face when he fucks you over good and proper, shits on you from a great height, then makes you lick his ass? Yeah, sure you do. But don't you be comin' the Little-Mr-Innocent with ol' Johnny-boy. What you go straight out an' do? Why, start bein' twice as mean to the guy workin' for you, fuck that tight little ass of his till you start feelin' like you're a man again. Now ain't that the truth or what?

Only difference in here is... that it ain't no m-e-t-a-p-h-o-r. There! That surprised ya, didn't it? Didn't think ol' Johnny-boy knew words like that, did ya? But then that's another reason yours truly is numero uno: he's a lot smarter than your average on-his-road-to-the-chair teenage fuck-up.

Anyways, like I started tellin' ya, lock-down and lights-out is at 9:30. That's when the entertainment starts. Ya see, Big Daddy gotta do Big Daddy things, gotta be seen by the guys doin' Big Daddy things, or he ain't gonna stay Big Daddy for long. This is when I takes centre stage and shows them all just how big Big Daddy is. Although it's only me gets to do the honours, the fag's really bein' fucked by all of us. For a short time, everyone gets the pleasure of feelin' there's someone lower than them, someone they can shit on after a long day bein' fucked over by the guards.

The room's in semi-darkness, three small, barred windows up near the ceiling catchin' some of the bright spotlights outside. Everyone's lyin' in their cots real quiet, waitin', some of them probably sportin' skin-stretchin' boners already. I throw off the blanket and stand where they can all see. I'm naked already 'cause we sleep naked. Pyjamas? What kind of pussies you think we are?

Within seconds Tony's there, standin' in front of me, head bent, lookin' ready and more than willin' to do as he's told. I spotted him straight off at induction: little guy, pretty, big moon eyes, started comin' on to me for protection the minute we met. Ever since then we've been an item. Him takin' care of my bodily needs, me lookin' out for him, makin' sure he don't have no hassles from no one else.

I see a couple of the guys already started bangin' their meat, imaginin' it was them that had a personal cocksucker to fuck over any which way that took their fancy. I feel my balls tightenin', my cock startin' to get heavier. I grab his shoulders, and push him down to his knees.

'Hey, Johnny! Make pussy-boy clean out your asshole.'

The idea gets some shouts of approval. A couple of wild hoots tell me some of the guys already shot off their first load of the night.

I smile, lookin' down at Tony. 'Think so? How many you guys think I should let pretty-boy here clean my asshole?'

Judgin' by the volume of noise, just about everybody. I see Tony shiverin' on the cold, stone floor. He jumps as my hand grabs his chin, forces his head backwards, makes him look at me. 'What about you, cocksucker? Wanna eat out my asshole, maybe see if there's somethin' else that mouth's good for?'

Tony nods, as much as he can, considerin' the grip I got on his chin.

'Speak up little fuck-boy, I can't hear you too well.'

'Yeah! ' His voice is all choked up, his face goin' scarlet. 'I wanna clean out your asshole.'

Some hollerin' tells me another few guys just released the pressure on their balls.

'Hey, Johnny, if he does good you ain't never gonna need ass-paper again!'

'Hey, Johnny, maybe we could suggest it to one of the guards, get pretty boy chained up in the can, give him a full-time job!'

'Yeah! That way he can look after all two hundred of us guys, back and front, every day!'

'Jesus! Talk about pussy-boy paradise!'

'Naw! The guards would never let us! They'd want to keep him for themselves.'

I wait for the talk and the laughin' to die down a bit. The sharp slap I give Tony across the ear takes him, and the guys, by surprise. There's a roar of approval, my own cock doin' a fair bit of jumpin' and twitchin' at the sight of him sprawled there, knocked flat, silky-smooth ass drawin' itself back into a kneelin' position. 'What did you forget?' I demand.

'I forgot to say... please.'

'That's better! There ain't nuthin' worse that an ungrateful pussy-boy who don't even know when a guy's tryin' to do him a favour.'

I turn round, grab my knees, his face level with my splayed ass cheeks, my hole level with his mouth. 'Start cleanin', fuck-boy!'

His tongue wets my ass cheeks but keeps clear of my shit-hole. I let him do this for a couple of minutes, quite likin' the gentle dabs on my butt, the little gasps of hot breath against my skin, his cock brushin' the back of my knees. But pretty quick I'm wantin' a bit more action.

'Marky!' I bark, since he's the guy on the cot nearest.

'Yeah, Johnny?'

I half turn, see the heavy-built black guy lumberin' towards us. His huge hard-on bounces off his stomach as he walks, several loads of spent spunk plastered across his torso.

'Get the pussy-boy's face up my ass!'

'Sure thing, Johnny,' he says, obviously relishin' the idea.

Marky's right arm grabs my waist, slippin' itself between my stomach and my skin-bustin' hard-on. Him holdin' me tight, I feel Tony's face rammed into my ass-crack, feel it held there, know Marky's left hand's got the back of pussy-boy's skull well under control. I can feel a nose wedged in there, a pair of tightly shut lips exactly where ol' Johnny-boy should be feelin' a certain cock-sucker's eager, slobberin' tongue.

After a few minutes, Marky's arm relaxes and I hear pussy-boy coughin' and splutterin', gaspin' for air. I turn my head sideways, just enough to look at Marky but keeping my ass starin' straight into pretty-boy's face. I'm laughin' but tryin' to sound real serious: 'I think we got ourselves a faulty pussy-boy here, Marky. Like, he's plugged in, but he ain't cleanin' properly.'

The other guys are lovin' this, a couple of them doubled-up with belly-achin' laughter, others shoutin' and hollerin' stuff I can't make out, most of them just grinnin' from ear-to-ear and beatin' their come-covered dicks.

Marky grabs hold of Tony's ears, pulls his face round so it's level with that standin'-to-attantion black cock of his. 'Listen, pussy-boy, you do like the man tells ya! Understand?'

'Yeah... OK.' Tony's voice ain't nuthin' but a whisper.

'Now, you get that pretty face of yours back in there and make like a good pussy-boy that does what's it's told!'

I turn away again. Marky slips his arm back round me, then pussy-boy's face slams into my ass-crack at speed. I feel the wetness, his tongue pushin' against my tight ring, sweepin' round and round, then up and down. Oh man, I'm tellin' ya, the sensation runnin' through me just ain't like no other, the solid lump of cock stickin' out in front of me revvin' itself up like some kind of turbo-charged engine.

Suddenly, the arm Marky's got around my waist relaxes, pussy-boy soundin' like he's just been saved from drownin'.

'How'd he do this time, Johnny?'

I gotta take some deep breaths before I can say anythin'. 'Don't know exactly, Marky. Still feels like it ain't workin' right. Take a look an' see.' Turnin' my head a bit, I see Marky bendin' down, peerin' up my ass, his cock bouncin' off the top of pussy-boy's head.

'Gee, Johnny, I ain't sure, but I think I see a bit of shit there that he might've missed.'

'Pedro,' I shouts over my shoulder, 'you got good eyesight. Come here.' I see the tall, thin shape comin' closer, his prick droolin' from a recent jerk-off. He bends down as well, standin' on the other side of pussy-boy, makin' like he's lookin' up my ass.

'Yeah,' Pedro tells me, 'I think Marky's right. The fuckin' useless fairy can't even clean an asshole proper.'

'Maybe,' I suggest, 'if the two of ya helped him?' I feel Marky's forearm wrappin' itself round me. Then Pedro does the same, but comin' from the opposite side, his arm restin' atop Marky's.

'You'd better get that tongue of yours fuckin' workin' this time, pretty-boy,' Marky says.

I feel the two guys' muscled forearms flexin' as they propel pussy-boy's face into my crack with nose-bustin' force. Oh Jeeze, I'm tellin' ya, they got him held in there so tight an' for so long, with that tongue of his burrowin' away like crazy, it seems like he gonna suffocate for sure. From the corner of my eye, I see Marky and Pedro are grindin' their hard-ons into as much of Tony's face as ain't disappeared up my butt. The guys on the cots are hootin' and whistlin', all at different stages of buildin' up and lettin' shoot.

Awe, man, I'm tellin' ya, I feel twenty-feet tall, like everyone else ain't nuthin' but a buncha fuckin' dummies who ain't fit for nuthin' 'cept lickin' my boots, kissin' my ass and maybe servicin' my dick.

'How's he doin' this time?' I hear Pedro ask, havin' to shout to be heard over the hullabaloo.

I realise that pussy-boy is hammering his fists against my buttocks, that he's havin' real breathin' problems, but that the guys are waitin' for me to give the nod. So I give it, not wantin' a dead pussy-boy to explain away tomorrow mornin'. I let go of my knees, straighten up and turn round. Marky and Pedro back away towards their cots, stiff cocks swayin' as they go. Tony's on his knees, chest heavin', tryin' to get some air in himself.

'I think you're gonna need some practice there, pretty-boy,' I tell him. He's lookin' at my crotch, starin' up into the towerin' shaft of flesh that he knows is comin' to him, one way or the other.

'Sorry...' he kind of mumbles.

'Well, sorry ain't good enough,' I roar, the way he flinches makin' my cock twitch. 'Maybe tomorrow I'll let the other guys take you to the john with them.' I like the idea of doin' that to him, feeling my balls tinglin' at the thought. The rest of the guys seem real enthusiastic about the idea too.

'Yeah!' I tell pussy-boy, 'you'd just love that! Wouldn't ya?'

He nods, knowin' better than to do anythin' else.

By this time, my cock's on fuckin' fire, feelin' like it could de-molish a brick wall no problems at all. Usually, I give it to him up the ass, but he squeals like a fuckin' happy pig the whole time. Naw, I decide, his mouth's almost as good, and it sure as hell is a lot damn quieter.

'Pedro, throw me a rubber.'

It lands a couple of feet away.

'Go get that, pussy-boy,' I tell him, my foot lashin' out and landin' on the side of his butt. He crawls over on his hands and knees and the other guys think this real funny.

'Go fetch!'

'Here, boy, here!'

Two-note dog whistles.

'Right,' I tell him, once he's back in position, kneelin' at my feet, 'get one on me.' Like I told you before, I'm smarter than your average teenage fuck-up: I ain't go no intention of takin' up resi-dence in a pine box before I gotta. His hands are shakin' as he pulls the plastic down over me.

'Open up!' I bark.

The other guys are gettin' real excited again.

'Cocksucker gonna take his medicine like a good little pussy-boy.'

'C'mon, Johnny, really give it to the fuckin' little pussy.'

'Yeah, Johnny, you spoon it to him, and spoon it to him good!'

His eyes have a kind of scared look as I grab a hold of myself, and push the head into his face-hole. It's like he can't open his jaw wide

Jack Dickson

enough, like there ain't enough room in there to accommodate what I gotta give him. But man, even I ain't ever seen it this pumped up.

The inside of his mouth feels real good: warm, wet, kind of invitin'. The length of my dick is throbbin' like the only thing that'd satisfy me is drilling holes in concrete. Thing is, I'm gonna treat his face-hole like it was a slab of concrete, and he can see that in my eyes, knows he's gonna get it good this time.

I manage to hold back a couple of seconds, give him time to fill his lungs, 'cause I know he's gonna need it later. I lock my fingers together on the back of his skull, him reachin' up and placin' little pussy-boy hands on each of my ass cheeks. The first couple of times I bang the back of his throat, I can almost feel the pain joltin' through him. That gets his little pussy-boy instincts workin' real fast, gets him re-anglin' his head, gets him relaxin' that throat.

Real soon most of my cock is all the way in, gripped real tight inside of his gut, and man, it ripples like no asshole or pussy-hole ever can. I just fuckin' ram myself in there, batter down full-force into that sweet pussy-boy mouth-hole, feel my balls touchin' his chin, my pubes grindin' against his upper lip. I'm still hearin' the guys way in the distance, still hearin' pussy-boy's choking gags, but really I've died and gone to heaven.

But I gotta look back down from heaven when pussy-boy finally manages to make me feel his nails diggin' into my behind. That's his way of tellin' me I'm killin' him, to make me notice his eyes are poppin' out of his head, that his face's turnin' blue. I gotta ease off a bit, just for a second, then he gets it twice as bad as before. I wanna punch it in further, wanna give the little cocksuckin' bastard a fuckin' he ain't never gonna forget, wanna drive it into him so deep he gonna piss in his pants every time he even hears my name.

Just before I shoot, my hands pull his head down hard on the rod wedged in his gullet. I hold him there and he's jerkin' forward with everythin' he's got. When the juice busts out, its like the top of my head got blown off at the same time – got blown off clean into space.

The cocksucker ain't movin' when ol' Johnny-boy's brain does finally kick back into gear, the hammerin' in my chest slowin'. I look down and see his eyelids are sort of flutterin', his eyeballs rolling about. There's a poppin' sound as I pull my dick out an' then push him away so he topples onto the floor. Flat on his back.

The guys are all cheerin' and clappin', a couple of stragglers still whackin' the last bit of life out of their cocks. I go to my cot, pull off the rubber and wipe myself with a towel. I feel real good, but kind of tired as well.

Pussy-boy drags himself off to the can for a good gargle, or maybe to powder his nose, or whatever it is he does in there. I settle into bed, the other guys startin' to get bunked down as well, the buzz of conversation slowly dyin'.

The room is completely silent by the time Tony comes back. He stops at the foot of my bunk, looks kind of longingly at it. Oh what the hell, I'm feelin' kind of generous on account of enjoyin' myself so much. I flick back the blanket and watch as he rushes round the side and clambers in. He puts his arm round me, his nose nestlin' in at my shoulder.

'I wish you weren't gettin' out tomorrow,' he says, soundin' sad.

'I told ya! Don't worry! I'll make sure you get set-up with someone else, someone who'll look after ya just as good as me.'

Despite me tellin' him this, I know he's startin' to cry. I feel the dampness on my skin, and his chest heavin'.

Jesus! I ask ya: pussy-boys!

# TERMINAL ORGASM

The thin, wiry boy of about twenty, with cropped hair and two gold studs through one ear, was on his knees, bent over the lower bunk. The well-built, muscular man with blond hair pulled back into a ponytail was kneeling on the floor behind him.

Mark pushed his arse back against Joe's distended cock, which was already all the way inside, gripped tight by a tunnel of rippling muscle. Both teetered precariously on the brink, locked together on the edge of a volcano, the build-up of pressure within both bodies becoming critical.

Joe breathed deeply. No, not now, he thought, not yet. He stopped thrusting; he gently ran the palm of his hand over the shaven nape of the other's neck, dispersed its collected rivulets of sweat.

Mark attempted to stifle his agonised moans by burying his face in the blanket. His body was wracked by the exquisite torment of possible release, yet again postponed. How often in the past few hours had he been brought to the point of shooting, only to feel the moment ebb away? He clenched his fists, every fibre of his being focused on the eight inches of solid flesh which now seemed to hold his very existence in its power.

Joe watched the flickering aura of his lover, watched it gradually move from flaming red to a warm orange, watched its orgiastic heat gradually dissipate. This would be their last time together; tonight had to be special, the best. 'Patience,' he whispered into the darkness. 'Patience.'

Mark's body began to tremble by way of reply.

Joe began thrusting again: long, deep, slow movements. He could feel the eagerness in the buttocks grinding backwards to meet him. The aura moved up-spectrum again with the speed of litmus paper in acid. It burned with a brightness which dazzled Joe, made his eyes squint: flashing gold, polished copper, searing pink, fluorescent white. The boy's aura was becoming ever more agitated: a kaleidoscopic, pyrotechnic display. Every so often a solar-flare would tear itself free and dance around the cell. Joe fucked the hungry little arse harder now, fucked it with a merciless and gratefully received ferocity.

They came together, a single orgasm shuddering through both their bodies. And in those few moments of cosmic union, they were more than just physically joined, they existed as one, were fused into a single nuclear consciousness which exploded with the power and brightness of a supernova.

All too quickly both were back in the gloom of their small, shared cell; and in their all-too-separate bodies. Neither moved, both panting, both reluctant to sever their physical connection.

Eventually, Joe did withdraw. Standing, he peeled off his condom, walked to the open toilet and flushed it away. Mark didn't move. After two years he knew the routine. Joe bent down and lightly parted Mark's arse, using his pinkie to gently check for tears or rips along the anal wall. After a few moments he lightly slapped Mark's buttocks. 'You're OK!' In a single bound, he launched his 6'2" of bulk onto the top bunk and stretched himself out.

Mark staggered to his feet, legs unsteady. He walked the few steps to the hand basin, ran the faucet, and strategically sat on the cold aluminium so his arse-crack hovered above the sink. He splashed the cooling water into his fuck-hole for several minutes before soaping it up.

'Hurry up,' came the voice from the top bunk.

Mark quickly towelled himself off. A few moments later, the

angular bones of his 5'8" frame were accommodating themselves round the solid and well-defined body on the top bunk. He felt himself encompassed in the powerful arms, rested his head against the broad chest still damp with sweat.

It wasn't long before Joe felt another dampness on his chest, felt the slow, steady trickle of quiet tears. He hugged the slender shoulders tighter.

'I don't want you to go,' Mark said, his voice low and sad.

'You know I've no choice.'

Joe's three-year sentence for hacking, 'illegal possession of information,' as it was officially known, had finally come to an end. Mark, on the other hand, was only two years into a life sentence.

Mark's pale blue eyes stared up at Joe's dimly lit face. He looked at the man who had taken care of him, protected him from the moment he had walked into this cell on the first night of his first custodial sentence. Everyone came in with expectations, but Mark had found the last thing he expected, something he'd never known before: warmth, caring, understanding... love. 'I want to come with you.'

'You can't.' Joe's voice was soft, but slightly chiding. There was no point in pretending; both had to accept the inevitable.

The sky outside the small barred window was turning crimson. Both were tired but determined not to squander these last few hours in sleep.

'Will you go back to doing what you did before?' Mark asked.

'I don't know anything else.'

'Have you ever met anyone else with your... abilities?'

'Nope. But there must be others out there, somewhere.'

Joe's 'abilities' had built him a formidable reputation on the outside. He was reckoned to be the best hacker in the business. But there was something only a select few, including Mark, knew: Joe was computer-illiterate; he didn't need the aid of technology to pursue his criminal activities.

The only tool Joe required was his own brain, the most advanced and sophisticated computer ever conceived. He had trained himself, developed the mental powers which lie latent in everyone. As well as seeing the aura of psychic energy which encompasses every living thing, his mind could reach out telepathically to that alternative time-space dimension called cyberspace and the databases stored there. He could even project his astral spirit into virtual-reality simulations.

The two talked on for a while, both nervously watching the ever-brightening sky, both determined to be strong, for the sake of the other. They fell asleep in each other's arms. But time marched on regardless.

The bus ride into the city took about an hour. The summer heat was brutal, oppressive. First things first, he thought – money.

'Harry's' was a small, non-descript bar in the yuppy end of town. It also served as a working office for several members of the criminal elite. Jenny was perched on her usual barstool.

'Well, hello stranger!' she said. The woman looked as though she had just stepped out of a Vogue fashion spread. Her poisonous-green aura, however, told a truer story.

'So what's going down?'

'For a man of your unique talents, there's always plenty.' The lips contorted into a smile, but the cold, grey eyes were hard as ice. Joe sat down and ordered a drink. Jenny lifted a hand-held terminal from the bar, hit a few buttons, then reeled off some potential customers. A Middle Eastern government interested in a detailed breakdown of a neighbour's military spending for the coming year, and a Swiss pharmaceutical group anxious for the formulae of a rival's new, wonder tranquilliser seemed the most promising.

'Usual terms,' she explained, 'cash on delivery. So the quicker you come up with the goods –'

'I'll know,' Joe said, finishing of his drink, 'tomorrow, maybe the day after.'

They talked about money and Joe watched as her aura shifted to a gangrene tone. He knew she was lying, deducting more than her supposed 10%. But what the hell, he wasn't exactly in a position to start lecturing on honesty.

They exchanged business-like smiles and Joe headed back towards the heat-baked streets. He weaved his way through the jostling crowd of smart, designer suits. Thoughts of a long, cold shower in his small apartment on the other side of town were suddenly interrupted. His head was pulled back by its ponytail, his right arm grabbed and forced halfway up his back. There were two of them, one either side.

'This way please,' the older of the two men said, almost civilly, as if Joe had any choice in the matter. Joe stood sandwiched between the two cops who had 'requested' he go with them.

The car journey to the station had been made in total silence. On arrival, they had bundled him through a door marked 'Detention Area'. It was a small, stark room with no furniture apart from a flimsy plywood chair. The fluorescent strip-lighting was harsh and a smell of disinfectant mingled with something distinctly less pleasant.

'So, what now?' Joe asked. He waited. No reply from either. Minutes passed. It was obvious the two cops' physical proximity was an intimidatory tactic: one stood a few inches behind him, the other so close in front Joe caught faint whiffs of his breath.

'Oh, come on! What the hell is this?'

The one behind spoke: 'You'll find out soon enough, asshole. Now stand there and keep your fuckin' mouth shut!'

Joe looked at the one in front: around twenty, his aura a bitter yellow.

'Joseph Johnstone,' the one behind began, 'we have reason to believe you are in possession of a Class A controlled drug. In accordance with the 1999 Control of Dangerous Substances Act, we intend to conduct a full body search. Do you understand?'

Joe nodded.

'A full body search,' the fresh-faced subordinate echoed.

Joe saw a goading glint in the brown eyes. He watched as the younger theatrically produced a pair of surgical gloves from his trouser pocket and then snapped them on.

'Remove your clothes slowly, one item at a time, and give them to the officer in front,' the older cop instructed.

Joe slipped off his leather bikers' jacket and handed it over. The polythene-clad fingers worked their way systematically round each pocket. Joe's impassive features didn't register his surprise when a small plastic bag of white powder was produced from an inside pocket. The jacket was thrown onto the chair and the strip continued. Nothing else was found.

Joe stood naked, his gaze meeting and holding the brown eyes opposite. He saw a small boy tormented and teased by an insecure, overbearing father; a childhood of hell at the hands of school and neighbourhood bullies; a policeman avenging himself for a life-time of petty hurts and insults. The cop seemed uncertain for a second, and looked away, as if he was the one exposed, vulnerable, self-conscious.

'Lift your balls and cock,' the voice from behind instructed.

Joe cupped his dangling genitalia with his right hand and pulled upwards. A PVC-encased digit explored the area between his inner thighs.

'Now turn round, face me, and grab your knees.'

Joe obeyed, waited a second, then a felt a sharp, penetrative stab delivered with far more force than necessary to confirm the anal passage clear.

'Nothin',' the young cop reported, sounding disappointed as he slowly retracted his finger with a stinging, hair-pulling twist.

'Bastard!' Joe mumbled as he straightened up.

'Stand there,' the one in charge said. 'Someone wants to have a word with you.'

Joe watched as his clothes and the cop-manufactured 'evidence' were swept up by the departing officers. He waited.

The 'someone' who wanted a word looked to be in his early thirties, had short black hair, an athletic build and a strong, aristocratic bone structure. He wore a crisp, white short-sleeved shirt, a black necktie and pinstripe flannel trousers belted with a narrow strip of tan leather. He carried a large manila envelope, which he carefully placed on the room's solitary chair.

'So, you're Joseph Johnstone?' The tone was educated, cultured and mildly mocking.

'Yes.'

'You're looking at six months inside, Johnstone.' The dark-brown eyes surveyed the naked man standing before them.

'That stuff was planted,' Joe said quietly, hands clasped behind back, staring straight ahead.

Someone's gaze had a cool, appraising quality as he slowly circled Joe's muscular, well-honed body. 'But there might be a possible... alternative. A way by which we might just conveniently lose the paperwork concerning this case.'

'What?'

'Well, there's a problem you might be able to help with. Your reputation as a computer-wiz is quite awesome.' Someone was stationary again, standing directly in Joe's line of vision.

'I'm listening.' Joe looked at Someone's aura: a rich, authoritative mahogany.

'This business with the drugs wasn't my first choice. I enquired about your 'going rate'. Unfortunately you charge more than my department's whole budget for the year. I even considered asking you as a 'concerned citizen'. However, I was assured that approach was unlikely to succeed.' Someone's hand shot out with such unexpected speed that Joe jumped. He gasped as his testicles were grabbed and squeezed with a firm, even pressure. 'So,' Someone continued, lessening his grip slightly, 'it seemed that a little coercive force was required.'

'OK... OK,' Joe rasped, 'I'll have a look at whatever it is for you.'

'I'm sure we'll work well together, Joseph. And look, I can see we share at least one taste in common.'

Joe looked down towards the hand still clutching his balls, looked at the eight hard, throbbing inches of proof that they did indeed share a taste in common.

'I think perhaps you might like a little example of what you can expect if I'm not entirely satisfied with your work. I can assure you, I'm a very hard taskmaster.'

Joe nodded his agreement.

'Assume the position!' Someone said with a faint chuckle in his voice.

Joe moved towards the near wall and spread-eagled himself against it. He felt Someone's shoes as they kicked his legs further apart. He heard the thin leather strap drawn free of its belt-loops, heard it whish through the air, heard the sharp crack as it impacted on his arse. A spasm of pleasure-pain convulsed his body, caused his back to arch, had his buttocks thrusting upwards eager for more. He shot his load against the wall on the sixth strike.

'I think you're going to enjoy working for me, Joseph,' Someone commented, producing a folded white linen handkerchief. 'Clean up your mess... and do try to control yourself the next time.'

Joe began wiping the wall and himself.

'All the information you need is in the envelope. I'll contact you in a few days to see how your investigation is progressing... And Joseph...'

Joe stopped his wall wiping and turned to see Someone standing by the door.

'I know you won't want to disappoint me...' Someone was fingering the brown belt now back around his waist. 'Will you?'

'No,' Joe agreed, attention returning to the almost-clean wall. 'I'll have your clothes brought back.'

Joe heard the door open then close. He was irked at the drugs plant and being blackmailed into 'volunteering' his services free of charge. But then again, he decided, thinking of Someone's rich, resonant aura, there was more to life than money.

Once back in his apartment, Joe spread the envelope's contents across the lounge floor. It didn't take him long to grasp Someone's problem. Two hundred and twenty people dead over the last year: all found on post-mortem to have suffered a brain haemorrhage; all hooked up to one of two Virt-Sex games – 'Army Camp' or 'Harem Nights'.

There were reams of documents from both government and industry scientists. The consensus of opinion seemed to be that it was a bug or virus in the programmes which caused the extensive neuro-cellular damage. Much effort had been expended investigating the possibility of either ultrasonic frequencies or epileptic strobing. There were detailed line-by-line breakdowns of the programmes as well as exhaustive frame-by-frame analysis. Their investigations had got precisely nowhere.

Joe considered the problem. As the eggheads had rightly concluded, it couldn't be the actual hardware – the VR suits and decoding boxes. There were millions of suits in use round the world and had been for over twenty years now. The technology itself was proven safe.

If not the hardware, then what?

Logic dictated the software. But that didn't ring true either. There were thousands of games – action, adventure, fantasy, educational – constructed on the same basic principals. And if it was the software, why just these 220 men and women? Their medical histories showed no prior abnormalities.

These two games had a combined hit rate of 80,000 a week in

North America alone. Every one of those eighty thousand users downloaded exactly the same version of the game. If the master-copy had a virus, then all accessors should have been exposed to its effects. No, it wasn't the hardware and it wasn't the software. Sadly, conventional thinking dictated that's all there was to computers. Luckily, psychic hackers were not constrained by conventional thinking.

Joe reluctantly swept the documents back into their envelope. He was annoyed at having to postpone further investigation into what was an intriguing mystery. But satisfying his curiosity would have to wait. What he needed now was money.

Joe lay stretched out and naked on his bed. His abilities stemmed from the synthesis of two very different and very ancient techniques: sex-magic and astral projection.

The first step was deep, controlled breathing. The mind must be focused exclusively on the inhalation and exhalation of air. It took about ten minutes for Joe to reach the required self-induced, trance-like state.

Next, the focus of his mind broadened, expanded to include his genitals. His right hand began massaging the ball sac, occasionally moving upwards in a sweeping-motion across a hardening cock. Encircling the foreskin with thumb and index finger, Joe began tugging on his eight inches of engorged flesh. The movement was slow and rhythmic, the upward pull synchronised exactly with the expansion of his lungs and abdomen, the downward stroke with their contraction.

After a while, his breathing and hard-on seemed to merge, and become indistinguishable, as if breathing-in was an action unachievable without the upward friction of foreskin against cockhead. Joe's concentration was intense: the build up of sexual tension had to be rigorously controlled. There must be no risk of over-stimulation or ejaculation.

Joe began to feel as if he were floating. At first, it was just a vague disorientation, a light dizziness. Gradually, the sensation became more pronounced. A separation had occurred: the husk of muscled meat on the bed was left behind as Joe gravitated towards the ceiling. He looked down and saw himself there: skin glistening, eyes closed, right hand moving up and down on his twitching hard-on. It was always an exhilarating experience: freeing the astral body from its prison of flesh. The liberation was powered by sexual energy. It was that force Joe had mastered and learned to control.

His studies had began with the mystic principles of Tantric Sex: the art of postponing orgasm. The arcane texts had explained how easily sexual energy could be redirected, sublimated, into its close relatives: magical and psychical energy. By controlling the flow of sexual energy within the body, by manipulating its point of release, an individual could unlock the door to other worlds, other dimensions.

Joe watched himself with a sense of satisfaction, pride even. He had trained his body well. The hand movement and breathing would continue automatically. The physical self would mechanically supply its astral counterpart with the necessary flow of psycho-sexual energy; it would keep itself at exactly the correct point of stimulation with a thermostat-like accuracy. The naked male animal lying on the bed was now a human dynamo, a biological generator of psychic and astral power.

Joe began his trans-dimensional travel. His consciousness shifted once again, began moving even further away from its meat-cage. There were streams of blinding, flashing, multi-coloured lights as he left the physical dimension, propelled himself along the space-time continuum, crashed through the multiplicity of realities separating realspace and cyberspace.

\*

People didn't understand about computers; didn't understand that the whole was more than the sum of the parts. Taken separately, each one was just what it seemed: a bunch of wires, circuits and microchips capable of reading and following a series of sequential instructions. It was when they were put together, linked into a structure very like the human brain's neural network, that something... magical happened. That something was consciousness. The Internet, now linking virtually every computer on the planet, was nothing less than a massive, self-aware, sentient brain.

Like all highly developed intelligences, the Internet had an astral presence which existed in a different dimension from the physical domain. Cyberspace was simply the spirit world of silicon-based life. Astrally, the Internet was a dazzling display of laser-like beams choreographed with mathematical precision. It was a mesh of ever-changing configurations, different patterns and formations emerging and dissolving by the second. It seemed to stretch for miles in all directions, a latticework of luminous mental energy suspended in the dark, infinite universe that was cyberspace.

Joe floated before the ever-shifting maze of linear lights. As always, he felt dwarfed, awed by its sheer enormity. He looked around and saw, twinkling like stars in the darkness, other Internet-like consciousnesses. Those, he felt sure, were the computer networks of alien civilisations. There was, he had noticed before, a web of light-threads connecting these disparate bodies: they were communicating with each other. He often wondered what they talked about, but had long ago decided it would probably be incomprehensible to any of the human or alien minds inadvertently responsible for creating this higher life form.

Time was running short: the non-orgasmic stimulation of his

physical self had a finite duration. He redirected his mind back to the radiant, complex thought patterns displayed before him. A shimmer of recognition rippled through the astral construct. It knew he was there. Joe didn't react as a beam of psychic energy moved slowly towards him. There was a moment of almost sexual pleasure as the cyberbeing penetrated him. But this intimacy went far beyond anything which occurred on the lowly biological plane. This union was a joining of consciousness, the ultimate mind fuck...

Within seconds, Joe was torn from the embrace of his ethereal lover, and was snapped back to his convulsing body. Come was shooting out of him with explosive force, volley after volley of thick, white viscous globules which splattered his upper chest, his neck, his face. Hours of pent-up tension were released within the space of seconds.

Panting, bathed in sweat, shaking, Joe swung his feet onto the bare wooden floor. The return was always so... sudden, so unexpected. But his meat had performed well, had energised the astral spirit just long enough to complete its role as the passive partner. But instead of body fluids, what had passed between the participants was pure, unadulterated information.

Now on his feet, Joe staggered to a small table which sat beneath the curtained window. His waning hard-on drooled long, white strings of spunk down his upper leg. He quickly scribbled the required details on a notepad.

Exhausted, Joe staggered back to the bed. He closed his eyes. It took several minutes for the room to stop spinning. Drying come tightened on his skin as he slipped into a long, deep sleep.

Joe woke to morning sunshine seeping in around the drawn curtains. After quickly showering and dressing, he made straight for 'Harry's'. Even this early, Jenny was propped on her usual stool. She took the sheet of paper filled with hastily scribbled chemical symbols and dollar amounts. 'Wait here,' she instructed, leaving.

Joe had a few drinks, chatted idly with the barman, and waited there. She returned two hours later, face flushed from the exhilaration of a successfully completed trade. The Swiss pharmaceutical company and the Arab government had both been grateful. Jenny handed over their payment, minus her highly elastic '10%'. Joe didn't argue, just took the money offered and left.

He was pleased the mundane problem of cash was, for the moment, solved. It left him free to concentrate exclusively on a far more intriguing problem – Someone's problem.

Curiosity dictated his first step: exploration of the non-psychic route into cyberspace. He was probably the only person alive who'd never experienced Virtual Reality via a computer terminal and VR suit. There was a hardware shop on his way home. He left loaded-down with several large boxes and relieved of at least half his ill-gotten gains.

Twenty minutes later he was admiring his new, matt-black, functionally designed cyberunit. It consisted of a built-in keyboard, a mini-screen and two jacks: one for the power-supply, one for the VR suit. As the salesman had promised, it hadn't been difficult to assemble or operate. The screen went from grey to black and announced: 'ARMY CAMP located and downloaded'.

Beginning to strip, Joe was surprised to find himself nervous, apprehensive. He was far too seasoned a cybernaut to be worried about the destination, or even the unfamiliar mode of transport. What played on his mind was the possibility of stumbling across a cause of spontaneous brain haemorrhage.

Pushing the thought from his mind, Joe, now naked, roughly shoved the expanda-foam butt-plug in place: four inches of rubbery, black plastic slid easily up his arse. Next, he put a condom over his still flaccid cock. He lifted and unzipped the VR suit. It was a one-piece item made from a thin, latex-like material which stretched to a skin-tight fit. Once the ski-mask-style hood was pulled over the face, his body was encased head to toe, except for the eyes.

It took him several minutes of manoeuvring to make sure the garment was properly positioned: the micro-thin metal filaments woven into the fabric were denser over the ears for sound; the nostrils for smell; the seat for butt-plug activation; the crotch for... the obvious. Lastly, Joe put the visor round his eyes. He was looking at, submerged in, a sea of endless blue.

Then the Virt-Sex game began.

'You sure you man enough to play?'

The questioned was posed by a close-shaven, crew-cutted man. He was in his mid-twenties with bulging forearms and biceps, which strained against the confines of a white string vest. His baggy camouflage trousers were tucked into thick-soled work boots.

'Yeah, 'course,' Joe replied, any other answer probably meaning a quick exit from the programme.

He had visited these cyber playscapes as a disembodied astral presence many times. The visual realism of the simulations had always impressed him. However, the physical sensations generated by the VR suit added a whole new dimension to the experience.

The barrack room had a row of neatly made beds down either side. There was a smell of sweat, socks, aftershave and polish. Sunlight and cooling air flooded in through the open window. Some distance away, out on the grass, a bellowing sergeant was mercilessly drilling a platoon of soldiers.

'Listen pal, don't go chicken on us once you're in there. We play for real.'

The computer-generated cybersoldier was convincingly lifelike. Yet, despite appearances, the man was really only several thousand lines of animated programming. He didn't have the aura which surrounded all truly living things. And, looking closer at the handsome face, Joe noticed the features had a slight cartoon quality, the skin an airbrushed flawlessness.

'I ain't never gone chicken in my life!' Joe protested, both in-trigued and vaguely aroused.

'Yeah, well... you wouldn't be the first who's gone apeshit when their luck ran out. Remember, eight sex-starved army-jocks ain't gonna take too kindly to havin' their R & R disrupted.'

'I hear what you're saying!' Joe insisted, now more than vaguely aroused.

'Right. Just so long as you get the picture. Give it a couple of minutes, then head down to the gym.' The soldier right-turned and marched briskly away.

Joe noticed a full-length mirror on the far wall. He was curious to see what the temporarily inhabited compu-sim body looked like. Staring back at him was a lightly tanned Nordic face, short, spiky blond hair, muscles bursting out from under army drag.

Now, he decided, seemed like a good-time to test the technol-ogy's fail-safe mechanism. All cybergames had a simple exit proce-dure: the player held their breath for a count of ten. Sensors in the VR suit took this as their signal to disconnect from the pro-gramme.

As he closed his eyes, inhaled, and started counting, Joe won-dered why this simple device hadn't been sufficient to save those other accessors from whatever had caused the blood vessels in their brains to rupture. No one – tied-up, bound, gagged, whatever – should find themselves 'trapped' in a simulation which had in some way gone wrong.

Exactly on the count of ten, Joe was once again aware of being encased in rubber, aware of the visor round his head, aware of being back in his own small apartment. The white lettering against the endless blue sky said: 'Game suspended. To continue, press button on left-hand side of visor'. Joe followed the instruction and instantly found himself returned to the barrack room.

No problem there, it seemed.

Not surprisingly, the gym was well sign-posted. He wandered through empty, military-grey corridors. Boisterous, playful voices seemed to echo from around every corner, their owners always just out of sight. The gym was large and well equipped. Eight uniformed men were grouped at the far end. Joe approached them.

'This, men, is the newest addition to our unit,' said the soldier from the barrack room.

Joe felt himself assessed and appraised by seven pairs of cold, calculating eyes. Every race and nationality seemed to be represented, each a perfect physical specimen, all wearing identical vests, camouflage trousers and boots.

'I'll run through the rules again, for the benefit of the newbie,' he continued, throwing a contemptuous glance in Joe's direction. 'We roll dice, lowest number gets what's coming to him. We all got the same odds, eight winners and one loser every night.'

Joe watched as the first man clenched his fist round a pair of dice, blew on them for luck, then threw. A pair of fives. He smiled, a look of relief spreading over his face. The dice were handed onto the next player.

The atmosphere was charged with sexual tension. Joe had to keep reminding himself that this wasn't real, that he was simply immersed in a sensory hallucination, that his fellow players were only pixel-drawn graphics. He looked at the smooth, deeply tanned Mediterranean who, so far, had thrown the lowest number – two twos.

Joe's cock twitched in anticipation. Despite the illusory nature of the scene, his own excitement was real enough. But what if he threw an even lower score, and 'got what was coming to him' from the other eight? His hard-on pulled again.

The dice were hot and damp when Joe cupped them in his hand. A three and a two: not the lowest. He sighed: happy but also, somehow, slightly disappointed.

The Mediterranean was looking decidedly worried as the last of the nine accepted the two cubes. Joe watched as the player, who'd seen so many others go 'apeshit', threw two ones. The man paled noticeably, his features drawn, his eyes darting from face to face, like a caged animal with no way out.

'You know the routine, man,' prompted a towering black man, his strikingly angular face as expressionless as his voice.

The loser stood motionless, like someone in shock. A whimper escaped his tightly pursed lips.

'Want us to remind you... ?' the man threatened, moving in unison with several of the others towards the reluctant player.

The group silently watched as the focus of their attention pulled off his vest, then bent down to untie shoe laces. He was almost shaking now. He was led naked to the press-bench, his erection already topped with a pearl of pre-come.

He lay face-down, his head projecting over one end. They tied his arms and legs securely to either side of the bench. His arse, splayed on the bench, was an open invitation.

The others stripped quickly, a buzz of conversation developing in tandem with an air of pack-like conspiracy. Joe quickly realised they were to take the man on the bench in pairs, the pecking order determined by their scores. He was coupled with the muscular, long-limbed black man. They were second in the running order. Joe looked at the ten-inched, fist-thick cock of his partner.

'Hey man, maybe you an' me could get together sometime, on our own.'

Joe nodded.

It was easy to see why the game was so popular. For a start, he noticed, this virtual body was several inches better endowed than his real meat. The dice throwing had actually been quite a tense, exciting affair. Presumably there was a genuine risk of 'losing' and finding oneself strapped to the bench. Added to that, there were possible variations in each game played in terms of which compu-sim got fucked; where you were in the getting-to-fuck queue; who you were partnering; and the option of having a separate scene with him.

Joe watched as the first pair set to work. One knelt on the floor and fucked the prostrate man's mouth while the other sat on the bench at the opposite end and started working his cock up the rounded, well-shaped arse. The wriggling, writhing receiver of these none-too-gentle hard-ons had already shot several loads by the time they swapped orifices.

Next came Joe and his new buddy. Joe took the arse. For the first time, the two-dimensional, unreal nature of the event struck home: there was no aura. When Joe fucked, the changes in his lover's astral glow were almost as important as the physical sensations. Nonetheless, he plunged his artificially enhanced member into the computer-generated image. The hole was wet and sticky from its previous two occupants. There were hoots and shouts of encouragement from the guys still waiting behind. Joe could see the programme wasn't designed for finesse and allowed himself to come quickly.

At the moment of orgasm he was snapped back to reality. The message read: 'Game over. Cost $300. If you want to play again please press button on left side of visor.' Joe pulled off the visor, his eyes taking several seconds to adjust from the virtual to the actual. The come in the condom was turning cold and he began unpeeling the VR suit from his body.

The game itself was nothing but good, clean, fantasy-fun. Whatever it was that had caused those players to haemorrhage, it wasn't intrinsic to the programme. The disruptive factor must have originated elsewhere in cyberspace and then invaded the individual playscape of each fatality. His approach to 'Harem Nights' would have to take a different tack. But first, a shower...

Joe, lying sprawled on the bed, glanced briefly down at his wet, naked meat. His right hand was slowly working its way up and down the length of his hard-on with rhythmic, clockwork repetition. Minutes later his astral-self was once again floating before the cyber-consciousness. Joe readied himself, opened his mind to the approaching beam of light, passively waited to be penetrated. The connecting experience was always intense. Joe knew the core of his being, his very essence, was at the mercy of the entity now driving itself deep inside him. But its intrusive embrace was always gentle, almost loving.

Six hundred and twenty people were at this moment playing 'Harem Nights', Joe learned. This time, however, he wanted something more than just information. His request was granted. He felt himself drawn into the kaleidoscopic matrix, absorbed into and made part of the crackling network of mental and spiritual energy which constituted this sentient, alien life-form.

Joe passed through array after array of dazzling, geometric light formations, went deeper and deeper into the very centre of the silicon-based intelligence. He felt himself guided, propelled along the mathematical maze of psycho-neural pathways.

The journey glided to a halt directly above a bulbous collection of nodules, each node containing a 'Harem-Nights' player locked in an individual playscape. With hypodermic-like swiftness, he was injected into one of the glowing spheres.

The room was Byzantine in design – a high-domed ceiling, mosaic walls and pillars. Scattered around the bare stone floor were piles of large, densely-embroidered silk cushions. Fleur-de-lis portals looked out onto desert sand the colour of rust. The blue-black sky was licked by tongues of flaming orange from a blood red, setting sun. Joe could guess the VR-suit-generated input which he was missing: balmy, sensuous heat-filled air; heavy Eastern scents; haunting, snake-charming musical notes.

He moved towards a stone archway and into a smaller antichamber. The scantily clothed woman lying on the luxurious Persian carpet was bound and gagged with chiffon scarves and obviously in some distress. She kept screwing her eyes tightly shut, pursing her lips, waiting, then looking around in disbelief. Joe realised she was attempting to use the exit procedure, holding her breath for longer and longer periods. Something, someone, was keeping her here, caging her within the simulation.

Joe looked around. It took his eyes several minutes to register what was there, and his mind several more to comprehend it – surely impossible, but standing only feet away: a 'living' computer-generated image.

The male compu-sim was covered with body-hair, muscularly overdeveloped, and very tall. His head was shaven, the scalp pink and shiny, the face mannequin-perfect. Its aura filled the room with a malignant, poisonous black. The locus of this power was a grotesque cock: a purple-veined enormity throbbing with undischarged electro-sexual static.

The man began taunting his captive, the player's consciousness held fast within his astral force field. He knelt on the carpet beside her, swivelled slightly at the hip, then lightly slapped her face. Each time his hand made contact, there was a display of sparks and a violent spasming of her limbs. The compu-sim shifted position, undid the scarves around the player's legs, then started running his hand up and down her inner thigh. His obscene hard-on pulsated. The victim, Joe realised, was about to be convulsed with a massive doze of negative psychic energy. The strength of the current would severely disrupt normal bio-mental stasis: and therefore cause the recipient's brain cells to burst and explode like so much popcorn.

Joe stepped forward, and walked into the swirling vortex of tormented sexuality emanating from the other man. The cloak of astral power swathing the compu-sim was like nothing he had ever encountered before; it threatened to suffocate him in its oppressive, claustrophobic folds. Common sense told him he should be afraid; that he should put maximum distance between himself and this monster.

Instead, he had decided to take a gamble. Both of them were, after all, intruders, interlopers, in this cyber playscape. It seemed probable the compu-sim would not be expecting to meet another disembodied free-radical. A few seconds' disruption to the imprisoning force-field might be just enough to let the terrified player beat a hasty retreat.

The man looked up, jumped to his feet, and was obviously startled. The pervasive, all-encompassing aura lightened to grey. Joe heaved a sigh of relief as he saw the woman take full advantage of her would-be murderer's confusion. She held her breath, waited, and then was gone, leaving an empty shell of skin-toned pixels behind.

Joe met and held the fury-filled eyes of the other man. It was a confrontation he had to win. The compu-sim's psychic-presence was now back at full strength, with Joe firmly trapped within its vicelike grip. One sign of weakness, he felt sure, and it would be him they found tomorrow morning, his brain the consistency of mush.

He noticed with some satisfaction that the fifteen inches of erectile tissue was beginning to wane. Joe decided to press home his advantage, exploit his successful bluff. He walked slowly towards the hirsute body. A moment of panic creased the smooth, plastic features. In a flash the man was gone, passing straight through the solid-looking, but illusory, wall behind.

Joe didn't hesitate, and immediately set off in pursuit. This might be his only chance to locate the killer's point of origin, to understand from where the computer-simulation drew its power, to devise some means of stopping it.

The two moved through the cluster of self-contained 'Harem Nights' playscapes. Joe kept his attention trained on the fleeing compu-sim ahead. The two passed unnoticed through version after version of the uncorrupted programme: the olive-skinned sheikh, the demure slave-girl receiving a variety of lessons in how to please her lord and master. They reached the perimeter of the game-space. Joe saw his quarry leap the black chasm onto an adjacent reality: another collection of individual fantasy nodes. He followed.

It shouldn't have been a surprise, but was: 'Army Camp'. Of course, the geographical proximity of the sites would explain why, out of the thousands of Virt-Sex options, only these two had been affected.

Players at different stages of the programme whirred past at an accelerating rate: the barrack room scene; the dice-throwing scene; a variety of compu-sims strapped to the bench; one where 'his' body of only hours ago was 'getting what was coming to him'. On and on they went, Joe managing to keep the naked shape in sight.

Ahead, at the edge of the technologically sustained dream world, he saw the compu-sim hurtle itself into the void. Below, Joe saw, a single mushroom-like construction: still a playscape, but different from the previous two. Joe leapt, breaking through the self-repairing, electro-astral membrane. Inside was a single, massive cyber-set. He was standing on a deserted main street: Westgate Public Library, Westgate Hardware Store, Westgate Visitors Centre. The virtual downtown shopping precinct apparently wasn't in use at the moment.

Joe scanned the two sunlit, desolate rows of plate-glass, thought he saw movement just ahead, started in that direction...

Shit!

A wrenching surge tore through his astral body, lifted him clean of the sidewalk. He was being pulled back to his physical meat, its output of psychic energy about to be terminated by orgastic release. There was no point in fighting, nothing that could be done. At high-speed, he felt himself retracting, pulled free of the mushroom-contained city. He glanced downwards and saw the three different virtual realities of 'Army Camp', 'Harem Nights' and 'Westgate'. They formed a small triangle of glowing light in the darkness.

'Westgate,' Joe thought, crashing back to oneness with his physical body, his own hot come raining down on him. 'Westgate' had to be the genesis of the mutant compu-sim.

Joe staggered towards the shower, his body tense, his head buzzing with mental static. He had slept most of the day, exhausted after the excesses of the previous night. Drifting in and out of half-sleep, he had decided upon his plan of action. There were only two ways the psychotic, murderous compu-sim could be stopped: Plan A and Plan B, as he had christened them.

The ice-cold water blasted Joe's naked skin. He untied his long blond hair from its ponytail and started massaging strawberry-scented shampoo into his scalp. The gentle motion had a calming effect. Next, he started working a bar of soap over his body, gently teasing out knots of tension trapped within the well-muscled physique. He winced as his lathered hand brushed over his cock. Its protective skin was red and swollen, inflamed from its hours of almost constant friction over the past twenty-four hours. The cyber-consciousness had told him all he needed to know about 'Westgate'. Joe now understood exactly who and what had caused those players to die.

'Westgate', it transpired, was a highly successful virtual soap opera. Millions of participants tuned in for an hour every week, hooked their VR suits up to the show's compu-sim stars and virtu-ally experienced the not-so-everyday lives of the town's varied in-habitants. The production, from scripting to story lining to computer programming was the work of one man: Jeffrey Holling. The world-wide hit had made him a millionaire overnight.

After rinsing off his suds-covered body, Joe quickly rubbed him-self dry. He felt refreshed, limbs warm and glowing, head clearer. Tonight of all nights, he was going to need his wits about him.

The one expensive suit he owned still managed, miraculously, to look good. Wearing a shirt and tie felt awkward, but 'Star 12' was that kind of place. Its computerised register showed Mr. Holling as a nightly patron. He tied back his hair and took a last glance in the mirror. The reflection staring back looked good, even if he did say so himself. Joe only hoped he was the TV mogul's type.

On the way out he opened a small, concealed drawer on his writing desk. The small Japanese ceremonial knife glinted in the light, its curved blade supported by a jewel-encrusted hilt. He carefully slipped the lethal weapon into his inside pocket.

The club was exactly as Joe had anticipated: smart, exclusive, expensive. He sat strategically positioned at the busy bar. From this vantage point, he watched both the writhing dancers in their sounded proofed, perspex cages and the more sedate restaurant area.

Joe recognised his target for the night instantly. The photograph held on First National's database was a good likeness: around thirty, pale, a sickly pall hovering over thin, boyish features. He didn't so much walk as shuffle. He had a gangling build and seemed physically ill at ease with himself. A waiter greeted him familiarly while handing over a menu. Apparently, the tycoon didn't come here to party: this was where Jeffrey Holling came to eat, every night, alone. Money didn't buy happiness, or even friends, it seemed.

Joe waited until dessert before beginning the pickup. Long, significant stares went unanswered. The object of his attention blushed, looked as though he wanted to disappear under the table. But Joe persisted.

An hour later they were unlocking the door to Jeffrey Holling's penthouse suite. Joe felt an involuntary shudder. He held human life sacred, inwardly rebelled at the very thought of murder. But if his plan failed, how else could the cyber-massacre be ended?

\*

'So, tell me about yourself, Jeff,' Joe said, sipping from an art-deco styled cup.

A smell of freshly ground coffee permeated the spacious, airy lounge. The host was painfully shy and kept fidgeting. He'd sat on a chair at the opposite end of the room, rather than where the guest had hoped: on the sofa beside him.

'Well, I work in television, the VR side and...'

Joe waited.

'And I don't go in for this kind of of thing much... getting it on with guys in bars.'

Joe believed him.

'I don't really know why; too hung up maybe. My parents were these born-again Christians, you know? Everything to do with sex was dirty, the devil's work...'

Figures, Joe thought.

'And anyway, I don't get that many offers. Guess I'm not the kind of guy that gets other guys hot. I couldn't believe it when you started coming on to me.'

'You ever picked anyone up before?' Joe asked.

'A couple of times... but nothing much happened, really. I think they left kind of disappointed. I certainly never saw any of them again.'

'Maybe,' Joe ventured, 'you just haven't been trying... the right things.'

'Right things?'

'Sure! Everyone needs to find their own special right things... maybe we can find yours.'

Joe finished off a last mouthful of coffee and led his nervous host through to the bedroom. Jeffrey stood just inside the bedroom door while Joe sprawled himself on the king-size mattress.

The Dr Frankenstein of cyberspace shuffled uneasily from foot to foot.

His monster had begun life as a character in the virt-soap 'Westgate'. Donald Marks was introduced to the show as a deranged sexual manic. The compu-sim had spent several episodes terrorising the town's inhabitants. Following a few suspected real-life copycat murders, the TV company had insisted the character be written out. However, as Joe could testify, the creation lived on.

One glance at Jeffrey, and Joe knew his suspicions were correct: his aura was a sickly yellow, severely anaemic, totally depleted of its baser hues. He was the source of the compu-sim's life force, its psychic energy. In creating Donald Marks, the soap-writer had given expression to a hidden, unacceptable part of himself. Feelings and emotions ruthlessly repressed within Jeffrey's mind had suppurated, turned septic, gone psychotic and become the powerhouse of his alter-ego.

'So, what are these right things then?' Jeffrey asked eventually, embarrassed by the silence.

'Come here and we'll find out.'

Jeffrey approached cautiously. His jaundiced aura flickered uncertainly.

'Don't be frightened,' Joe said quietly.

Jeffrey said nothing, eyes riveted to his shoes.

'Why don't you undress me?'

'Undress you?'

Joe waited. After a long hesitation, two trembling hands reached down, and started unbuttoning a tight-fitting shirt. The strip was accompanied by a tense, nervous silence. Joe levered himself this way and that as Jeffrey removed item after item. Down to white briefs, Jeffrey stopped, his breathing heavy, anxiety all but extinguishing the already weak aura.

'Go on,' Joe gently encouraged.

'I'm no good at this kinda thing,' Jeffrey protested.

'Course you are,' Joe reassured. 'You just need to relax a little, find yourself.' He lifted his arse off the bed slightly, his right eyebrow cocked somewhere between an invitation and a challenge.

Tremulously, Jeffrey peeled the stretch fabric over the levitated buttocks and down the muscular, hair-covered legs. His eyes consumed the naked body stretched out before him.

Joe saw a response in the pallid aura: a sunburst flash of orange. He felt his own cock harden, his balls tingle. 'You like my body Jeff, don't you?'

'Yes.' The reply was almost a whisper.

'Why don't you touch it?'

The orange reappeared: this time a slow, steady, diffuse flame. Tentatively, Jeff's hands ran across the glistening torso, and the black-coated upper thighs. Joe felt himself respond to the touching and the deepening colour of the toucher's aura. Gradually the hands became more confident, more assured. With increasing boldness, they fondled his balls, gripped his erect and twitching cock, found their way round to his arse-crack and solidly packed butt. Joe gave a low moan. Jeff flinched.

'Hey, it's okay,' Joe reassured. The orange, he now saw, was a deep burnished copper, rich and sensuous. 'Jeff,' he continued, slowly turning onto his stomach, 'look at me, look at my arse, tell me what you see.'

'I see... something that gives me pleasure, makes my insides turn over, something that makes me hard... but frightens me at the same time.'

'Don't you see something else, Jeff?' Joe asked, aware his butt was gently undulating. 'Don't you see what this arse wants, what it's begging for, pleading for?'

No answer.

'For a few hours, Jeff, it wants to belong to you. It wants to give itself to you, wants you to exercise your rights of ownership.'

'But, how?'

'This arse needs to understand, Jeff, needs to understand that it's now your property. It wants to taste the sting of your belt.'

The first couple of lashes were awkward, unfocused. The next couple were better: well-spaced, deliberate. After a few minutes the strokes began to take on form, structure: hard-hard-soft, hard-hard-soft, hard-hard-soft.

Joe's body movements became synchronised with the beats. He arched backwards on the down stroke, his hard-on flexing in counterpoint. The tempo picked up, the interval between impacts shortening. Joe groaned in appreciation, gave himself over to the innate rhythm of control for so long buried in the man's id. He felt the sexual current flowing between them, locking them together, ionising the air around them. He craned his neck for an instant, looking at the man standing behind him. The aura was ablaze, pulsating, exploding in a rainbow of colours each time the strap landed on its target.

His plan seemed to be working. Relief hastened the incipient orgasm trapped within Joe's writhing body. It exploded in an animal howl, a torrent of ejected white, an ecstasy of contorted muscle. Jeff walked round to the side of the bed, panting heavily, drenched in sweat from the beating he had just delivered. Joe looked up, saw the brightly burning aura, alive, drawing its energy from the whole personality.

'That was incredible, Joe. I've never experienced anything like it.'

Joe found Jeff's previously elusive gaze meeting and holding his. The eyes, he registered for the first time, were grey. They seemed lit-up from within, empowered.

'We've all got these feelings inside us, Jeff. I don't think anyone really understands how or why. They're not bad or evil. It's only when they're refused existence that they become something dangerously uncontrollable, something that needs to find expression through another means, another channel.'

Jeff nodded.

'These feelings, this need for domination and submission, everybody experiences them in a different way. Take me, for example. I only feel it with other men. But I'm sort of in the middle: top some guys, bottom for others. But you... you might find you only want to top, and that you want to do it with both men and women.'

Jeff nodded again.

'Now, look at my arsehole and tell me what you see.' Joe felt his arse-cheeks forcefully parted.

'It's kind of... opening and closing.'

'That's because it wants you inside it, wants its owner to take full possession of his property.'

Ball lightening ricocheted within Jeff's field of psychic light. His aura seemed barely able to contain the force of astral energy released as the final prison walls of repression and denial were blown away. The power that previously flowed from this man's subconscious into his fictional creation had been successfully re-routed. It was now actual rather than virtual. Donald Marks was dead.

A smile twitched at the corners of Jeff's lips: a knowing smile, an understanding smile. 'I'll go get a condom.'

Joe shivered slightly, lying on his stomach, waiting. He'd entered this room with a nervous, insecure man. He was going to leave it well and truly fucked by a born master.

Joe was back at the police station, back in the Detention Area. He was naked, on his knees, eagerly sucking on his reward for a job well done. The cock projected up and out from pinstriped pants, entered his open mouth and reached deep into his throat. But Joe's pleasure went beyond the merely physical. He felt himself held fast, encompassed in the strong, authoritative aura. It encircled him, bathed him, possessed him.

Suddenly, Joe felt a tightening in the orgasmic field of energy which surrounded him. His eyes strained upwards. Someone looked down, gave a slight, almost imperceptible shake of the head. Joe slowly drew his lips from the saliva-coated hard-on's base, lifted his mouth to the dark red summit. His tongue explored the bulbous mound which crowned the tightly stretched pink skin. The centre of his universe quivered, a droplet of pre-come rising from deep within the volcanic edifice. The tension within their shared psychic space lessened: the moment of crisis, of premature ejaculation had passed. Joe took the full length of rigid flesh back into his mouth. He vaguely wondered how many hours Someone would allow him to continue. However long it was, it wouldn't be long enough.

After several more postponements, Someone finally nodded his okay. The hot white lava erupted with explosive force, spewed out as if under geological pressure, solidifying even as Joe gulped it back. The positively charged ions enveloping them vibrated as a unified mass, producing a single, crystal-clear celestial note of ear-splitting clarity. The astral glow around the two men coalesced, transmuted itself into a living membrane, allowed them to exist for the briefest of seconds as a single, unified entity.

Joe got to his feet, legs sore and cramped. He looked down at his own hard and aching cock.

'I once told you, Joseph, I was a very hard taskmaster. I should have added I am also very generous to those who complete their allocated tasks.'

Joe stole a glance at Someone's ocean-blue eyes.

'And right at this moment, I'm very favourably disposed toward you. So, if there's anything you want to ask me for?'

Joe asked.

Someone smiled. 'Going away on a drugs-rap wasn't really a threat, then. Tell me, why did you do it? Why did you help us?'

'Because,' Joe answered, struggling to find the words, 'there's nothing I wouldn't do... for you.' He felt himself embraced, an arm around his waist, the other across his shoulders, and pulled tight against Someone's chest. He basked for a few moments in the deep, woody tones of the other man's aura.

As he dressed, Joe listened to Someone talking on a cell-phone, heard him arrange the requested reward.

'You'll go straight from here. They're expecting you,' Someone said in a sad, farewell sort of voice.

'Hi!'

Mark jumped at the sound of the voice he most wanted to hear but least expected. He turned from the cell's small hand basin, face wet, water dripping. Movement seemed impossible, a threat to the continuation of the precious hallucination.

Joe watched his lover's aura convey emotions temporarily surprise-locked within the smooth, beautiful face, the thin, supple body. The light around him danced and fizzed, filling the small space with its sparkling offshoots and enveloping them both in a shower of shooting stars.

Mark rediscovered the use of his legs, threw himself into the open arms of his lover. 'How long are you in for, this time?' he asked, swallowing back tears. His hardening cock found another in the groin pressed tight against him.

'Years, Mark. Years and years and years.'

# PLUS ÇA CHANGE

It's Saturday night – Neil and Jimmy's fifth anniversary party. They've hired a suite at the new Hilton, down by Washington Street, and as my Docs hit that plush carpet, I grin at the doorman.

He can't seem to decide who's here for the live satellite relay of the World Heavyweight fight in the Rob Roy Room and who's going to the private event in the Glencoe Suite. He eventually waves me towards Rob Roy, muttering:

'No trouble – you're all gonna be good boys tonight, eh?'

I salute, and take the stairs two at a time. Good boy? Am I not always?

Neil meets me at the door of Glencoe. 'Tam! Ye made it!' He hugs me.

I hug him back and give him his present, 'cause I'm more his friend than Jimmy's, really. Me and Neil go way back: he taught me a lot. 'Who's all here?' My head's craning over his shoulder into the room behind.

'Man, ye shouldn't have.'

I turn my face and I see he's fingering the edge of this mint-condition Queen Vic guinea that I went into overdraft and hundreds of damp, dusty coin-shops to get for him. 'Ye like it? It's not one ye've got already?'

Neil laughs and winks. 'You should know!'

I try to laugh back. But I'm remembering the hours I spent staring at coins just like that, one balanced on each of my fingers while Neil gave me hell... and the heaven that would come if I let any of them drop.

Neil still knows what I like. His big hand slips down onto my arse, which he pats – 'Aye, Tam – I love it. You knew I would.' – then a squeeze. Then: 'Michael! And who's this?'

My prick's just starting to respond when Neil moves away to greet a couple of guys I half recognise. So I go on into the party.

There's about twenty here already. Jimmy, Neil's boy, is standing in the middle of a crowd, holding forth, as usual, and as I walk across to the bar he grins, and catches my eye. I smile back, give him a wave, then order a bottle of Caledonian Clear from the barman and start to check out the talent. Then everything goes black. There's something warm and soft over my eyes and this laugh in my ear.

'Guess who?'

I almost stop breathing... then start gulping for air. I'm grabbing at the hands, clawing them away and turning round at the same time. 'Wullie, ya stupit bastard! What do ye... ?'

'Christ, Tam! Sorry!' His big face is staring at me.

I thrust the bottle of mineral water at him, my heart still pounding. 'Get us something a wee bit stronger, eh? This stuff's rats' piss!'

Wullie takes the bottle, and looks at me kind of awkward. But not as awkward as I feel. He makes his way back to the bar and I find a wall, and lean against it while my breathing gets back to normal. See... I'm scared of the dark. Bit weird for a leather-boy, eh? All those shadowy corners, backrooms and artistically lit dungeons: bet you're thinking I don't get much action if I'll only sub under spotlights! Well, you'd be wrong. Totally wrong.

So where did the being scared of the dark come from? Fucked if I know... my mum says it's to do with the asthma I had as a kid: it was worst at night. Grew out of that years ago... but darkness – even dim light-bulbs... I know I should – what's the trendy word? – 'explore' it with someone. But for most tops where I will go more than compensates for where I won't... and that suits me just fine.

'Here ye go, pal. You OK?'

Wullie's back with the something stronger. My head's a bit clearer now, and I wish I hadn't bothered to switch my drink. But I take the glass anyway, knock the whiskey back in a gulp and change the subject. 'Didn't expect to see you here.'

Wullie was Neil's after me and just before Jimmy. He wasn't too happy when it was made clear he was either gonny have to share his master or forget the whole thing. Wullie did neither: oh, him and Neil called it a day, all right, but Wullie's got a memory to match his prick and he's never really taken to his replacement.

'Water under the bridge, Tam – so the tarot cards say. Time to move on.' He smiles.

I laugh. Wullie's into all sorts: tea-leaves, astrological charts, reincarnation – the works. 'About time, pal.' I don't believe any of that shite, but I'm pleased for him all the same so I get a hold of his ponytail and give it a tug. 'On the prowl then, are ye?' I pull his head way back... 'cause Wullie always did bring out the dom in me.

He grabs my hand, digs his big fingers in. 'Hey, as if you're not here for exactly the same thing.'

And I let go. 'Cause he's right. The Glasgow scene's... well, 'small and intimate' is how the UK SM Guide puts it: that fuckin' small and intimate everyone knows everyone else real well and things get kind of stale from time to time. But Neil's work takes him abroad a lot, and he always tries to bring us a wee pressie back from foreign lands. A bit of... new blood, he calls it. So a good turn-out's always guaranteed at anything he's involved in.

I grin, slap Wullie's arse and look around the room. It's filling up. Neil's still at the door, welcoming everyone. Jimmy's moved from his entourage, and he's doing the hostess-with-the-mostest bit now, chatting and laughing with everyone. Wullie's leaning on my shoulder, gazing with me.

'Fuckin' toe-rag. What the hell does Neil see in him?'

'Never could work out what he saw in you, man,' I say, 'least Jimmy's easy on the eyes.' I turn my head a wee bit and look at him.

The scars I know criss-cross Wullie's broad back are nothing to the big one that runs from just under his left eye to the corner of his mouth. Wullie's from Possil. Ye grow up queer in that bit of Glasgow, ye grow up fast.

He laughs, plants a wet one on my cheek. "It's not my face anyone's interested in, Tam.'

And I laugh back and give him a hug. 'Cause Wullie takes his punishment like the hard man he is... and I respect that.

'Is this a private scene or can anyone join in?'

Me and Wullie disentangle ourselves, and there's Jimmy and... My heart's beating a tattoo in my chest and my prick's up and about. But Wullie's in there first.

'Good turn-out, Jimmy...'

And there's not a trace of anything in his voice, thanks to whatever rubbish his tarot cards told him this week.

'Oh, and congratulations to you both, man.'

Wullie sticks out his hand. I know Jimmy'll take it out of politeness, but I'm not really watching him. I'm watching the other guy... and he's watching me, sort of eyeing me up and down. I blink, and look at my boots. 'Cause actions speak louder than words... and anyway, he's already imprinted on my mind. Tall – at least my height, maybe taller. And broad... a lot bigger built than me, and I'm no Kate Moss! Solid looking... densely packed muscle. Cropped black hair, bushy black brows, smooth face... big mouth. And something about that mouth is kind of... familiar.

There's talking in the background, but I'm not really listening. And I know he's not either. I can feel those arrogant-looking dark eyes boring into the top of my head. All my eyes need to see is the hem of that long, leather army-style coat and those big work boots. Everything's starting to fizzle around me. My balls spasm as I close my eyes and let the dark surround that tall, dark body.

Then there's an elbow in my ribs. 'Christ, I think I'm in love!'

I open my eyes and he's gone.

Wullie nudges me again. 'Man, oh man!'

I raise my head.

Wullie's looking star-struck. 'Elijah.' He whispers the word.

'What?' I give myself a shake.

'Mister Elijah Deville. It means "of the town", according to fuckin' know-it-all Jimmy. He's from –' Wullie tries an accent '– Noo Or-lee-ong. Half African, half French. Over here to do some business with Neil... fuck, Tam... and to think I almost didn't come here tonight!'

My throat's too dry to answer. I watch Wullie watch Jimmy steer Mr Elijah Deville towards the buffet table, and I'm still trying to work out where I know him from.


It's about an hour later. Wullie's eaten most of the vol-au-vents and come on to half the guys in the room. I'm feeling sick with lust and I'm – subtly, I hope – pumping Neil for info on his new business-contact.

He smiles. 'I know as much as you do, Tam. We flew over from JFK together, couple of days ago. Elijah's into the usual import-export stuff: artsy-crafty, from what I can gather, and he doesn't seem to be short of a bob or two.'

Elijah... I repeat the name over and over in my head until it becomes a kind of mantra.

'Says he's got... contacts over there that might be useful to me. He's looking for new markets over here.' Neil laughs. 'All you gotta do is mention Glasgow these days, and after the European City of Culture year, the world and his father thinks we're all really cosmopolitan!'

Elijah could be a fuckin' dustman for all I could care! 'What's he really into?'

This time Neil laughs and I know he's been teasing me, making me wait. 'Can you not work that one out, even yet, Tam? Christ, half the room was watching when Jimmy brought him over to you and Wullie.'

My cheeks are hot and sweat's trickling from my pits.

'I think Elijah might be just what you need, Tam... but you'd better get in there quick.' His eyes flick over my shoulder.

I turn, just in time to see Wullie and a tall, dark figure walking towards the door. But Neil's there for me, like the good pal he is.

'Elijah! Wullie! You can't leave yet – the cake's not arrived!'

I watch them both turn then as, if on demand, Jimmy appears from a wee door at the rear of the room. The place falls silent and they all move back to against the walls. Every eye's on Jimmy. The guy really knows how to make an entrance. He's wearing a thong and a wee padlocked chain round his neck – like the one Neil put on me, all those years ago. Everyone's stopped talking and I can hear Jimmy's bare feet on the thick carpet. Neil walks forward to the middle of the room.

Jimmy stops about a foot away from his master and kneels, holding out this chocolate-covered, boot-shaped cake, complete with fourteen angelica eyelets and five candles. 'Thank you, Sir.' He lowers his head and the words echo round the room.

Neil lays a big hand on the back of Jimmy's shaved neck. 'Thank YOU.'

Then this big cheer starts. Neil's hauled Jimmy to his feet and he's got his arm round him. They're each holding a side of the cake, both blowing out the candles. I'm clapping too, whistling through my fingers. But when I finally tear my eyes away from the floor show and look over to where Wullie and Elijah were standing, the space is empty, and the door's just closing.

\*

Another half hour or so passes. I've had a slice of the boot cake and I'm getting talked at by this guy whose name I didn't catch about this new company he's starting up. But my eyes are watching Neil. He's lounging in one of these big, comfy chairs and Jimmy's sitting at his feet, head on Neil's thigh, getting his ear stroked.

And they seem so... right together – more right than me and Neil ever were – that I couldn't be jealous. And I'm not – not of them, anyway. But maybe of what they've got.

And this guy's still talking. 'Aye, we're needing backing – loans, grants and the like. You're something to do with the... enterprise thing, yeah?'

I look away from Neil and back to this guy. 'Enterprise thing?' Maybe he really doesn't know I've just been given a budget of five million to promote innovation and investment in the greater Glasgow metropolitan area; maybe he's just making conversation and doesn't give a fuck what I do for a living. Maybe he's interested. Am I?

I give him the once-over: 25-ish, too-new leather jeans and vest, ponytail like Wullie but nowhere near a fraction of Wullie's style. I smile, and cross him off my list. 'Aye... I'm involved with GGEF.' I smile. 'Geez a ring, I'll see what I can do.' And I wander over to the bar... 'cause business advice is all this one'll ever get from me.

The night's wearing on, and I'm beginning to wish I hadn't bothered coming. Everyone seems to have someone – even Mr Too-New-Leather's found himself old Pat, who likes his tops fresh and malleable.

Still, the blond barman's kind of hot, and maybe if I hadn't already scened with or knocked back the seven tops in the room, me and Blondie could have drummed up a three-way. But it would have to be back at his place or mine. 'Cause I'm a bit too long in the tooth for the open-air stuff, even if the weather was up to it.

And 'cause Neil's got rules: no public scening.

For Jimmy's birthday in March, he managed to hire this old warehouse down by the docks. The landlord was just letting him and me in early to get things ready when some dickhead turned up in full leathers, leading his spectacularly scarred sub on a chain. That was the end of that!

So Blondie hands me another Caledonian Clear and I find myself thinking about Wullie and... Mr Elijah Deville.

Christ, I never even found out from Neil where the guy's staying... 'cause Glasgow's not Noo-or-lee-ong, and some hotels are funny about two guys – one in full combat gear with a scar he didn't get in the Gulf War – getting up to all sorts in one of their rooms. I'm thinking maybe they've gone back to Wullie's place, and I'm trying to remember if he's still sharing a flat with that student, when:

'Double vodka! Straight!'

I turn and grin at him. 'It'll be the only straight thing about you!' I pretend to look at my watch. 'That was quick – Mister Elijah Deville turn you down?' It's meant to be a joke – hell, they were away for a good two hours – but I'm thinking I might have hit a nerve 'cause Wullie's not laughing, just staring at a spot above the barman's blond head.

'Get a move on, son!'

I raise my hand, turn Wullie's face to mine, then wait until the barman goes off to refill the optic. 'Well? I want all the details!'

Wullie's face is ashen, the scar almost glowing against his too-pale skin, and his eyes are lowered.

'What's wrong?' My guts start twisting. 'Did he hurt ye, Wullie?' A wave of protectiveness breaks over me. 'Was he too heavy for –'

'Leave it, Tam.'

He tries to move away but I hold that clammy face firmly. 'Man, if he's hurt you I'll –'

'I said leave it!'

He grabs my wrist and pulls my hand away. Then Blondie's back with more vodka. Wullie drinks in silence, then orders another. I stay there, my hand resting on the small of his back now and I can feel the tension in his skin.

But I do as he asks. Wullie'll tell me in his own time.

It's nearly midnight and, as far as the celebrations are concerned, things should be starting to ease off. But I see Neil's ushering another six or seven into the room, and Jimmy's still doing the rounds with what's left of the boot cake. I'm circling again, saying hello to folk that weren't here the last time I circled, though I glance back at the bar every now and then. Wullie's still there, still drinking. I'm gonny have to take him home soon, and I'm just about to track down Neil and make our excuses when it feels like someone's opened a door and let in the cold air. I turn and find myself staring into a wide, black face and a wider smile.

'Elijah Deville. We met earlier, I believe.'

I blink at the hand he's stretched out towards me, then grasp it... and it's icy. I'm trying to smile back, trying to speak but my mind's full of cotton-wool and my prick's twitching against well-worn leather. Fingers tighten around mine and it's like a signal, like some sort of masonic handshake. Something tingles between us. I DO know him, though Christ knows from where. But more important, I know what he wants.

We've moved to the other side of the room, though I've no idea how we got here. He's still gripping my hand, still talking. His voice is deep, rich – a sort of mixture of accents and not as Yank or French as I would have thought – and it's filling my fuzzy head.

For some reason I'm not looking away now, but focusing on those arrogant eyes, which are sort of sparkling. I catch the odd question once in a while, and hope my answers are intelligible. Eventually, I even find myself asking some of my own, but not the ones I really want answers to. 'Neil – Mister McLeod – tells me you're over here on... business.' I'm back against a window, him in front of me blocking out the rest of the room.

He laughs, and the sound rips through me, turning my guts to mush. 'Your accent is rather... heavy, Thomas...'

I flinch: my mum's the only one still calls me that.

'You must forgive my lack of understanding.'

And I know I'd forgive him anything – everything! But I switch to my work voice all the same. 'Perhaps my department at the Glasgow Enterprise Trust can help.' I'm fumbling in the pockets of my jacket for business cards. He's laughing again, and my face is a furnace.

'As versatile as ever, Thomas. Let's discuss how we can... help each other – but somewhere more... private, I think.'

My heart's hammering. My hand catches on the teeth of one of the zip pockets and I curse, jamming a bleeding finger into my mouth. Then there's a soft black hand on my wrist.

'Let it flow, Thomas – helps cleanse the wound...'

My mind's miles away, and I'm thinking about the cleansing strokes I want Mr Elijah Deville to rain onto my back, thinking about those strong hands wrapped round the handle of a heavy flogger, him pushing me to my limits.

'Give me a minute with Neil. I'll meet you outside.'

I watch him walk across the room – slowly and quickly at the same time – sort of gliding, weaving in and out of groups of guys. You wouldn't think someone his size could move so... smoothly.

Then there's an arm round my shoulder and slurring in my ear. 'Don't go, Tam... don't go with him...'

Wullie's some weight when he's sober; tanked up like he is now, it's like tryin' to prop up a tower-block! I push him back against the wall. 'I'm getting you a taxi, pal... time for beddy-byes.'

His arms are round my neck, pulling me against him. 'Don't go, man... for me, eh?'

I'm holding him there, looking at 6'4" of hulking Glasweigan – 6'4" of frustrated manmeat who, for reasons best known to himself, didn't click with the hottest top either of us have seen in a long time. I shiver. 'What you on about?'

He mumbles something about bad vibes. Then my mind starts to work... and I'm remembering other times – times me and Wullie nearly came to blows over his wee tricks to put me off guys. We're good mates, me and Wullie, but when it comes to men...

I manage to haul him onto his feet, and sort of drag him across the room towards Jimmy. 'Get this mad bastard into a taxi for me, eh?' I know Wullie'll hate the fact that he's so out of control in front of his arch-rival, but I've better things to do than baby-sit him, right now.

Jimmy smirks. 'Never could hold his drink, that one.'

Wullie the Dead-Weight's still mumbling, starting to stir a bit when Neil and Mr Elijah Deville appear.

'Is he OK?'

The concern in that deep, accentless voice makes the hairs on my arms stand up on end.

Wullie manages to raise his head from my neck and I feel that shiver again. 'Leave him alone!'

Christ, I want to hit the fucker! Just 'cause his scene didn't work out, fuckin' Wullie Dalgleish grudges me having a go. And that does it. I let go his arm and he slides to the floor like the big lump of jelly he is. 'Ready?' I smile at Mr Deville, then follow him out.

A cheer from behind the doors of the Rob Roy suit tells me the fight's still in progress. An empty foyer tells me the doorman's in there watching. I'm walking a couple of paces behind Mr Elijah Deville, waiting for him to swerve towards the lifts that go up to the guest-rooms... but he just keeps on taking those big easy strides of his across the carpet, through the automatic doors and out into the cold night.

It's well after midnight now, but as we walk through the car park I can still hear traffic thundering over the Kingston Bridge above my head. I fall further behind, trying to work out which car's gonny be his, guess which hotel he's gonny be staying at when he stops, like he's waiting for me to catch up. So I oblige, my breath steaming. When I reach him, he's looking across Argyle Street to down past the old bonded warehouses towards the river.

'*Plus ça change.*'

'Come again?' My French isn't what it should be, though I kind of recognise what he says as part of some quote.

'The more things change, the more they stay the same, Thomas. Cities don't alter much.'

I smile, then laugh into a cloud of my own breath. 'You've been here before?'

He's still staring towards the docks. 'No... just somewhere very like this.'

I'm hugging myself to try to keep warm. 'Glasgow's changing all the time these days.' My eyes sweep over the flyover, towards the new Finnistoun headquarters of the Daily Record and the derelict warehouses, then back to Mr Deville. 'Couple more years and this'll be gone too... and good riddance!'

He turns, and his eyes shine under sodium street lights. 'Then I'd better see it, Thomas... take a piece of old Glasgow back with me to the New World before it disappears for ever. Could be my last chance.'

Christ, I'm shivering again. Mr Deville sounds a wee bit weird. But I smile, 'cause I can imagine the look on Wullie's face if he got this routine too. And... what the hell: I'm game. 'Sure, Mister Deville: I kind of like a walk myself, this time of night.'

'Elijah, please.'

His hand's on the sleeve of my jacket, and I wish I'd worn something warmer 'cause the cold's seeping through to my bones.

I grin. 'OK... Elijah it is. But can we drop the Thomas stuff?

Make it Tam?'

He grins back. 'Sure... what's in a name, anyway?'

And my prick's slamming itself against the leather of my jeans. OK: it's gonny be dark down there, but if he wants a tour of old Glasgow he's got it... 'cause I've a feeling the guide's tip at the end's gonny be worth waiting for.

Washington Street's deserted, part from a couple of coffin-dodgers dead drunk in a doorway. I'm walking in front, giving Mr Elijah the full number: knew that secondment to The Glasgow Preservation Trust would come in handy some day. I'm telling him about our part in the slave trade, about why Washington Street was named after the first president, about the connections there's always been between Glasgow and the New World. We've done all that's left of the big tobacco warehouse that got burnt out in the 1920s, and I'm just about to start on the merits of Alexander Greek Thomson's architecture when I realise Elijah's not behind me any more.

My heart gives a wee stutter. Christ, I've lost him! Neil's gonny go daft if him and Jimmy's fifth anniversary party ends in a house-to-house search for his new American business-associate! So I retrace my steps back up past shadowy hulks of buildings and rotting loading-bays. Nothing. I go to nudge one the winos with my boot, ask if they've seen him, but they're away too... and it's just me and the traffic in the distance... and the dark.

'Elijah?' His name sounds weird when I shout: no echo. My heart's making up for lost time, and I'm racing up and down the street like a kid that's lost its mammy, peering through cracked windows, kicking boarded-up doors – looking in places I know fine well there's no way he could be. The dark's not really bothering me any more. All I can think about is finding Elijah.

Then I hear something. I stop dead and listen, my ears tingling with the cold. Aye... I can just hear it over the noise my lungs are making. A sort of... moaning. Faint, but definitely there. And it's coming from the old rope works.

I'm belting across the street, heaving bits of corrugated iron out the way with my shoulder. Then I'm inside... and I'm shivering again. At least outside there were a couple of street lights in the distance. In here, I can't see a fuckin' thing, not even the dark any more. But I feel it pushing against me, like it's almost alive.

'Elijah?' I'm standing there, blinking back tears, and for some reason my prick's still hard.

'Thomas.'

The voice is behind me, and I spin round. 'Elijah! Thank Christ! I thought –' But he's not there – least, not as far as I can tell.

'The sisal works.'

His voice is behind me again, so I turn back, my fingers grabbing handfuls of dark, thick air. 'Elijah! Where... ?'

'Remember the fibres, Thomas – remember how they clogged up your lungs and made you cough?'

His voice is circling around me: it's either that whiskey finally hitting my system or some kind of weird acoustics. Something's tickling the back of my throat and I start to wheeze. Dusty fuckin' death-trap of a place is bringing on my asthma.

'You got it worse than most, Thomas. I nursed you for three nights, thought you were gonna make it...'

I'm trying to walk towards the sound, 'cause the words are making no fuckin' sense.

'But they dragged you dying from my arms, just before dawn...'

I'm gasping for breath, coughing and choking, and shivering all at the same time, wanting him to stop rabbiting on and let us get out of here.

'They dumped your beautiful body in the swamps, Thomas, like they did with the others. We never got to say goodbye.'

'Oh, fuck!' I'm just managing to get my wind when my foot

catches in something and I'm sprawling amongst lager cans and pigeon shite. My head's spinning with all his stupid ranting and I feel like I'm suffocating again. Then there are strong hands on my shoulders, dragging me up. Before I know what's happening, I'm on my knees, jacket and T-shirt being ripped off my back.

'I'm sorry, Thomas...'

He's rubbing my tits and my nipples are wee icebergs.

'I'm sorry I denied you – denied our love. I'm sorry keeping my job as plantation-manager meant more to me than you did. Not a day, a year has gone past when I haven't looked for you...'

He's crouching behind me, working my tits till I almost scream.

'I've missed you, Thomas – missed this.'

He kisses my neck and my whole body's shaking again.

'I thought I'd found you so many times... in Rome, Rio... Berlin... Chicago...'

His hands slip down over my belly and start to loosen my belt.

'They were you... but not you...'

He's unzipping me now, and my prick's fair leaping into his hand. Then he laughs, breathing Siberia onto my neck.

'I should have known it would be Glasgow. Our main port for... distribution. Second city of the empire, if my memory serves me correctly.'

His hands move to under my arms, pulling me to my feet. Leather's bagging round the tops of my boots and I can feel his fingers back on my prick.

'And this is what remains of the very factory where the raw sisal that killed you was manufactured into rope. I'm repaying a debt, Thomas. Saying goodbye.'

It's flashing through my mind that Mr Elijah Deville fuckin' likes his wee games, then the last thing I expect to happen happens. Something wet and icy's slipping down over my prick, covering it with liquid frost. And it finally dawns on me what's going on here... but when he grabs my balls and starts to knead I don't fuckin' care. One of my hands is on his shoulder, the other one pushing his face further into my pubes. Then I'm really fucking that face, using both hands to move that refrigerator mouth up and down my aching prick.

Over my moans and the sounds of him sucking me off there's more sounds and other words... inside my head.

'I know you hate the dark, Thomas. I used to laugh, but I always brought a candle to the shack at night. I can still see the shadow your ebony body cast on the tar-paper wall... still imagine your fear as the swamp water closed over your frightened eyes...'

His big hands are gripping the cheeks of my arse and he's trying to get my balls into his mouth too. My hands are just resting on the sides of his head now, 'cause my mind's really starting to play tricks. I'm... hearing things. Weird things – insects sounds, and I don't know if it's all the spunk that's gathering in my balls or something else but I'm feeling really warm and tingly. Sunshiny warm – like a hot summer's day in the park. I'm sweating, even though it's fuckin' freezing in here and his mouth isn't much warmer.

Then he's moving... and I throw back my head and bite my lip as a hand grips my waist and a tongue like an icicle plunges into my hole. His other hand's on my prick now, just holding it, not pumping or anything. And the voice in my head's back.

'I can still feel your hot tongue inside me, Thomas, lighting me up. You gave me so much.'

And I know what I want... and I know what Wullie turned down and why: not a rubber in sight. 'Fuck me, Elijah!' The sound of my voice is inside my head and soaring round the dusty building. Everything goes fuzzy again... until I'm on my knees, gripping handfuls a pigeon shite and he's ramming the head of his big black prick into my arse. I'm half-thinking this is the weirdest scene I've ever had and I'm taking a hell of a risk. The other half somehow knows Elijah would never hurt me.

Christ, he must be eight or nine inches! And thick with it! But my arse gulps it down in one go, takes it all, and I'm moaning through the pain as his big hairy balls slap against my frozen cheeks. He's leaning over me, fingers working my tits again, lips flicking snow-kisses on my neck. My eyes are closed and I'm ramming back onto him, pigeon shite and worse melting on my sweating palms. He's fucking me hard, but there's a sort of... gentleness to it and he's saying my name, his hands slipping up from my tits to hold me under the arms.

'Come with me, Thomas...'

And I'm thinking maybe if he starts to work my prick again I just might manage it, at that! But the voice is in my head – must be in my head, 'cause he's still repeating my name and kissing my neck.

'Come back with me. Come home. We can be together for ever... I won't deny you again.'

I finally get what the voice is on about now. America: good weather, good attitude, thriving SM scene... all those clubs... My iron prick's slapping aff my belly with each thrust and my balls are starting to spasm. I'm groaning, squeezing my arse-muscles, working his big black cock and mumbling. 'Yes... yes... yes... yes...'

But he's slowing, holding back... and I want his cock filling my arse like I never wanted anything in my life. 'Come on, man... give it to me!'

'You really want this, Thomas?'

The words are in my ear this time, not my head.

And I'm shoutin: 'Aye! Come on, Elijah! Fuck me! Let's go!'

'You know what you're saying?'

Do I? Fuck knows... but something tells me this is right... this is the way it's got to be. And if he wants me to beg, I'll beg. 'Please...'

Then he's pulled me up off my hands and knees and I'm balanced on the balls of my feet, kind of crouching in his lap. His cock's buried deep in my arse and one of his hands is pumping me while the other's round my chest, holding me tight. Wee lights are sparkling on my eyelids and I'm in this weird head-space, sort of... floating...

Elijah's flexing inside me and I'm clenching my sphincter around the root of him as he works my prick. Something's rushing in my ears and it's not just blood. Fuck, when I come my whole body jerks forward and my eyes fly open... and it's not dark anymore. Christ, it's not even Glasgow!

I'm on my back, my legs wrapped round this big blond guy's waist and I'm staring up into blue eyes, which twinkle at me, then close.

What a head-fuck! My first thought's that Wullie must have slipped something into my mineral water. Then I wonder if maybe Mr Elijah Deville moonlights with a hypnotist act.

I peer over this big shoulder, and there are... trees and grass and things around us. I can hear... insect-noise, and water and behind that, way in the distance, some sort of... machinery, like a factory. There's smells too... the smell of our sweat and something sweet, like flowers, and worst of all, there's... feelings. Real feelings. The stickiness on my belly and the emptiness in my balls that tell me I've just come, and... other feelings, like... love and things...

But it's Elijah's voice that's moaning my name, Elijah's big arms that're raising me up off the warm grass, Elijah's cock I feel as it plunges between my thighs... my dark thighs!

Then I'm pushing him off me, fighting him, trying to get up, I'm sobbing like a baby, tears streaming down my face 'cause this is all a bit too weird – even for me. 'Naw, man... no way! Use a rubber... or get out of me!'

Last thing I see is big, blue confused eyes staring into mine. Last thing I hear is Elijah's rich voice as he kisses my wet cheeks. 'Sorry, Thomas... I'm being selfish again.'

Then I'm back in the dark.

*

Wullie tells me it was the two coffin-dodgers that found me, trousers at my ankles, covered in pigeon shite and come. Neil had already organised a search-party, when me and Elijah didn't reappear, and he and Wullie got me home, gave me the once-over – handy that the big lump of jelly's a nurse – then put me to bed.

Found out later Neil's business-deal with Elijah fell through – their interests weren't... compatible – and he left Glasgow the next day.

Wullie's still not let me in on what went on with him and Mr Elijah Deville, and I've told no one about my... out-of-body experience.

I was showing this Japanese guy round the old rope works, couple of weeks later. He's with a big electronics company – circuit-boards and the like – and although I'm meant to be encouraging investment and regeneration, the thought of this place refurbished up and in use again makes me shiver, so I quote Mr Fujiyama a ridiculous price and he changes his mind – and after the GGEF have paid for a new door and good locks to be put on the place too!

'Cause it belongs to Elijah. Elijah and Thomas. I keep the keys with me all the time, hear them jangling in the pocket of my leathers when I come here at night, to sit in the dark and be with him, fuck with him.

'Cause... *plus ça change*... but this time he doesn't just own me.

I own him too. I finally belong... and I'm not afraid of the dark any more.

# TRIPPING

'My name's Mac and I'm a tripper.'

A ripple of applause, punctuated by low 'Hey, Mac's.

In his pocket, strength-seeking fingers rubbed along metal. 'It's been two years since my last trip.'

The ripple surged into a wave.

'Did eighteen months in rehab. Almost got sent down, but –' his voice cracked; Mac swallowed '– ten weeks tomorrow I've had it – ten weeks, two journeys a day, five days a week and I've been –' fingers rubbed harder at the talisman in his pocket '– fine, so far.'

Applause crashed over his head and broke around him. Someone stood up. Then someone else. He was surrounded by a storm of clapping, supportive hands. Mac's face reddened. In his pocket, wetness flowed freely from ripped fingers. His legs began to buckle. With a slight nod of his head, he sat down before he fell down.


After the meeting, he tossed the usual dollar into the usual box and took a coffee from the table. Eric, his sponsor, had noticed the bleeding, and asked if everything was OK.

Mac had smiled the practised smile and taken the offered handkerchief which now bound his gashed fingers. Sipping scalding instant, he scanned the room. He recognised few faces: addicts came and went like the seasons. His eyes lingered on a figure leaning against the back wall.

Late twenties, maybe thirty. Gangly. Long limbs encased in loose-fitting nylon. Cropped hair. More facial piercings than Mac had seen in a while. Wild eyes bounced off his then darted around the room. Could be a skim-freak – definitely pale enough – or an acid-casual: AA handled every kick that was in the book...and some that weren't.

Mac remembered his first time at a meeting. What was it Eric said about helping yourself by helping others? He took another sip of the coffee and strolled over. 'Hey there!'

Cropped head flicked up.

Mac extended his bandaged hand. 'Rennie MacIntosh – call me Mac.'

Calloused, work-gnarled fingers gripped his. 'Chev.'

Tension pulsed from the man's knuckles into his own. 'Unusual name...'

Wild eyes glinted, lit up from inside. 'Short for Chevrolet...' Fingers tightened, pressing into the make-shift bandage. 'One of the greatest achievements of twentieth-century combustion-engineering...'

Mac tried to pull away. He couldn't.

'Pure power...'

The coffee cup fell to the floor. Mac wanted to pick it up. He couldn't. He dragged his eyes from blazing irises and stared down at their linked hands. Blood from the cuts was oozing through the handkerchief, dripping onto hard, rough skin.

'Pure energy...'

Mac wrenched his fingers free. 'Sorry... got to go.' He walked unsteadily from the room. Outside, it took every shred of strength he possessed to go straight home.

In front, the stream of cars slowed to a surly crawl.

Mac focused on a nodding toy dog in the back window of the vehicle in front. The pink and white of a make-shift crash-barrier flashed on the periphery of his vision. Under his hand, the plastic-coated knob of the gear-shift quivered. Ten weeks of nothing, and now...?

The car was too warm. He wound down the window, inhaling what passed for morning air on the freeway. And other smells. Gasoline. Oil.

The nodding dog lurched. Mac pressed his foot to the accelerator and inched forward. The approaching whine of the emergency services changed pitch. He wound the window down completely. Underneath the gas and oil, something else. Not so much a smell as a taste.

He shifted into neutral, eyes moving from the nodding dog to the asbestos roofs of the warehouses which lined the left side of the freeway. Mouth open, he drew the odour onto his tongue and rolled it around. The siren dropped a semitone and sped past. Mac closed his eyes. Furious honking from behind. Eyelids shot open. He shifted gear, closing the gap between himself and the nodding dog.

Out of the corner of his eye, chrome glinted through early morning smog. Like a wink, the gleaming shard invited his gaze. Mac stared straight ahead. Fingers tightened over the gear-shift's vibrating knob. His right eyelid began to twitch. The leatherette under his back and arse was hot and damp. Seconds dragged by, stretching into minutes that could have been hours. His stiffening cock ticked its way up the inside of his thigh.

'Fuckin' trippers, eh? No consideration for other people!'

Whiplash tingled down his neck. Mac stared through the open window at the back of the man leaning on his hood. Behind, other drivers had left their vehicles and were standing around, bemoaning the inconvenience in loose groups.

The man switched his gaze from the coned area of the freeway and scowled at him. 'They're sayin' it's an illness now – can ya believe it? Some crap about cadmium-contaminated breast-milk!

Fuckin' sick all right – sick fucks, if ya ask me!'

No one had. Mac stared at the scene to his right – two bemused drivers, shaken but uninjured; three vehicles – two at opposite sides of the road, hoods and radiators crumpled by impact with a road-sign and a wall respectively. The third was upside down, wheels still kicking like the useless legs of some shelled invertebrate. Rainbow liquid bled from a perforated gas-tank and shimmered blue and pink in the cop-car's revolving light. The trail snaked across the tarmac, then split, trying to connect with each of its injured companions.

'Why do they do it, eh?' The face turned and blared into his.

Mac flinched. He knew the driver didn't really want answers; which was just as well, because he didn't have any. A single roar punctured his thoughts. The head of his cock nudged the buckle of his safety-belt. Mac released the gear-shift, unbuckled and scrambled out of the car. More drivers were moving towards the pink and white crash-barrier.

Mac peered beyond two firemen holding chain-saws to the source of the roar. Blood-spidered hands gripped the shattered roof-frame. A paramedic was attempting to apply a gauze pad to the gaping wound in a bare, blood-freckled shoulder. Two uniformed figures tried unsuccessfully to grab flailing legs which pumped and kicked like pistons. The roar subsided into an agonised moan.

Mac felt the sound deep in his guts. His skin prickled as chain-saws buzzed into life, hacking at already-damaged body-work and ripping the man from the arms of his metal lover. The moan became a series of sobs, rising over the screech of disintegrating vehicle. Mac thought of the sound a ship made when breaking-up in a storm. He stared at a sheen of gasoline which slicked pale, scarred skin.

'There's the culprit! If I had ten minutes with one of them, one of those drivers, I'd –'

Mac screened out the end of the rant. Not a driver – not any-one who entered and left the vehicle at the beginning or end of each journey. Not even a journey – not in the conventional sense. A trip.

He followed the procession to the back of a waiting ambulance. The sobs were almost inaudible now, the sheened, naked limbs writhing less. Mac's eyes travelled down onto the tarmac, and the remnants of a blood-trail trickling its way into the iridescent pool at his feet.

Seconds before the cops managed to bundle the now-limp fig-ure into the back of the ambulance, he glimpsed the face. Under multi-pierced eyebrows, tears sparkled in Chev's bruising eyes. The smooth forehead was peppered with crushed glass, tiny punctures weeping red. The pain of defeat trembled in Mac's guts. The ambulance doors slammed shut. Tremors beneath his feet told him the wrecking-crew had arrived to dispose of the de-bris.

Voice at his side: 'Lock 'em up an' throw away the key, that's what I'd do!'

Shaking, Mac returned to his car.

He stared at the white-coated night-nurse. 'No, I'm not a relative, just a...' Friend? Acquaintance? Fellow-sufferer? Brother-beneath-the-skin? Having rehearsed this speech all day, Mac cleared his throat and made way for the half-lie. 'Er, but I was there at the... accident. I work with people like Chev.'

'Well, you can't see him!' Harassed frown. 'But at least we've got a name now – he's still unconscious and his ID-tag won't scan!'

Mac instinctively rubbed the titanium identification-plate be-hind his own ear: the authorities had no idea when they'd insti-tuted mandatory tagging they were giving a generation their first taste of body-modification, and a lust for metal. 'He OK?'

'Apart from the coma?' A deeper frown. 'Mainly superficial

stuff – we'll patch him up, keep him here for a day or so...' Her eyes flicked over his shoulder. Mac followed her gaze to the two cops lounging against a 'Pepsi' dispenser. 'Then he's not our problem anymore.'

'If I can't see him, tell him Mac was here – and tell him I'll be back.' The metal amulet was warm in his pocket.

He knew he should go to a meeting. Or phone Eric. Crawling on his stomach through mud and petro-chemicals, Mac listened to the distant barking of the wreckers' guard-dogs.

Just once.

Just this once. It was a lie, and he knew it. There was no 'just once'. When the metal got back into your blood you were a goner. Mac inhaled the stench of oil and grease and stared at the twisted heap.

Security-lights illuminated tall piles of kinked fenders and concertina-ed radiator-grills. He crept forward, hands slipping in pools of sump-oil.

Trips... lots of different trips.

He'd known a chick who could only get wet in new cars. The cops caught her in a Hyundai-dealership at four in the morning, wouldn't believe she was only there to breathe in the smell. Couple of years later, the big car companies caught on, started bottling the stuff to sniff in the comfort of your own home. Too late for Lisa: a six-to-ten for attempted auto-larceny had turned her on to other pleasures.

Mac raised himself onto all fours, skirting a tower of buckled steering-columns. Grease-monkeys, chrome-chasers, rust-raunchers: lots of different trips. Some got it up for interiors, others exteriors. Some didn't even drive... garage-cases, sneaking down just to look and wank, once a week.

Mac edged past a heap of crank-shafts. He thought about Chev's naked legs as the cops had dragged him from the wreckage, and the steel knee-pins which had twinkled in the sunlight. The man had at least two pounds of metal in him already. A total body tripper.

In the security lights' blind-spot, Mac stood up and scanned the recent-arrivals' area, searching for the caved-in roof of a Peugot 260. And found it. The metal skeleton had been crumpled further by the wreckers' claws. Mac hoped the inside would be intact. He laughed aloud.

The dogs barked once, then fell silent.

His own detachment surprised him. Two years ago he'd been unable to pass a parking-lot without getting hard. These days, he was driving one of the things, ten times a week, no sweat... once a tripper, always a tripper?

Oily mud squelched under his feet. He walked over to the vehicle. The engine had been removed – Mac knew that. But if his instinct was right, there was life inside. He stuck his head though a jagged space, groping in the darkness. Fingers contacted with metal. Cold metal. Cold, hard metal.

The denuded hand-brake was at an almost ninety-degree angle. Mac's balls tightened as he fumbled towards the shattered dashboard. Dry. Crystalline. He raised shaking fingers to his lips and tasted... saltiness. Not blood-saltiness, though he could smell there was plenty of that around. Another more intimate, equally vital body-fluid. Mac's guts turned over. Licking dried spunk from his fingers, he closed his eyes.

Skinned metal rubbed his thigh. His cock started to stretch inside his pants. Mac groaned, leaning back further. He inhaled the smell of two spent life-forces. One drilled from deep in the ground. The other fucked from deep in a man's balls.

Before he knew what he was doing, his pants were down and cold metal was pressing against his hole. Mac gripped the edge of the roof-frame and began to gyrate. His fingers slipped a couple of times as he circled the hand-brake, teasing himself. Re-adjusting his hold, he swung back, raising his legs and planting his feet on the dashboard. Crushed safety-glass crunched under his boots. He hung there, suspended, then began to bear down.

His thighs spasmed uncontrollably. Mac stared through the shattered windscreen into darkness as the hand-brake pushed past his sphincter. He hovered there, the first inch of hard, solid steel inside his arse. Mac savoured the invasion, the way the muscle clenched around the cold shaft. He could feel the bevelled finger-indentations, feel his sphincter tighten around the first... then second... third... at the fourth finger-grip, Mac's right hand released the roof-frame and grabbed his cock.

He was out of condition. The muscles in his left arm screamed as he used his feet to lever himself back up the hand-brake... then down again. He closed his eyes, inhaling the freeway smell of blood and gas and sweat and spunk. Mac fucked himself harder and faster, jacking his cock as the steel shaft buried and reburied itself in his arse.

The car moved beneath him, grating and grinding. Mac blinked back another saltiness as the pain in his left arm became almost unbearable. His cock was agony, his balls knitting to-gether... he howled when he came, splattering the dashboard with another layer of milky liquid. And the wreckers' dogs howled with him.

He'd forgotten how easy it was, how plausible he could be. A phone-call to Eric had resulted in their meeting for a drink. It had taken imagination to divert his sponsor's attention... and only sec-onds to slip the official ID from the pocket of Eric's jacket into his own.

Mac flipped the stolen wallet open at one of the two cops who flanked the door to Chev's hospital room. He watched sleep-de-prived eyes register the Official Counsellor's symbol, then blink him forward.

Inside, the rhythmic bleep of a heart-monitoring device punched holes in a wall of silence. Mac stared at the inert figure. Chev's pale face was almost grey against the white sheets. Mac strode across the room and sat on the edge of the bed.

Beneath metal porcupines, eyes were closed. Mac counted the eyebrow-piercings: six in each. Tiny slats running from left-to-right in one, right-to-left in the other. He was pleased the medics had at least learned not to try to remove the metal. His own nipples and foreskin were a mass of numb scar-tissue, after eighteen months in rehab, the doctors believing out-of-body meant out-of-mind.

He studied the lip-piercings at each side of Chev's mouth. Mac shivered at this tripper's alliance with the trip. Nothing hidden, nothing shrouded in shame – like something parents thought their kids would grow out of.

He glanced at the door, then beyond to a uniformed sleeve which was just visible through the plexi-glass panel. Now tripping was a Code One Offence. There would be no rehab-alternative for Chev... He stared down at the unconscious figure... not that rehab would do any good.

During his own therapy, his case-worker had shown him endless pictures of naked women, naked men, rutting animals. After a year of trying to will himself hard Mac had finally succeeded. If only the medics had realised it was the '56 T-Bird behind the well-muscled black guy which was responsible for his eventual erection. He laid a damp palm on Chev's glass-pocked forehead.

Eyebrows darted towards hairline. Eye-lids sprang open. 'Hey! What ya...?' Panicked pupils darting. Shoulders and chest straining up from the bed. Then eyebrows V-ing in suspicious recognition.

Mac withdrew his palm. 'Keep quiet – the longer you're unconscious, the longer the cops gotta leave you here.'

The pale body sank back onto paler sheets. The heart monitor stuttered, then resumed its tracking. Mac stood up, moved round to the other side of the bed, blocking any view of Chev from the door's plexi-glass panel.

'What you want?' The suspicion remained.

Mac's guts turned over. 'Listen, I can –'

'What's it to you, man? What do you care?' His mouth scowled.

Adrenalin shot through his veins. Chev was right: what was it to him? He had a new life now, a normal future of nine-to-five with a nice pension at the end – a future filled with meetings and Eric's ever-reliable, unquestioning support. He stroked the chain of stitch-clips in Chev's right shoulder. 'Let me help...'

'Save your sermons, man – I don't need your help –'

'You've not got a lot of choice – me or the cops.'

The lip-piercings curled into a sneer. 'I'll take my chances, thanks!' Chev twisted away.

Mac's cock was throbbing against the fly of his pants. He focused on the jagged metal teeth surrounding the gash just above Chev's left buttock. 'I can get you out of here. I can get you a car. I can show you a couple of tricks –'

Chev turned his head.

Mac stared into glittering eyes. 'You need an alternator connected to the transmission – that'll cut out the engine when you reach the desired speed – and an extra gas-tank, maybe two...' He was dizzy, light-headed as blood fled from his brain and rushed to his already-swollen cock.

'That works?' Chev's eyes shone. 'I mean, I've heard guys talk about –'

'I almost scored, but I was alone –' Mac frowned '– that was my mistake – yours too. It's got to be a –'

The head shook slowly. 'I'm strictly a two-way man –'

'Let me be there – what you got to lose?'

Chev pushed himself up and leant on an elbow. Mac stared at the bulge which was tenting the sheet just above Chev's groin and pressed home the advantage. 'You can't do it without me.'

Bandaged hand groped for bandaged hand. Mac lowered his head and kissed steel sutures.

A low moan. Bloody fingers squeezed his.

Mac's brain was working so fast he could hardly speak. He'd lain awake all night, then called in sick as soon as the switchboard was manned.

Oh, he was sick all right – a sick fuck, just like they'd always said.

Getting the car was easy – hell, he owned one, didn't he? Body-Shop Johnny was surprised to see him. And curious. Two thousand dollars had considerably diminished both responses. Mac had left the list of modifications, with strict instructions the car be ready by midnight.

Getting Chev past his cop-guard and out of the hospital wasn't going to be quite as easy.

Mac smiled at the night-nurse. 'Sorry to be so late tonight.' He sat the small hold-all blatantly on the counter.

She returned the smile this time. 'Five minutes, then – the doctor'll be round at ten.'

Mac nodded benignly. 'Ah, good – I hoped to have a word with his consultant.' He smiled and walked on. The cops barely acknowledged his presence as he opened the door and slipped inside.

Chev lay on his back, the sheet lowered to waist-level. Mac could see the shoulder wound was healing nicely: more skin bonding with more metal. He sat on the side of the bed, between Chev and the door. His voice was low. 'Disposable slippers, surgical mask and head-cap are in the bag. Don't say anything. Just follow me.'

He spent the next ten minutes moving furniture and exploring metal-meshed flesh with his tongue.

If the doctor thought it strange the segregation-screen was in place around the bed, he made no initial comment... and no further comment, after one swift blow rendered him unconscious.

Luckily, the surgical greens were a good fit. Luckily, the two cops and the receptionist only registered an addiction-counsellor and a doctor leaving the room. Mac knew luck had little to do with it. The metal was in their blood.

Body-shop Johnny's workmanship was as reliable as ever. Mac closed the hood. On the other side of the car, Chev was tearing off baggy green shift and pants. Mac stared at the scarred, bruised body, then dragged his eyes beyond.

He'd driven to a long-abandoned feeder-road – close enough to smell other vehicles, distant enough to avoid cop-detection. It had taken all his concentration to stop Chev grabbing the controls and tripping right there and then. A quarter of a mile away, the city's main freeway streamed with motor-life. Mac turned. Chev was inches away, his damage-modified body-work strong and glistening in the head-lights.

Mac's balls were sweating. He forced himself to look. Even in semi-darkness he could see the darker hollows in Chev's thighs, where gear-shifts and steering columns had impacted over the years. Titanium winked at him from the tibia-pins. Mac groaned, wanting to fall to his knees and nuzzle the implants. His eyes came to rest on the wiry V of hair between bruised thighs and the half-hard member nestling there. Mac stretched out one hand, touching the shoulder wound. The other met the smooth metal of the car's vibrating hood. Fingers on his cheek told him Chev was doing the same. Three skins. Three hearts.

A frisson of expectation glimmered over his body. He withdrew his hands and began to undress. Jacket, pants, shirt and shoes fell away. He felt Chev's eyes on him. Mac stood naked, body-hair erect as heady exhaust emissions surged into his nostrils.

A three-way. He'd waited a lifetime for this. Chev was leaning over now, both hands clamped against pulsing metal. Lip piercings contacted with the hood in scraping kisses. Mac moved behind Chev's body and edged between splayed thighs. Vibrations resonated up through the fleshy conductor into his own tissue. Fingers resting on titanium sutures, his cock brushed Chev's arse, the sensitive head a second contact with the power-source.

Chev moaned more loudly, face pressed side-on to the hood. Metal porcupines shivered against each other. The moan lowered in pitch, became a hum which hovered in unison with the life-force beneath the metal skin. Mac heard the tone, felt it deep in his guts. His cock trembled, his arse-hole spaced in rhythm with the timbre. He opened his mouth and let the note escape into the night.

Chev pressed back against him, hard arse-cheeks pulsating with the sound. Mac allowed his cock to stroke Chev's quivering pucker, then wrenched himself away and pulled open the driver's door.

Body-shop Johnny had done a good job. He fingered the straps of the double body-harness – reinforced polymer silica. No chain-saw could cut through that. A voice in his ear:

'Let's do it – do it now!'

Mac glanced past a cropped head to the road in front.

Chev was facing him, suspended just above the drivers' seat. One leg brushed his. Mac's thighs spanned the root of the hand-brake. He could feel engine-tremors shooting up through the vibrating stick and into his tight balls. He stared at their two cocks, stiff with expectation, then at the projectile which stuck up between them.

Chev's breath on his forehead, Mac shifted into first. The car roared its annoyance. Mac pressed a bare foot to the gas, increasing the sound. He raised his face to Chev's, fingers gripping the metal shaft between their legs. Another hand on his.

The lip piercings were inches away from Mac's mouth. Metal curled into a smile. Cock pulsing, Mac leant forward and tasted adrenalin. Ten fingers tightened on the hand-brake. Beneath, the car was barely held in check.

Two hands began to pull as two mouths continued to kiss. On the periphery of sensation, Mac felt the double alternator kick in. The harnesses left them both an arm free. He encircled Chev's hard, scarred waist, drawing the man closer to the quivering shaft.

The engine was screaming now, begging for release. Mac yanked the hand-brake up another inch. Chev's mouth gnawed at his; he longed to gnaw back, but knew he had to concentrate, pace the act. The passion itself would last nano-seconds, if they were lucky. Anticipation was all.

Mac had made this trip in his head so many times. He didn't need to check the instruments to know the speedometer was about to hit ninety. His eyes flicked open. Chev stared back, pupils swollen. Mac noticed the irises for the first time: rings of iridescent petrol-blue all but eclipsed by the oily depths of ever-expanding pupils. Strapped between the front seats of a vehicle he had owned less than three months, staring into the eyes of a man he had known less than forty-eight hours, Mac felt complete. Almost.

Above Chev's eyes, twelve shards of metal quivered. Then V-ed. A harsh laugh. 'Enough shit – let's trip!'

The smell of burning fossil-fuels and sweat hot in his nostrils, Mac threw back his head and released the hand-brake.

They were discovered two weeks later, by a couple in a Winnebago who had taken a wrong exit. According to the medical examiner's report, the heat of the post-impact inferno – caused mainly by the extra three gas-tanks – had fused what was eventually identified as the bodies of the two male passengers with the surrounding metalwork of the vehicle.

Separation for the purposes of internment was not deemed feasible.

## THROUGH THE LOOKING GLASS

The south of France. I wander on to the balcony of our room and take long, deep breaths of the warm, salty air. The luxury hotel overlooks the sun-drenched beach. I watch white-ridged waves ripple on a sea of sparkling indigo.

Hard to believe that only two weeks ago I was standing on a street corner in London, the only thing I owned up for sale. And, as usual, it was a buyers' market...

I wasn't having a good night. In fact, that whole week had been capital B, capital A, capital D. I won't bore you with the details. Let's just say I was down to my last three smokes and trying hard not to think about money for food, rent – luxuries like that.

September, and already cold enough to shrink a cock. Meddina, across the street, was back waiting for her fourth trick of the night. Shivering, I dug out a cigarette and lit it. Shit! Demand for the boy-next-door type seemed to be at an all-time low. The smoke felt good as it hit my lungs. I watched Meddina haggle with a guy in a flash sports car. Meddina won. The car roared off. I lit up another cigarette – one left. Possible nicotine depravation added itself to my list of worries. I waited. And waited.

Eventually: a john. The guy had driven past three, maybe four times. He drew in, stopped, engine still running.

'Hey!'

'Who? Me?'

'Yeah, you,' he said, in a sharp cut-the-bull tone.

Jack Dickson

I sauntered up to the open window. 'What?' I asked.

The guy inside looked to be in his forties, really built, cropped hair, blunt features.

'Let me see your face!'

I bent down, and stuck my head in the window. Noses inches apart, we stared at each other. His eyes were dark brown.

'OK,' he said.

I straightened up, waiting for the usual 'how much?'

It didn't come. Instead, he opened the car door.

'Get in!' he told me.

'Hey! Wait a minute. What about...?'

'Just fucking shut up and get in!'

I hesitated. Like they say, it's a free market. Free to go or starve. I got in. For a couple of minutes we just sat there. Him, staring straight ahead, knuckles white around the steering wheel.

Finally: 'Well?'

'Well what?' I asked him.

He let out a long sigh. 'Are you gonna put on that seat belt or are we just gonna sit here all night?'

'Oh, right,' I said, drawing the harness across my chest.

He started up the engine. 'Seventy-five percent of all road accident fatalities could be avoided by passengers wearing their safety belts,' he told me.

'Oh, right,' I said again. Something was starting to tell me this might be a mistake.

He pulled out into the road and set off at a speed well below the limit.

Silence.

'We going to a hotel?'

More silence, my heart pounding.

Slowly: 'Just sit there and keep it shut.'

'Oh, right,' I said for a third time. Something told me this was definitely a mistake.

A few minutes later: 'OK if I smoke?' My hands were shaking.

Instant answer: 'No, it fuckin' isn't!'

'Oh, right,' I said for the... Who the hell was counting?

'Fifty-two percent of all fires are started by carelessly discarded cigarette ends,' he told me.

'Oh, right,' I said. 'Didn't know that.'

'Yeah, well, you know it now.'

'Oh, right.'

The lights up ahead changed to red. I decided to act on what something was telling me.

'Fuck you!' I shouted, elbowing him hard in the ribs, unfastening the safety belt, fumbling at the handle.

The car shuddered to a halt. Him, bent double, gasping for air. Me, still fumbling at the door handle. Him, still bent double, still gasping for air. Me, still fumbling at the door handle. Him, straightening up. Me, still fumbling at the door handle. Him, turning. Me, giving up with the door handle.

Him: 'It's called central locking.'

Me, like an idiot: 'Oh, right.'

Him, an open-handed smack across my face. Me, the taste of blood in my mouth.

'Don't try that again!'

I nodded, tongue finding a cut on my lower lip, fingers finding a rapidly swelling bruise on my right cheek. I should have known what was coming next:

'Three percent of all road fatalities are caused by passengers attempting to leave a moving vehicle.'

'Milton Keynes – named after the two most famous economists of the twentieth centaury: Milton Friedman and John Maynard Keynes. Know that?'

I shook my head.

He parked the car, then said, 'Get out!'

I got out, stood there, paralysed.

'In there!' he said, nodding towards a semi-detached villa identical to every other one in the street.

'Milton Keynes is one of the safest places on the whole country. It has a homicide rate eighty percent below the national average, a burglary rate eighty-seven percent lower, an overall road accident rate of only seven percent, and, even more impressive, a road fatality rate of ONLY two percent!'

I tried to look impressed.

He fumbled with keys and eventually got the door open. Inside was a dark hallway. Straight ahead was a brightly lit kitchen. A woman appeared, a flimsy dressing gown tied loosely around herself.

'Move it, kid!' he barked, giving me a helping shove.

The woman was about the same age as the man, but a good deal more ragged round the edges; straggly peroxide hair; no make up, but you could see she must have been a real looker, once.

'Sit down,' she slurred, pointing to one of the three chairs strewn around a circular breakfast table.

Looking at her blue eyes, I realised she was drunk. I sat.

She turned to Mr Facts-and-Figures. 'What've you done to him? Look at his face!'

He shrugged.

'Let me put some ice on that for you, sonny.'

She opened the freezer door and began packing cubes into a dishcloth. He sat down and glowered.

'There we go, sonny,' she said, pressing the ice-pack against my cheek.

As she bent over, the none-too-secure dressing gown gaped open. I could see her left tit, the large nipple standing erect. My cock responded, started pushing inside jeans that weren't cut for expanding members.

'My God, where did you find him? He's perfect!' she said,

breath heavy with alcohol.

'Round Kings Cross way. The kid's a male prostitute.'

She didn't respond.

He continued. 'All these months of searching finally paid off.'

He dug deep into the inside pocket of his jacket and produced a black leather wallet. From inside, he pulled out a small snap shot, gazed at it, then at me, then back at it.

'I couldn't believe it. Had to drive past four times.'

He sat the photograph on the table facing me and my ministering, drunk, tit-flashing angel. It was a head-and-shoulders shot. A woman. My eyes, my colouring, my hair, my bone structure.

'Suppose you want an explanation?' he asked.

I couldn't wait.

'I'm Mick Stein and this is my wife, Marigold.'

I smiled over the table at Mrs Stein.

'Get you a drink, sonny? Some gin maybe?' she asked, filling up her glass.

I shook my head.

'You drink too much!' her husband told her.

'Yeah, yeah,' she said, 'you told me a hundred times...'

Both of them together: 'Sixty-two percent of heavy drinkers die from an alcohol-related illness before the age of seventy.'

'We,' he continued, 'don't really care who you are.'

I tried not to look too offended.

'I'm in insurance. Spend my life working out probabilities of death and then selling policies.'

I nodded: so far, so good.

'A couple of months ago, I was asked to do the paperwork for a routine policy renewal. Turns out it was for an old lady – a very, very rich old lady. The sum itself was chicken-feed, twenty thousand pounds. What took my attention was the terms...'

I noticed Marigold's dressing gown had fallen open again. The half-exposed tit looked firm and hard. I imagined my hand closing round it...

'In the event of her death, the money was to go to Battersea Dog Home. Unless, that is, her long-lost grandson has been located. The same for the rest of her three-million estate.'

He pointed at the photograph still lying face up on the table.

'That's the old dame's daughter, Mary. Got herself pregnant. The family made her put it up for adoption. Not long after, Mary died and the old lady has been suffering from a bad conscience ever since.

'And you want me to play the grandson?'

'You're the right age, got the right kind of looks.'

Suddenly, I realised Marigold was looking at me looking at her tit. She smiled and made a half-hearted attempt at pulling the flimsy fabric tighter, then threw me a 'you-cheeky-little-devil' glance. It pumped my half hard-on into a full one. And in those jeans that was no mean feat.

He talked on some more, but I was already convinced. It was to be a three-way split, a million each. They'd put me up for a couple of days while we sorted out a story about where I'd been and what I'd been doing for the last nineteen years.

Marigold finished her drink and went to bed.

'Tea?' her husband asked.

'Yeah, sure.'

Out came a pot, strainer, cosy, matching china cups and saucers.

'Nothing beats a good brew,' he told me.

I nodded.

He poured me some, then himself. He avoided looking at me as he took a sip of the steaming, dark liquid.

'Any milk?'

He nodded, stood, and went to the freezer. 'You know, there's a .0005% chance that Mad Cow Disease might be passed to humans through milk.'

'What the hell. I like living dangerously,' I told him, pouring a generous slosh from the bottle into the cup.

Silence.

He seemed to be almost blushing, awkward, shifting in his seat. It's not what you expect from someone who's 6'4", built like a brick shit-house and has the features of a psychopath.

'So, kid,' he still couldn't bring himself to look at me, 'you're a prostitute, a rent boy?'

'Yes,' I said, sipping the tea.

'You do it with... with... both –'

'Both guys and women.'

'How much you usually charge?' He shot me a quick glance.

No 'almost blushing' about him now: scarlet. And a pound to a penny it wasn't only his face experiencing a change in blood flow.

'Oh, about a hundred.' Only a slight exaggeration.

He stood up slowly. 'Well, seeing as you're getting a million thanks to me, I guess that entitles me to quite a bit of your, er, time.'

I saw the bulge as he took the two steps towards me. The hard-on looked in proportion to the rest of him.

Towering above me, crotch level with my face, he said, 'You know, I've always wondered how it would feel with a guy. I mean, I've screwed plenty of women up the arse.'

I felt his hand run over my chest, grab the belt round my jeans, and haul me to my feet. My hard-on ached for release from its prison of too-tight denim. With a couple of quick, abrupt movements he obliged it.

'Jesus! The idea of being fucked by another guy really turns you on,' he said, leering – the idea of the idea really turning him on, too.

'Turn round and bend over!' he barked.

Deftly, I did as he said, managing to reach down into the pocket of the jeans at my ankles for a condom. He didn't say anything when I handed it to him. I heard the foil paper tear, and the sound of rubber stretched over something long, thick and very hard. My own cock, sandwiched between stomach and the tablecloth, gave a spasm of twitches. Next, I felt his fingers jabbing.

'Jesus, I bet you just can't get enough. Probably want that hole of yours plugged day and night. How many other guys have you had up there?'

'Too many.'

He laughed, a low guttural snigger. 'I bet being fucked by someone like me must be paradise for a little cocksucking fairy like you?'

I whimpered my agreement.

'Well, now you're gonna get it and get it good!'

I felt his cockhead press against my ring. He started to push in, a hard aggressive thrust. Something told me there would be nothing subtle about what was going to happen.

Something was absolutely correct.

Next morning, it was 11am when I finally shook myself awake. The bedroom was sparse but functional: a bed, obviously, a wardrobe and a dressing table. Downstairs I could hear a TV.

The bathroom had a small shower. I stood under its needle-point stream of tepid water for a good twenty minutes. The towels were soft and fluffy and smelt of fabric conditioner. Everything had a slightly unreal quality. Apart from the pain in my arse: that was all too real. Mr Facts-and-Figures fucked like a machine: cold, hard, rhythmic, unemotional. I dressed slowly and went downstairs.

Marigold was on the lounge sitting in front of some morning chat show. She was wearing the same flimsy dressing gown of the previous night. In her hand, a half-full glass.

'Hi,' she said.

'Hi,' I replied.

She switched off the television.

'You don't have to –'

'Of course I do. A growing boy like you needs a good breakfast.'

She ushered me through to the kitchen and sat me down at the table.

'Bacon and eggs OK?'

'Yes, fine, thanks,' I said, stomach rumbling.

She flapped around, clattering pans, breaking eggs, unpeeling rashers, all the time pulling at that dressing gown.

'Bet a big hulking lad like you enjoys his food,' she said, setting down four slices of buttered bread and popping the cosy over the tea pot. After placing the plate of fried food in front of me, she poured herself another drink. I ate in silence. She drank in silence.

Then:

'So... you're a prostitute, a rent boy?'

'Yes,' I said, pouring myself some tea.

'You do it with... with... both –'

'Both guys and women.'

'How much do you usually... charge?'

'Oh, about a hundred.'

She stood up slowly. 'Well, seeing as you're getting a million thanks to me, I guess that entitles me to quite a bit of your, er, time.'

I watched as the dressing gown slid to the floor. The body beneath was plump and curved.

I felt her hand run over my chest, grab the belt round my jeans, and haul me to my feet. My hard-on ached for release from its prison of too-tight denim.

'Turn round and bend over!' I barked.

Deftly, she did as I said.

After unzipping myself, I encased my hard cock in a sheath of glistening rubber. I poked my fingers in and around her juicy cunt. 'Jesus, bet you just can't get enough. Probably want that hole of yours plugged day and night. How many other guys have you had up there?'

'Not nearly enough,' she said.

I laughed, a low guttural snigger. 'I bet being fucked by someone like me must be paradise for an old slapper like you?'

She whimpered her agreement.

'Well, now you're gonna get it and get it good!'

I pressed my cockhead against the soft folds of her cunt. Something told me there would be nothing subtle about what was going to happen.

Something was absolutely correct.

The south of France. I wander on to the balcony of our room and take long, deep breaths of the warm, salty air. The luxury hotel overlooks the sun-drenched beach. I watch white-ridged waves ripple on a sea of sparkling indigo,

Of course, the old lady rumbled me within minutes. I blurted out the truth in a long, confused confession.

She just smiled.

'So... you're a prostitute, a rent boy?'

'Yes,' I said.

'You do it with... with... both –'

'Both guys and women.'

'How much you usually... charge?'

'Oh, about a hundred.'

She stood up slowly. 'Well, seeing as I'll be taking you on as a paid companion, I guess that entitles me to quite a bit of your, er, time.'

I watched as she produced a strap-on dildo from a drawer. Her hand ran over my chest, grabbed the belt round my jeans, and hauled me to my feet. My hard-on ached for release from its prison of too-tight denim. With a couple of quick, abrupt movements she obliged it.

'Turn round and bend over!' she rasped.

Deftly, I did as she said.

'Jesus, bet you just can't get enough. Probably want that hole of yours plugged day and night. How many other rich old ladies have you had up there?'

'None,' I said.

She laughed, a low guttural snigger. 'I bet being fucked by someone like me must be paradise for a whore like you?'

I whimpered my agreement.

'Well, now you're gonna get it and get it good!'

I felt her cockhead press against my ring. She started to push in, a hard aggressive thrust. Something told me there would be nothing subtle about what was going to happen.

Something was absolutely correct.

# WILDLIFE

Wanna hear something weird? Wanna hear how ya can know someone and... not know them?

Me and Jim joined the Federal Park Rangers on the same day, six months ago. Turns out we were both in the Marines: Jim for ten years, till he busted his arm, me for two – till they busted my ass!

I sort of messed around between the Marines and rangering: pumped gas, bussed, that kind of thing. Did drugs for a while, lived with a chick for another while. Suppose I was kind of drifting, trying this and that till I found what felt right. Tell the truth, don't suppose I knew what I wanted – hell, who does at nineteen?

Me and Jim hit it off straight away. He's a big guy: 6'4" in his socks, 280 pounds of pure muscle, and when he's wearing his rangers' boots, hat and waxed, padded jacket, he looks like the jolly green giant – only not so jolly.

I'm kind of skinny – 'least, was till Jim got a hold of me. Two weeks into the job, he had me workin' out till the sweat poured off me in buckets. Sit-ups, chin-ups, bench-presses – you name it, Jim had me doing fifty of each before I knew where I was! And not in a gym, before you accuse us of being a pair of those candy-assed types that spends all their time in spandex pussy-drawers. Nope, Jim trained me in the open air, right in the heart of Alexandra Park, in this real quiet clearing.

So that's how I ended up with the build I got now – and that's how me and Jim got to know each other real well. Or so I thought.

When it comes to late shifts, most of the guys start crying-off. Me and Jim don't mind the graveyard shift. Tell the truth, we kind of like playing with the... wildlife. The critters we look after during the day ain't got nothing on what appears at night: glue-sniffers, crack-smokers, guys with guys, guys with chicks, chicks with chicks – even a guy playing with his labrador.

Now, me and Jim kind of got into the habit of having a bit of fun with this wildlife – you know the kind of thing: come on all heavy-like, make 'police-report' noises and see what they're gonna offer us. Sure helps with the crap wages this job pays: we've had watches, money, cars – jeez, there ain't nothing some folks won't do to avoid getting busted.

Sometimes we even get paid in kind. The guy with the labrador? Turns out he was a congressman or something, real dyed-in-the-wool Republican – a family man, the types what legis- lates for traditional values and all that crap. Yeah, well, wasn't his wife's name he was moaning when my dick was up his ass and Jim was slapping his pink, bible-thumping face in time to my thrusts.

Anyway, this particular night was quiet. Nothing out of the or- dinary. Must have been about two-ish. Jim was checking the east perimeter fence and I was having a smoke.

Then I hears a noise. You work nights in the park, you get kind of sensitive 'bout noises. First couple of weeks on the job, I couldn't tell a polecat from a pine marten, a grizzly from a gopher. I was jumping at shadows, trigger-finger itching to blast the leaves off the trees. Then I learned to judge things better, got to know what was ordinary and what wasn't. And this wasn't no ordinary noise. So I pull on my jacket and go to investigate.

I got night-eyes as well as night-ears, these days. Couple of yards into the undergrowth and I can see this shape, hugging this big old elm and sort of rubbing itself up and down the trunk. Only it's a sort of weird shape with arms in the wrong place. The arms sort of twist, and it's then I move a bit closer and see the arms are legs; real white legs, and they're wrapping themselves around the middle of the shape.

I'm skirting round past a clump of bushes to get a closer look. A bit of a moon kind of peeks out from behind a cloud and reflects off skin. A young guy: skinny, the nobbles of his spine glinting as he uses his lats to brace himself against that big ol' elm. I move round some more.

The noises are louder now: two sets of breathing, low grunts and sharper moans synched into one. I shift a bit and my foot catches in something. I look down and sees this heap of clothes all tangled round my work boot: couple of leather jackets, well-cut pants, an expensive-looking designer shirt.

I sort of laugh. A pair of princesses in Alexandra Park – boy, are me and Jim gonna have some fun here! Then I duck down and shut up real quick. Not that the kids seem to notice – jeez, they was really into it! Soon my hand's on my crotch and I'm stroking myself real easy-like. I stay like that, craning my head to get a better look. Then:

'Whatcha up to, over there?'

Jeez, my heart jumped!

The kids sort of freeze under the beam of Jim's flashlight and so does my hand. Christ, felt like I did when my mom caught me beating off over her Sears catalogue when I was ten! I stagger out of the bushes just in time to see Jim appear in the clearing, shotgun over his shoulder, holding a coil of rope. His steel-toed boots are planted a yard apart, flashlight focused on these two kids who look like they'd been turned to stone. 'Hey man,' I says, trying to sound normal, 'wondered were ya'd got to!'

Jim don't say nothing back, just keeps his beam trained on the trunk of that big ol' elm. The noises have stopped; well, not stopped so much as changed. I move my eyes from this sort of four-legged kid. 'Looks like a new kind of critter, don't it?' I say.

Jim turns his head and looks at me.

Something clutches in my guts... 'cause I know that look... the same look Jim gets when he's working me real hard, pushing me way past my limits. My cock twitches and I'm thinking real fast as I walk towards the tree. 'Yer mommies know yer out, girls? Ain't this a school-night?' I say.

Jim laughs.

The kids don't move. The bigger one with the long, tangly hair's still inside the other kid – though there can't be much holding them together now!

'Let's see some ID!' Jim moves forward.

I start to circle round, making sure we ain't gonna be interrupted, and when no ID seems to be forthcoming, Jim grabs the tangly-haired kid and pulls him out of the other one.

I'm a couple of feet away. Jim's holding the kid real tight – got him by the arm, the fingers of his big leather work glove digging into bare flesh. He's shaking him hard – so hard I can hear teeth rattling. Long, tangly hair's flying everywhere and the kid's struggling, writhing about like an eel. Ain't saying much, though, just sort of mumbling, trying to roll off his rubber and stuff his softening dick back into his well-cut pants and get away from Jim at the same time.

'Leave him alone!'

The beam of Jim's flashlight moves to where the new voice is coming from, and I see this blond, pale shape sitting at the root of the tree rubbing its butt, where I guess it hit the ground real sudden-like.

Jim must have loosened his grip on the tangly-haired kid 'cause there's a sort of scuffle. The kid rushes past me, and grabs one of the leather jackets. So I grab him, but he's slipperier than a snake. He throws the jacket to the blond kid, elbowing me in the process, then runs back towards the elm... well, must have been the elm, though I couldn't see too well, being all doubled-up and trying to get my wind back and all.

'So ya wanna play rough?' There's an edge to Jim's voice.

I look up. The two kids are standing by the tree. Blondie's wearing the leather jacket but nothing else. Tangly-hair's bare-chested, one arm around Blondie's waist. Jim's a couple of feet away, training the flashlight on two chalk faces.

'ID, boys,' I say, picking up back where we left off.

Musta been the way I said it, 'cause Tangly-hair fumbles in the pocket of those well-cut pants then holds something out. Blondie just stands there, staring at Jim, real arrogant-like.

I'm squinting at this driver's licence. Tangly-hair turns out to be a John Nixon: also turns out to be twenty-three. I look at the picture, then up, then back again. Kids fake these things all the time – Christ, I had ID said I was twenty-one, three years before I could drink! Maybe fright's making Tangly-hair aka John Nixon look younger, so I take off my glove and run my fingers over the plastic. Seems OK. I scowl, laughing inside. 'Ya just assaulted a Federal Park Ranger, boy – what's yer mommy gonna say when's she's got to come bail ya out of jail?' I stuff the licence into my pocket.

'Let's see something from you!' Jim's sort of circled round behind me. He's looking Blondie up and down and Blondie's, like, leaning against the big ol' elm, shifting his weight from one pale leg to the other and pushing his hair back from his face like a real princess.

I catch the Nixon kid's eye, and he looks like he's about to shit himself. 'No way you're twenny-three, boy, you look more like eighteen to me,' I growl, hooking my thumbs into my belt and sort of swaggering a bit. 'So that's –' I count off the charges on my fingers '– fake ID, assaultin' a Federal Officer –'

'Hey, man – chill out!'

I grin, 'cause The Nixon kid's looking anything but chilled himself.

'Sorry I hit ya – it was an accident. I didn't mean –'

'Got myself a witness, boy – it look like an accident to you, Jim?' I say.

'Aw... please, man – come on! Just let us go!'

I looks over at Jim. He don't look like he wants anyone to go anywhere. And I guess he's got the same feeling I have... that maybe someone's gonna need to be taught a lesson.

The Nixon kid moves his arm from around Blondie's waist and I can almost see the pink finger-marks he's left on smooth, white skin. He moves in front, kind of shielding his pal. 'Look, guys,' he says, trying to sound cool but I can hear the tremor in his voice, 'we're not hurtin' anyone or anythin'. We'll just get out of your way an'...'

'How old's he?'

Jim's voice is real quiet. I start to shiver, even though it's a warm night.

'Old enough!' Blondie's reappeared from behind the other kid, resting an arm on his pal's shoulder, real casual-like. And he's soundin' sort of... lippy.

Now, if there's one thing really gets Jim's goat, it's lippy kids.

Jim likes his respect. I give him respect, 'cause I know he's worth respecting. I also know Blondie is biting off a lot more than that cute mouth of his is ever gonna be capable of chewing.

The Nixon kid's sounding real worried now. 'C'mon, man,' he says, 'give him your ID an' we can get –'

'Sure I'll give it to him...' Blondie's still smiling. The hand that's not around his pal's shoulder reaches slowly into the jacket's top zip pocket. I start to grin... then I see the gun. A hand-gun. Looks like a foreign-job. Maybe a Glock. Jim's fingers are inching towards his shotgun. Blondie's sounding lippier than ever. 'Give it to him good!' He's talking to his pal but the eyes and the gun are trained on Jim.

'Man, we don't want no trouble. Let's just –' The Nixon kid's staring at the gun.

'He wants trouble.' Blondie flicks the barrel towards Jim's head and steps forward.

Christ, he's still hard, and there's two barrels pointing at Jim, who's just standing there not saying nothing, hand resting on the strap of his shotgun. And I remember mine is back in the truck.

'And he's gonna get it. Drop it, big guy – and the rope!'

Now Jim usually takes shit like this from no one. But no one usually has a gun... 'cept us. So he does as Blondie says, slides the shotgun from his shoulder real easy-like, then throws it and the rope on the ground between us and the kids.

'Get it, Jack!'

His pal darts down, snatches at the shotgun like it's a rattler.

'Hands behind your head, big guy – you too, man!'

I'm peering at the Glock. There are a lot of replicas around these days. 'You gonna make us, princess?'

The Nixon kid freezes, still holding the shotgun. Blondie smiles, real sweet:

'Sure I'm gonna make you, man... an' I'm gonna enjoy every minute of it!'

I decide to humour him. My arms move up, fingers lacing behind my neck. 'You been watching too many Tarantino movies, kid. You ever used one of those things?'

Blondie's moving forward, hard-on bouncing off his pale belly. 'Sure – my daddy showed me!'

Jim's voice cuts in. 'Aw... his daddy showed him! Well, ain't that the cutest thing you ever heard? His...'

I don't catch the rest of the sentence – don't know yet if Jim even got anything else out. 'Cause when I hear a bullet whiz past my ear that old Marine-training comes back real fast and my face is in the dirt, no questions asked. The sound echoes around a bit, and I wait to make sure nothing else is coming before I raise my head. I see leather – and bare legs. I look up the length of the work boots, up waxed pants and jacket and I see Jim's holding his hat, sort of staring at this hole just above the brim.

'Oh fuck, oh fuck, oh fuck, oh...' The Nixon kid's mouth's hanging open, and he's gibbering like a baboon.

'Want another demonstration?'

'Leave it, man!' The Nixon-kid's staring at Blondie, throwing his weight from one foot to the other, sort of jittery-like.

'I said, want another demonstration, big guy?' Blondie strolls over to Jim, the gun in both hands.

'I guess you know what you're doin'...'

'Now let's see some ID from you.'

Jim drops his hat and he's tossing his rangers' badge and wallet onto the ground. So I do likewise.

'C'mon, man – leave it!' The Nixon-kid's hopping about now, eyes flicking between Blondie and Jim. And he's not holding the shotgun anymore.

'No way!'

The moon suddenly breaks through a bank of cloud and I can see a bit better. Jim's fingers are linked back behind his head.

'Huh?' The Nixon-kid's sounding confused – and he ain't the only one.

'You wanna go? Go!'

He looks from Blondie to me and back again, then grabs his shoes and he's off. The flashlight's lying on the ground where Jim dropped it and, what with the light from the moon, the clearing's real illuminated. And there's a quiet, like just before manoeuvres.

Then Jim breaks it. 'What ya want?'

Blondie sniggers. 'That jacket – for starters. Always fancied one of those waxed-jobs.'

Jim doesn't move. There's less than an inch between his fore-head and the barrel of the gun. A click tells me the safety's been released.

'Take it off!'

I know Jim, and I know his padded wax is more than just a jacket to him. He lowers his hands, real slow-like. Then he's popping fasteners, unzipping and easing his big arms out of the sleeves. He throws the jacket onto the ground.

At this point, I could have done any of three things: made a grab for Blondie, made a grab for the shotgun – which must be around somewhere, 'cause I know the Nixon kid didn't take it with him – or high-tail it back to the truck.

I do the first... but don't count on the speed of Blondie's reflexes. Before I know it, he's kneed me in the nuts and I'm writhing around on the ground. At first there's nothing but white stars... then I throw up.

After a while the pain lessens a bit, and when I finally unscrew my eyelids there's a pair of bare feet inches from my nose.

'Tie him up!'

I blink a couple of times, my head still spinning. Then something hits the back of my neck and I know it's Jim's rope. A toe prods my cheek.

'Do it!'

I stagger onto one knee, and look over at Jim. The work shirt's gone the same way as the jacket. I raise my head a bit more, and I don't think I've ever seen that expression on Jim's face. Then my brain gets into gear, and I scan the ground for the shotgun: nothing. So I haul myself up, take the rope and walk towards Jim, wondering what the hell I'm gonna do.

'To the tree, man – tie him to the tree.'

Something makes me not wanna look at Jim, and he seems to feel the same 'cause his head's lowered as we both start towards the elm. Blondie's behind with the gun, and sweat's pouring from my pits. Jim stops, back to the tree, and I'm thinking about the best sort of knot to fake when Blondie laughs:

'Kneel, big guy – I want you on your knees!'

Now I got to look at Jim. And he looks at me. Then we're both looking at Blondie... who's staring back, buck-naked from the waist down. Guess it's his age or something, 'cause he's still hard.

I can't take my eyes off his cock, and I'm real grateful when Jim slides down the tree, knees apart, back resting against the trunk. I duck round, do a quick slip-knot over his wrists and ankles, then move to the front, wanting to check I'm not cutting off his circulation or anything.

'Take his dick out while you're there, man.'

I almost laugh. 'Hey, princess – you wanna suck on his cock, all ya hadda do was ask!'

'Just do it!' Jim's voice sounds weird and my hands are shaking. I undo the webbing belt, then lower the zipper. His cock pulses against my fingers and I flinch.

'Pull his pants down, man!'

'Cause of the way Jim's legs are spread, this ain't too easy. But with a bit of a struggle I manage to drag the waxed pants down over his thighs. I move back and look at him, his arms behind that big ol' elm, his torso gleaming.

In the background I hear the click-click of a safety catch released then replaced. Jim's cock's poking out of the front of his boxers like some shy, half-tamed critter. My nuts are still aching from Blondie's kick, but there's another sort of ache there too. And it's making my face all flush up. I close my eyes so I don't need to look at Jim.

'You want it, don't you?'

I'm thinking about the shotgun, both our wallets, two sets of federal ID – not to mention our reps if someone comes along and sees all this.

'You want my dick, big guy!'

I open my eyes, glance to the side and see a pair of pale legs and a white ass. The gun's still gripped in Blondie's hand, but that hand's hanging by his side now. Guess this is my chance to clobber him, or run. But I do neither, 'cause the ache in my nuts is spreading up into my cock and I'm still kind of frozen with fear. So I shuffle a bit until I'm crouching side on to them and then I just freeze there like a coward, waiting to see this Scarsdale princess try to make Jim do something he don't wanna do.

Blondie's got a hold of his hard-on, and he's running his fist up and down the shaft. The moon shifts, and his shadow falls across Jim's face. He takes a step closer, legs planted two feet apart. Then he leans forward, sort of drops himself onto the tree, supporting his weight with his arms. Jim's head's disappeared completely now, but I can see his belly and the waistband of his boxers between Blondie's pale legs.

'Oh yeah... you want it bad, big guy!'

I'm staring at Jim's crotch through the white V and I see his cock stretching up and out of his boxers and I realise Blondie's been telling the truth all along about Jim wanting his dick. Blondie's having to stand on tippy-toe to get his crotch at lip-level, and when that smooth white ass starts to swivel and pump, my own cock takes a leap into action.

There's a long, soft sigh – could have come from any of three mouths – well, maybe not Jim's, seeing as his is pretty full at the moment. The moon's shining on Blondie's twitching back and I notice a couple of scrapes and scratches from when he was under the other kid. He grinds his hips for a couple of minutes, then jerks. And I stare at the marks... 'cause I don't wanna think about the heat in my face and the throbbing in my cock.

Blondie pulls out and turns. I'm staring past him at Jim. His eyes are closed, nose and lips all smeary. The rest of his face is as scarlet as mine.

'You want him, man?'

Blondie's dick – all wet with come and Jim's spit – is still standing straight up against his belly, sort of glistening in the moonlight. My stomach gives a lurch.

Blondie grins, nods over his shoulder. 'He's begging for it...'

I'm still staring at Jim – his cock, leastways, and it's like one of those new saplings we planted last week: strong and thrusting up towards the sky. My guts lurch again, 'cause Jim looks so different, his big ol' body tied to that big ol' elm.

'Aren't you, baby?' Blondie walks over to Jim, nudges his hard-on with the barrel of the gun.

Now, I ain't ever heard anyone call Jim 'baby' before, and I never thought I would. The word makes me shiver. I get up, half-stagger towards him, tripping over his jacket, hat, belt, our IDs... even the shotgun's still there. Guess it must have been hidden by the jacket. Jim groans – 'Come on, man,' – and it's like when that lot came off, something else came off with it, 'cause – don't ask me why – but before I know it my zipper's down and I'm holding Jim's head still, cramming my aching cock between his lips.

His mouth's all warm and slimy – Blondie's come, I guess. His 'tache and beard are scratching my thighs and I sort of moan: I've had blow-jobs before, but there's something about the way Jim's beard's rubbing my nuts that's driving me wild.

First couple of minutes I'm too busy grinding to think much about Jim – till something sharp nicks my shaft. I howl, grab his ears and try to drag my cock out of his mouth. But he sheaths those teeth and his lips change to firm cushions that hold me there. Then he really starts to skim my shaft with just the right pressure. He's cradling the head of my cock with his tongue each time I thrust, pressing down with his lips each time I withdraw. Minutes later, my balls are pulled up tight and I know I'm gonna shoot real soon.

'Good, cocksucker!'

I only realise my eyes are closed when the lids spring open. Blondie's crouched beside me, stroking Jim's hair... and Jim's making this moaning sound through his nose, which turns into a sort of choke as I thrust deep into his mouth, the head of my cock near enough hitting the back of his throat.

Blondie's hands move away, doing something I can't see. Then Jim's gag kicks in, massaging my shaft and I don't care about seeing.

Couple more thrusts and I'm almost there, but I don't wanna come 'cause Jim's mouth feels so damn good. So I ease back a bit, try to pull my cock out of that warm, sloppy cave.

Then there are hands on my ass, gripping me tight and pulling me forward. My nuts tighten and knot together. Over my groans I can hear Blondie jacking himself again, but not for long. 'Cause when I explode inside Jim's mouth, there ain't nothing I wanna hear 'cept that deep sigh and the splattering against my legs that lets me know he's come too. He holds me there, hands massaging my ass-cheeks, sucking every last drop from my slit.

By the time I've gone soft and my cock slips from Jim's cummy mouth, Blondie's long gone – as are our IDs, wallets and the rifle. But I still think we got the best deal – and so does Jim. Turns out the hottest bit of parklife was hiding beneath layers of waxed cotton and a federal rangers' badge all along.

# MICK AND THE MANIMAL

He peered through the bars and scanned the inside of the cage.

Nothing. Just a dark, smelly cube with a heap of dirty straw in the back right-hand corner. Mick scowled. These intergalactic zoos were all the same. The handbill had claimed 'Creatures Captured and Collected from all Corners of the Cosmos'. The other trailers had contained the usual disappointing array of genetically altered waifs and strays from no further afield than the nearest bio-engineering lab. This cage was empty – unless that stench indicated some sort of exotic bacteria.

Mick backed away from the bars as an acrid whiff assaulted his nostrils. The whole thing was a con. He looked around for someone to complain to: $5 was $5, and he wasn't about to –

A low growl split the silence. Mick's head flipped back to the bars. There *was* something in there! He narrowed his eyes in the gloom. Inside the cage everything was shades of darkness. Mick squinted.

A patch of darkness moved. Another growl. He inched nearer, then leapt back as a hand from behind grasped his shoulder.

'Don't get too close, buddy – that's a manimal in there!'

Mick stared through dusky half-light at a peaked cap and the face beneath.

'Obtained at great personal expense on Clotho, in Omega Quadrant. The only specimen in captivity – killed three of my men with its bare hands!'

Mick smiled. He had heard it all before.

The ZM laughed. 'Think I'm kidding?' He picked up a small rock and ran it along the bars. The sound reverberated inside the metal cage. Another growl. Louder this time.

Despite his scepticism, Mick shivered. 'OK, OK – you've convinced me.' He had to shout over the dying echoes of stone-on-metal. 'What is a... manimal, exactly?'

The ZM dropped the rock, draped an arm around Mick's shoulder and led him away from the cage. 'What is a manimal?'

Mick could still hear soft growling as they walked towards the exit.

'Now there's a question.'

'Is it... X or Y?' His interest surprised him. The twitch of his cock surprised him even more.

'Y. Triple Y!' Under the xenon exit sign the ZM stopped.

Mick stared at the seven-inch scar which bisected the weather-beaten face. The man laughed, fingers tracing the knobbles of toughened skin. 'Yeah – it gave me this little memento. Come back tomorrow, buddy – take the tour.'

As the ZM unlocked the gate and guided him through, low growls still echoed in Mick's ears.

He left work earlier than usual next day, choosing the long way home which took in the park and the travelling zoo. Beneath sixteen-ounce Ortarian silk, Mick's nipples began to tingle. Approaching the gate he saw the ZM, resplendent in daylight and a scarlet outfit, holding forth to a group of children:

'Freaks of nature! A glimpse of the future... or what links us to the beasts!'

Mick suppressed a smile as he caught the man's eye. The ZM beckoned. Seconds later he was part of the group. Walking far enough behind to segregate himself from the awe-struck children but close enough to follow the master's commentary, Mick noticed 'The Tour' pointedly avoided the cage at the far end of the exhibition area – the cage which housed the manimal. The noise from No.18 made his stomach churn.

As he neared the cage, Mick saw movement behind the heavy bars. The shouting was louder, accompanied by low, rumbling sounds. There was a keeper inside the cage. Mick stopped, a yard away and watched a sweating figure in overalls probe and prod a long metal pole into shadows at the rear. The man was red-faced. 'Eat, damn you!' The other hand held a slab of dripping flesh.

Mick's stomach lurched again. He took a step closer. A hair-covered limb snapped out of the darkness and seized the pole, heaving the weapon at the opposite wall. Mick's jaw dropped. The keeper was retreating towards the far side of the cage, stalked by a hulking, four-limbed... man? Animal?

The manimal paused in the middle of the space, raised itself from all-fours onto two legs. The creature was a mass of straggling, matted fur, longer on the head area and mellowing out to fuzz over its back and well-muscled hindquarters. Mick grasped a bar with one hand and stared at the only hairless area of the manimal's body. A thick, brownish cock curved upwards from between iron thighs.

Under sixteen-ounce Ortarian silk another cock twitched in response. Mick squeezed the cage bar between sweating fingers. Manimal moved slowly forwards. The keeper dropped the food and fumbled in overall-pockets. Manimal paused a second time. Keys appeared. Manimal growled. Keys fell to the floor. Mick stood spellbound. Silently, the manimal raised a hair-swathed arm. Fuzzy fingers flexed...

'No!' Mick seized the cage bars with both hands.

The manimal froze, arm in mid-air, and turned a shaggy head.

The sweating keeper grabbed the keys, unlocked the door and beat a retreat.

Mick's eyes scanned the strangely pale skin of the manimal's face, the thick whiskers, the bushy eyebrows and then travelled down to the densely fuzzed torso to the turgid cock head which strained beneath the tight foreskin. He dragged his gaze back to feral, yellow eyes. Mick stared at the manimal. The manimal stared at Mick. Beneath coarse facial hair, pink lips seemed to smile. Then the manimal reached over and picked up the pole.

From behind, Mick could hear the keeper's voice but not the words. His eyes were trained on the manimal, who was now running sharply clawed paws up and down the pole's thick shaft. Mick's gaze flicked to the other thick shaft which sprouted from a wiry bush. The head of the creature's manimalhood shone with a glaze of pre-come.

Manimal turned. Mick stared at densely fuzzed, muscular haunches. A hairy arm reached round and began to rub the length of the rod between bristling ass-cheeks. Mick's heart was beating in his ears. Bracing one end of the pole against the floor, manimal dragged himself up and down its length. The yellow eyes were lowered. Breath steamed from flaring nostrils.

Mick's own rod was throbbing now. One hand dropped from the railing to stroke sixteen-ounce Ortarian silk just as, a few feet away, a larger, hairier fist moved to grip ten inches of quivering manimalhood. Then there was water everywhere. Mick flinched as an icy jet shot past him. Suddenly Manimal was a shaking, snarling mass of wet fur and sinew.

'This'll cool it down!'

Mick's hard-on waned. He watched Manimal forced back against the rear wall as the keeper opened the hose up to full. He watched Manimal claw against the wall of water, then hurl the pole against the bars. The air was full of snarls, splashes and wet, dripping frustration.

Later that evening, Mick sat before his vid console skimming a bio-encyclopaedia. The Ortarian silk suit was a crumpled heap on the floor, his protein-tab uneaten, still in its dispenser. He scanned index after index, every 'man' prefix in every category. Nothing. No manimal – was that even its real name? He tried the 'o's. Plenty on Omega. Little on Clotho's indigenous flora and fauna.

He flipped to the 'h' subsection, and dropped the cursor to 'history'.

The screen flickered. Mick noted the size: five hundred bits. The document began to load. A visual was appearing.

Mick stared. Cave-art. He paused the screen at an ancient line-drawing which depicted a ritual between a pair of trees, then fast-forwarded through a variety of other primitive paintings. Comets. Suns. The arrival of sky-visitors. Changing seasons...

Mick flicked faster. He was sweating now, fingers slicking the console-buttons. Then it appeared: a dark, blurry form began to fill the monitor. Manimal. The same long, thick head hair, pale face, broad shoulders... Mick's hand slipped from the console. Fingers crawled over his own smooth torso... the mass of fur, coating the well-developed muscle of chest and abdomen.

Mick's index fingers traced a line of meagre stomach fuzz. The sketch had caught every detail of the manimal's hard body. His vision blinked in and out of focus. He froze the frame. Manimal was no bio-engineered creation of hapless mutation. Manimal was real!

Mick dragged his eyes from the image and searched for text. Nothing... but more sketches. More manimals. Alone. In groups. Adult manimals with smaller, less mature manimals. Hunting large creatures with spears. Paying homage to a bright, sky-bound object.

A final set of artwork downloaded. Manimals in pairs. Manimals copulating. Proud, erect manimals. Mick moved closer to the monitor. On the screen, a thick manimalhood was buried deep in the ass of another beast. Mick shivered and tried to will himself into the cave painting. He could almost hear the groans, smell the thick foetid manimal sex-stink, feel ten inches of iron manimalhood thrusting up into another beast's guts.

Mick was still shaking when the screen-blanker activated itself.

He logged in sick at 6am that morning.

At 7am he stood outside the locked zoo. His body was sore from lack of sleep. Half an hour later the ZM appeared, affable as ever. 'What can I do for you, buddy?'

Mick's throat was dry.

The ZM rubbed a stubbly chin. 'Tell me while I shave!'

'Why is he – it – so violent?'

They were standing in the ZM's quarters. Around them, the travelling exhibition was stirring into life.

The ZM smiled, patting balm onto his smooth face. 'It wants to get laid!'

Mick's heart began to race.

The master grabbed a shirt. 'We get three weeks of this every year! Last night was the worst so far – howling and grunting for hours, throwing itself against the bars...'

'Why don't you get him a mate?'

The ZM shrugged on his jacket. 'Hell – I know most of my spiel is junk, but one thing's true: our manimal is the only specimen in captivity. Think I'm risking more lives, just so it can get its rocks off?'

Mick's mind was back with the cave paintings.

'I tried to mate it, last time this happened. Sigma Sabre-tooth: they're close, genetically.' The scarred face frowned. 'Ripped the bitch to shreds then tried to eat her – I can't afford to lose exhibits. This is a cut-throat business, buddy!' He laughed. 'You a bio-anthropologist or something? Maybe –'

From the far end of the cages an angry growl cut into the conversation. The sound reverberated in Mick's chest. The master slapped his shoulder.

'Better get that hose out again, I suppose – don't know why the bugger can't just jerk off!'

Mick watched the ZM leave the trailer. His eyes fell on a small board of keys on the wall. Irate growls and water jets filled his head. Key No. 18 was clearly marked. His fingers shook as he reached over, grabbed the object and walked from the trailer.

Eight hours later, he was back. Skin prickling, Mick vaulted the security fence. The zoo was a grey mass of sleep noise. As he passed the other cages, an occasional exhibit stirred. Mick quickened his pace, rubbing the palms of damp hands on his thighs. He walked on until he reached Cage No. 18. Sex sweat soaked the nightsuit. He stopped, and stared. Yellow irises stared back.

Mick fingered the slender key. The eyes held him; the smell drew him to the bars. He could hear the manimal's shallow breathing, see the darkness quiver. The strong, furry body moved closer, towards the front of the cage. Two clouds of breath condensed in the freezing air as a band of light from a nearby security scanner flicked across, illuminating the tall shape with the wild eyes... and the ten inches of manimalhood which protruded from between two rusting bars.

Mick swallowed a dry lump in his throat. Sex sweat trickled from his pits. He stretched out a hand and touched the hard cock. A low growl. The surface was moist and smooth-feeling. Mick ran his finger up and down the shaft, pausing at the piss-slit to spread strong-smelling pre-come over the taut skin.

The growl became a low, rhythmic moan as he continued to stroke the manimalhood, which flexed and convulsed under his hand. Mick moaned in response, grasped the bristling root and moved closer. He wanted the rough hair of the manimal's whiskers against his face. But all he felt was the sterile coldness of cage bars. His own cock was twitching uncontrollably now. Part of Mick's mind remembered the Sigma Sabre-tooth. He loosened his grasp.

Moans changed to whimpers as he withdrew his hands. An ear-splitting howl shattered the silence. A hairy arm shot from the blackness. Mick almost screamed as four strong fingers cupped his balls and began to squeeze. He pulled away from the probing pads. The key was slippery in his wet fingers.

Mick closed the door and began to tear at the nightsuit. The cage was surprisingly warm. As he stripped in thick blackness, a dark outline circled him. He heard the tread of feet on straw, then metal, then back to straw again. Breath stroked his face. Soft finger pads traced his hairless jaw line. An unfamiliar sensation burned in his cock, travelling up through his body. Mick threw back his head and howled. Iron claws seized his shoulders, dragging him down onto the wet floor.

Two slick bodies thrashed in a morass of hair, sweat and pre-come. Mick almost shot then and there, as a warm, dripping mouth encased the length of him. A rough tongue urgently probed his piss-slit, coaxing other lube from his aching cock.

Mick howled a second time, fingers scrabbling over matted fur towards the hole between the manimal's hard ass-cheeks. Before he knew what was happening, the manimal was on all fours in front of him and Mick was pressing the swollen head of his spit-soaked cock against a hard body. Tangled hair rasped his thighs. Mick gripped shoulder tufts and pushed ball-deep into the manimal's hot ass. Tight muscle stretched to embrace his length, clamping him in a painful vice. Mick laced the thick mane between white-knuckled fingers and gasped.

They were both growling now, the sounds synched with Mick's short jabs. He crouched behind the manimal, hands slipping to clutch the fuzzy waist. His legs trembled as his cock was manipulated, squeezed and pummelled. Musky manimal-sweat rose from the beast and filled his head.

The tight tunnel of muscle continued to fuck Mick's cock until his brain, then his balls, exploded. His fingers dug into furry muscle and he found himself pumping floods of hot come into a slick,

fleshy vice. Manimal roared in response to Mick's low moan of release. They remained joined until Manimal had milked every last
droplet from Mick's cock. Instinctively, his hand slipped down
from a quivering waist to grasp ten swollen inches of manimalhood.

The security light flashed on. Other howls shattered his after-
glow. Other animals were awake, shrieking and baying. Mick
caught a fleeting glimpse of Manimal's sweat-drenched back. He
wrenched his cock out, grabbed the nightsuit and fled.

'Wanna buy shares, buddy?' The ZM grinned.

Mick barely registered the words and headed straight for
Manimal's cage.

On returning to the single-occupancy apartment, he had lain
naked on the bed, shoulders lacerated. The nightsuit was a torn rag
under his aching body as he writhed, luxuriating in manimal sex-
stink and his own salty odour. Holding his limp, bruised cock,
Mick had noticed several livid, circular indentations – souvenirs of
those tight manimal ass-muscles. And a streak of dried blood. The
release had drawn more than come from his body...

As he neared the cage, footsteps echoed behind him.

'The bugger was at it again last night – screaming like a ban-
shee. Woke up the whole damn zoo. And some idiot's lost the key
to its cage!'

Mick frowned as the ZM fell in step with him. When they
reached the cage he stopped, and stared through the bars.
Manimal was sleeping, the long furry body stretched out on a
heap of straw. Mick smiled, longing to reach out and stroke the
fuzzy coat.

'Hmmm.... must've tired itself out!'

Mick scanned the fuzzy face then travelled down the relaxed
haunches to the manimalhood, which lay snoozing on a hairy
thigh. His own bruised cock managed a twitch: Manimal was almost

as impressive flaccid as hard. Mick laughed. 'He looks... happier.'

Yellow eyes snapped open. Mick watched as the manimal raised a shaggy head, lowered a hairy hand to his groin and scratched heavy balls with long claws, then clambered to his feet.

The ZM laughed. 'Don't know why... or what it thinks it's saving itself for!'

Mick stared. Manimal stretched well-muscled arms above the mane of hair, the thick cock swinging lazily between his legs. Manimal yawned, displaying an armoury of razor-sharp teeth.

The ZM moved back. 'Keep clear, buddy – it's a deceitful bugger. That mouth can kill!'

Mick remained where he was and continued to smile. That mouth had coated his cock with thick saliva: he had nothing to fear from Manimal. They stood there for a while, watching each other. Eventually, Manimal turned away.

'Well, blow me! What's it up to now?'

Mick continued to watch as Manimal walked to the pile of straw, crouched and began to lick himself.

He visited the zoo again that night.

Nights became weeks. Weeks became months.

There was no more fucking, but together they explored other pleasures. Hour after hour Manimal lay between Mick's thighs, feasting on his swollen organ while Mick's fingers played with the long tangled shoulder-tufts. The beast's pelt was becoming glossy and thick-feeling. On other nights, Mick found himself submitting to grooming which, on his smooth body, didn't take long. Following his lover's lead, Mick spent hours licking and cleaning every inch of the hard hairy body. He learned to appreciate the low moans which crept from Manimal's throat as he finger-combed the thick, straggling mane and licked the fuzzy, rough-feeling manimal crack. He learned Manimal's ways.

Occasionally, he visited in daylight. The ZM never allowed him to pay these days. Manimal was still far from docile, but the manic ferocity had abated and his cage was now regularly included in the ZM's tour. Mick especially liked to join a tour which coincided with Manimal's feeding-time. The audience would gasp in awe as the ZM piled on the exaggeration, Manimal crouching patiently in one corner of the cage, while an unbelievably brave keeper reached in, filled the water trough and deposited lumps of dead flesh which Manimal fell on... well, like an animal.

Mick was happier than he'd ever been, until one night, while stroking the dense fuzz on Manimal's chest and abdomen, he detected... movement.

'He's got worms.'

'Rubbish – it's as healthy as a sabre tooth. Look at that coat!'

Mick and the keeper were standing a little away from the cage, not really listening to the ZM's elaborate claims for manimal prowess.

'It's as happy as a pig in shit, buddy!'

Mick stared. He couldn't tell the keeper about the changes only he could feel in Manimal's body: the swellings, the strange thickening of the long manimalhood. He couldn't tell the keeper that Manimal never came, regardless of how much cock he fucked or how vigorously Mick tongue-fucked that manimal ass. 'Is there a... vet?'

The keeper laughed. 'What good would that do? No one knows anything about the bugger – what point of comparison could there be?'

Mick scowled. 'There must be some record of the physiology. Somewhere.'

'Maybe. We'll ask on Pluto.'

Mick blinked.

'Didn't you know? We're moving on tomorrow.'

Mick tried to take in the keeper's words. He stared into the cage.

Manimal rose from a crouch and turned to face him. Mick caught those bright, yellow eyes.

Tonight had to be special.

Mick knelt behind his manimal, the thick hair on the beast's back stroking his chest. He reached round, ran his hands over the hard, corrugated abdomen to the thickening cock. Manimal purred. There was no sign of discomfort. Mick's own cock lay along the length of Manimal's ass-crack, gripped by iron haunches. He felt a combination of frustration and irritation. Three months. Three months of his own pleasure.

Slowly, he eased his legs out on either side of the hairy form and pulled the beast back against his chest. One hand gripped the fat cock loosely, the other wandering down to caress the hard, heavy balls which were always pulled up tight. Those balls were definitely filled with something, as was that taut belly, which seemed to ripple as Mick gazed down over Manimal's shoulder. He buried his face in the thick mane and inhaled a new smell – musky, still feral but with an undertone of sweetness. His hands travelled up from the cock to cup the beast's hairy pecs. He squeezed one engorged nipple. Manimal whimpered as Mick's fingers slicked with a warm, viscous liquid. He shuddered, raised a hand and licked a fingernail. Salty sweet. Manimal's body was oozing.

Mick's cock stretched. Manimal shifted back against him, rubbing a hairy ass-crack along the length of him. The beast shivered, tensing and relaxing by turns. Mick kissed the bristling neck. Manimal moved in his lap, edging round to face him. Amber irises shone in the half-dark, closing in as the hair on Manimal's upper lip tore against his own and an urgent tongue probed his mouth.

Mick wrapped a smooth arm around a quivering back and pulled the beast to him, tasting musky sweet-saltiness on the warm, feral breath. Eyes closed, and moaning, he reached down blindly for those hard inches of manimalhood. The other mouth pulled away and a thickening cock slipped from his grasp.

Mick opened his eyes. Manimal was arranging a pile of straw, making a sort of bed. He watched as Manimal crouched at one side of the heap. Manimal smiled. Mick smiled back. Manimal began.

The wank was slow, deliberate – like a ritual. Through the half-light, Mick watched hands-that-had-killed roam over the strong, shaggy body. He watched one hairy fist settle around ten inches of swollen manimalhood, which was thickening further before his eyes. The beast whimpered. Soft rhythmic sounds from deep in the manimal's chest filled the cage. Long, drooling strings of pre-come leaked from the bursting, uncut cock onto the heap of straw.

Mick gasped as retracted claws sprang from finger pads, quickly severing the foreskin. Wrinkles of flesh peeled back, revealing a bulbous, engorged head in the middle of which the beast's piss-slit yawned, impossibly dilated. Mick watched Manimal spread a mixture of thick pre-come and blood along the swelling length.

The manimalhood was almost as thick as an arm now, stretching further without the hindrance of the foreskin. The beast was swaying, the long mane flicking from side to side across a contorted face. Waves flashed over his torso, rippling the hair like wheat in a summer's breeze. Manimal's fist moved faster. The ripples spread lower, becoming visible pulses which spasmed in sync with the manimal's strokes. A warm, foetid smell was flooding the cage. Milky trickles streamed down from bullet nipples, matting the forest of chest hair as the whimpers increased in volume, becoming more pain than pleasure.

Heat from the two bodies condensed and ran down steel walls. Manimal's wank continued. The pile of straw between them was a mess of pre-come. Mick stared, his own fist holding his now-hard cock, drawn into Manimal's ecstasy.

The beast was panting now. Yellow eyes closed as the motion of the fist changed. The hairy hand moved down to cup large balls.

A tremor vibrated through the convulsing body. Manimal fell forward onto his knees and began to howl. Mick shivered at the sound of terrible agony mated with exquisite pleasure. Ten tumescent inches of burgeoning manimal meat were aimed at the pile of straw. Mick could see the heavy balls contract in rhythm with the waves on the beast's chest and belly. A rope of sticky come shot onto the straw.

Mick's gasps were obliterated by the roar which accompanied each volley. He began to panic. He had no idea what was... Manimal paused, breathing heavily. Then another howl ripped loose from his hairy throat as more come pumped from the trembling cock. Mick's awe turned to fear: the pool of steaming come was dotted with blood. He crawled over to the howling, shivering mass of hair, helpless and terrified.

Outside, the zoo was waking up. Screeches, growls, low bays of sympathy echoed in Mick's ears. Something was wrong... it shouldn't be like this. Manimal opened his eyes, mouth twisted somewhere between a grin and a grimace, then threw back his shaggy head and roared. Mick watched, tears streaming down his face as the swollen, distorted manimalhood disgorged a final sticky burst of come... and something else.

The zoo moved on. Twice. Each planet was very much like the last, from this side of the bars.

At least the cage was bigger, these days. Family-sized.

Mick looked over to where his alien mate was blunting sharp claws on clean, matt-steel walls. Then he lowered his eyes to the small, smooth manimal playing happily between strong, furred legs. He noticed the already large cock swaying between slender, lightly muscled thighs.

Like father, like...?

Mick smiled. Oh well... maybe the hair would come later.